PAUL CARR

A veteran of the U.S. Navy, Paul Carr spent his months at sea reading classic mystery and detective novels. He studied economics at Mercer University and worked in financial and computer-related positions before authoring six crime novels, including four Sam Mackenzie thrillers and two Detective Michael Dalton Florida Keys mysteries. He lives with his wife, Elaine, on a lake in Georgia, where he is busy on his next novel.

THE CAYMAN SWITCH

PAUL CARR

W🌐RLDWIDE

TORONTO • NEW YORK • LONDON
AMSTERDAM • PARIS • SYDNEY • HAMBURG
STOCKHOLM • ATHENS • TOKYO • MILAN
MADRID • WARSAW • BUDAPEST • AUCKLAND

WORLDWIDE™

ISBN-13: 978-1-335-14725-7

The Cayman Switch

First published in 2013 by Paul Carr.
This edition published in 2020.

Copyright © 2013 by Paul Carr

Recycling programs
for this product may
not exist in your area.

This edition published by arrangement with Harlequin Books S.A.

For questions and comments about the quality of this book,
please contact us at CustomerService@Harlequin.com.

Harlequin Enterprises ULC
22 Adelaide St. West, 40th Floor
Toronto, Ontario M5H 4E3, Canada
www.ReaderService.com

Printed in U.S.A.

THE CAYMAN
SWITCH

ONE

A BEAD OF perspiration slid down Jackson Craft's neck. He fought an impulse to loosen his tie. The man he knew only as "Baxter" stood a couple of feet from his chair as they waited in front of the massive desk. Baxter nodded at him, flashing a grin that said, *They know what you did.*

Ruben Vale stood at the window, gazing out at the Gulf of Mexico, talking on the phone. Jack could hear little of what he said. After a couple of minutes, Vale closed the phone and turned around. Glancing at Jack as if he might be a piece of furniture, he buttoned his suit coat, stepped behind the desk, and sat in the executive chair.

The room screamed Early Billionaire: original paintings from the Sixteenth Century, vases from a dynasty that used swords as weapons of war, tables that might have once been owned by Henry VIII or one of his queens. It looked like old money, but Jack knew better.

"What's your real name?" Vale asked.

"You know my name."

Vale picked up a folder from the desk and opened it.

"Yes, you said you're Daniel Reston, but the Reston you claim to be died five years ago in South America." He smiled, revealing a gleaming set of perfect teeth.

Jack crossed his legs. He had broken his own cardinal rule and gotten too close.

"Must have been another Daniel Reston," Jack said. "It's a fairly common name."

"My people found several, but none of them fit your description."

"Then there must be some mistake in your information."

Vale's smile leaked away.

"No. I'm afraid you made the mistake in taking our money."

He nodded to Baxter, who pulled a handgun from inside his coat and reached for Jack's arm. "Let's go, old man."

Jack stood and pulled his arm away. "I'm sure we can work this out," he said to Vale.

"I'm afraid not. When Baxter's finished, you'll be most eager to tell him anything he wants to know."

Jack shrugged and started to turn, but stopped and looked back. "Okay, you win."

The oldest trick in the book, but Baxter fell for it and glanced at Vale. Jack smacked the gun hand with his right forearm, knocking it away, then grabbed Baxter's wrist and twisted downward, leveraging his elbow with his other hand. Like snapping a tree limb. Baxter screamed and dropped to his knees. The gun fired wild and the smell of hot sulfur bit into Jack's nostrils. He ripped the weapon away, stepped to the door, and heard what sounded like an army running down the hall toward the office. Pulling his phone from his pocket, he pressed two buttons.

SAM MACKENZIE DROVE across the MacArthur Causeway toward the Miami Beach marina where he lived. He had ridden all over town looking for a water pump for his boat. The last time he'd taken it out, the pump had stopped discharging water, which ran the engine hot, and he'd had to get a tow in from Government Cut. A lot of trouble, but better than burning up the engine.

He turned into the marina and parked, then strode to his boat under the July sun. Inside, he went straight to the fridge and pulled out a cold Corona. Sitting down in the lounge, he uncapped the bottle, drank a third of the beer, and took the pump out of the box. It didn't look like it would be difficult to replace. He'd never done it before, but thought he could figure it out. Besides, he didn't have anything better to do.

The cell phone chirped. Glancing at the display, he saw Jack Craft's number and punched the answer button. Before he could say anything, he heard the voice of a man: "Lay the gun on the floor."

Sam heard a clatter, then the same voice again. "Okay, lean against the desk, real easy."

A moaning sound issued from the background.

"Shut up, Baxter!"

"I think Reston broke his arm." Sam thought he'd heard this new voice somewhere before. Deep and practiced, like someone who gave speeches for a living.

"That's too bad. He should have seen it coming."

Next, Sam recognized Jack's voice: "I wasn't expecting to have someone pull a gun on me in the Outpost Mariner."

"Hey, you shut up, too, Reston!" First voice again. "You trying to call somebody? Give me the phone." A couple of tones sounded, as if someone grabbed the phone and pressed some keys by accident, and the connection died.

Sam wondered what Jack had gotten himself into. One of the voices had referred to Jack as "Reston." He had used that name before. Wondering about the reference to the Outpost Mariner, Sam punched in the number for John Templeton Smith III. J.T. answered on the first ring.

"Sammy, I was hoping you'd call."

"How's it going?"

"Not bad. Just getting a little bored."

That meant he needed money. He always did; his debts were endless. Dangerous people were constantly after him. Consequently, he didn't stay in one place very long. Surprisingly, it didn't seem to bother him in the least.

Sam told J.T. about Jack and the phone call.

"That doesn't sound good. When did you last see him?"

"About three weeks ago, when he canceled out on us for that Schmidt job he'd been planning. He wouldn't say why, just that he had something important to take care of."

"Yeah, I was counting on that money. I wasn't too happy when he called it off."

Sam remembered. Jack told him J.T. blew his top and said don't call on him again.

"Yeah, I heard."

J.T. chuckled. "I'm over that now, though. You want me to find out what I can about this 'Outpost Mariner' Jack mentioned?"

"Yes, please."

"Sure, hold on."

Sam heard keys clicking on J.T.'s computer.

"There's a hotel by that name in Key West."

"Do you have the telephone number?"

J.T. read it off and Sam said he would get back to him in a few minutes.

He called the hotel and an operator answered after a couple of rings. Sam asked to speak with Mr. Reston. The operator said to hold and she would connect him. The phone rang several times before it went to voice-mail. He hung up.

Sam leaned back in the chair and rubbed his eyes, wondering what he should do. Pretty typical for Jack, always pulling the strings. No one figures out what's going on until the puppets stop dancing, but then it's too late. It looked as if he might have been caught this time. If so, he probably deserved the consequences. Sam ran his fingers through his hair and sighed. He found his spare cell phone—the untraceable one—and called Jack's number.

"Hello." It sounded like the man who had taken the phone from Jack.

"Is this Reston?"

"Uh, yeah, this is Reston, who is this?"

"You don't sound like him."

"Yeah, I know. I caught a cold, okay?"

"Okay, no need to get snappy. This is Charlie. I got the information you wanted."

"The information…oh, yeah, so you got it, huh?"

"That's right. Give me the address and I'll drop it off."

"I'm at the Outpost Mariner. How soon can you get here?"

"How about seven o'clock?"

"Okay, meet me in the hotel bar, corner booth."

After hanging up, Sam called J.T. back and told him about the calls.

"What are you going to do?" J.T. asked.

"I guess I'll go down there."

ERNIE PRESSED THE red button on the phone, closing the call.

Ruben looked nervous. "Who was that?" He wasn't used to this kind of thing, especially when the guns came out.

"A guy named Charlie. Said he had some information for Reston. I'm supposed to meet him in the bar tonight."

"What did they do with Reston?"

"They took him to the empty office down the hall. We'll move him after dark."

Ruben nodded, an odd look on his face, then smiled and said, "I've got an appointment with a TV person from Miami this evening."

"For what?"

"To discuss doing a show about me."

Ernie could feel his blood pressure rising.

"We've been over all that. You can't go on TV. They'll ask a lot of questions."

"The world deserves to see how successful I've become."

Ernie rolled his eyes. "You mean the people in Hollywood, don't you?"

"Well…them, too. They shouldn't have canceled my show."

"That was a long time ago. Besides, you probably shouldn't have gotten caught with the director's wife."

Ruben waved the comment away and pulled a mirror from the middle drawer of his desk. He looked at his reflection and smoothed his hair over one ear.

"How'd I do today? Did I look tough? I've played a tough guy before, you know."

Ernie shook his head and sighed.

"You did fine, Ruben."

Ernie had wanted to meet with Reston himself, but Ruben insisted on playing his role. Ernie watched on the remote camera, waiting for something to go wrong. He supposed what happened wasn't actually Ruben's fault. Baxter had gotten careless. Reston might look like somebody's rich father, but that didn't make him any less dangerous. Ernie had zoomed in on the old guy's face and had seen it in his eyes. Baxter should have seen it, too.

It had been more than seven years since Ruben lost his show. He tried to get other work, but nobody would hire him. Several months had passed before he called Ernie.

"What do you want me to do?" Ernie had asked.

"Well, you know, you always seemed to have a lot of money in college, and I don't remember you ever working for it."

Ernie thought about some Rolex watches that were too hot to sell and asked Ruben if he could unload them on his friends.

"I never sold anything before, but I'll give it a try."

Ruben turned out to have quite a flair for moving stolen merchandise. They made a lot of money, and in recent years had even turned some of their business into a legitimate enterprise. Lately, though, Ruben just complained about their having to run under the radar, constantly, and pined for the limelight that had been ripped from him. Ernie had had enough of it. Especially with this TV lunacy, which had the potential to land them both in jail. If Ruben persisted, Ernie would have to do something about it.

SAM GLANCED AT the water pump. He'd have to get to it later. The boat would be here when he returned. He packed a bag, got some cash from the lock box in his stateroom closet, and drove out of the marina.

The trip to Key West took less than three hours, but seemed longer. The panorama of nothing but water and sky, so large and blue, gave one the impression of being suspended in time.

J.T.'s plane landed on schedule, and he came out of the terminal rolling an overnighter and carrying a laptop bag. He had put on a few pounds since the last time Sam had seen him, but he looked fit, as if he might have been working out with weights. Towering above most of the travelers, they tended to step aside for him to pass. The ponytail remained, and had some gray in it, even though he was only in his mid-thirties. He spotted Sam's car, ambled over and got in.

They drove to The Mean Manatee, a restaurant on Duval, where they ordered fish sandwiches and beer. Seated on the patio, they ate their sandwiches beneath ceiling fans that dropped the temperature down to about ninety. Reggae played from a speaker close to their table.

"What've you been up to?" Sam asked.

"Did some work in California for a consulting firm."

Sam raised an eyebrow and said, "No kidding? You mean legitimate computer work?"

J.T. chuckled. "Yeah, I lasted about a week before I told them where to go. After that, I went back to hacking. It can pay pretty well if you get the right clients."

He told Sam about a couple of jobs he'd done for a man who had served time for selling bad bonds.

Sam heard only a fraction of what he said, wondering what to do about Jack Craft.

"How's Carling these days?" J.T. asked, bringing Sam back into the conversation.

Carling and Sam had seen each other regularly for a few weeks, and then drifted apart. She ran Carling Research, a company that dissected cadavers and produced human-tissue study aids preserved in acrylic for use in medical schools. The facility also served as an underground emergency room for the few who knew about it. Her clientele consisted mostly of men injured during some type of criminal activity. Sam and J.T. had both been patients there at one time or another. Carling ran the operation alone. On the job twelve to fifteen hours a day, her schedule left little time for romance.

"Doing fine. I haven't seen her for a while, though. She stays busy."

J.T. nodded. He knew Carling pretty well.

A cottage that looked like something from *Hansel and Gretel* sat on the side street next to the restaurant. Several colorful chickens pecked at something in the small, immaculate lawn.

"How about Amy?" Sam asked.

Grimacing, J.T. said, "Nah, didn't work out. Lifestyle issues. You know."

"Yeah."

A rotund woman in a housedress came down the steps from the cottage porch, swinging a broom.

"Shoo! Shoo! Get gone!"

The birds clucked, flapped their wings, and scampered to the street.

A man with long, oily hair and filthy clothes stopped on the sidewalk next to the yard. "Hey! They got as much right to be here as you do!"

The woman's eyes narrowed and she pointed the broom at him. "You get gone, too."

"So, what's the plan?" J.T. asked.

Sam glanced at him, drank the last of his beer and set the glass on the table. He shrugged and said, "I thought we'd check out that hotel bar and see if the guy shows up looking for Charlie."

"Sounds okay to me."

After dropping some bills on the table for the meal, they went to the car, and Sam got his associate a Glock 9mm from the trunk. J.T. entered the address of the Outpost Mariner into the GPS system. It led them up Duval almost to its end. They passed inns and restaurants, and then turned right and drove another couple of blocks before arriving at the resort. The sign in front boasted 200 rooms, a restaurant, and conference facilities.

Sam parked his car and they went inside. It looked like an upscale hotel from a different generation, with lots of wicker furniture and palms in the lobby's cool expanse. Soft music played in the background while lazy fans whirred overhead.

They entered the hotel lounge and took seats at the bar where Sam could see the table in the corner. A man sat there with a near-empty glass in front of him. His thinning blond hair gave him the look of a tennis pro who had crested the hill, ready to slide down the other side. Glancing up as they entered, he seemed to decide they were there just to drink, and motioned for the waiter to bring him a refill. He looked at his watch every few minutes and ordered two more drinks while he waited. Sam and J.T. had a couple of beers each. At seven-thirty, the man in the corner answered a call on his phone. After talking for a minute, he got up and left.

TWO

RUBEN SAT AT the table with Mona Miles, the Miami news anchor, in the private dining room of his favorite waterfront restaurant. They'd had dinner and were on their third drink. The meeting couldn't have been going better, except for the fact that Mona hadn't said anything about his appearance. He had given her his best on-camera smile, and hoped for something like, "You look terrific, and you haven't aged a bit since your television show." Instead, she had just glanced at him when she shook his hand and started talking about all the traffic on the Overseas Highway. She did seem a little nervous from the trip, and that could account for her oversight.

It sounded as if Mona would do the show herself. She probably saw it as a steppingstone to a network position in New York. Big star like Ruben Vale, how could she miss?

Mona dabbed a napkin to her lips and said, "Okay, let's talk about some specifics. We'll have an hour of airtime, so we need a lot of material."

"I thought we'd start by touring my house on the Gulf. I could take you there tonight."

"Uh, no, not tonight, maybe tomorrow."

Ruben wondered if she thought he was hitting on her. He was, but didn't want it to sound that way. Anyway, she must have been too tired, otherwise why would she have passed up a visit to Ruben Vale's house on the Gulf?

"Tomorrow's okay."

"Good. Say we tour the house for a few minutes. Then I can ask what you've been up to these last few years and you can talk about your projects."

"Projects?"

"You know, the work you've been doing that made your fortune."

"Uh, can't we just say I'm rich and talk about my art collection and travels, things like that?"

Mona took a sip of her drink. "Well, yes, we can do that, but the viewers will want to know how you bounced back after your show got canceled."

Again with the canceled show! Why did they keep bringing that up? Ruben almost rolled his eyes, but decided that might not be a good idea.

"It wasn't exactly canceled. I had some other commitments."

Ruben felt like he might have something stuck between his two front teeth. He had been worried this might happen and had suggested they just have drinks. Mona said she hadn't eaten since early morning and would prefer to have dinner. He'd given in, because he didn't want to start off on the wrong foot, but now he had this problem.

Mona shrugged. "I heard it got canceled because of something between you and the director's wife."

Ruben didn't like where this was going. And that thing in his teeth...surely she had to see it when he opened his mouth.

"Well, why do we have to go into any of that, anyway?" He tried to keep his lips together when he spoke.

Frowning, Mona stared for a moment. "Okay, let's skip that part for now. We'll talk about how you've made your money. You must have been producing or directing, doing something in the background."

Ruben hadn't considered that.

"Sure, I've been making some independent films."

Mona's eyes widened. "Okay, now we're getting somewhere. You can tell us about those."

"Well, I really couldn't talk about any of that, since the films haven't been released yet."

Mona leaned back in her chair and crossed her arms, the frown back on her face. Could it be the thing in his teeth, or was she getting annoyed? Ruben really wanted to go to the men's room and check his teeth, but feared she might not be there when he got back. He turned his head and coughed while he raked his fingernail between his two middle incisors. There didn't appear to be anything there. Had it been his imagination? He covered his mouth, coughed again, and turned back to face Mona.

"Are you okay?"

"Oh, sure. Something must have gone down the wrong pipe."

Mona nodded. "Anyway, we were talking about your independent films. Ruben, I'm going to level with you. We'll need some material to do this special. If all we talk about is your house and how well you're living, that'll be about ten minutes' worth. This kind of show, people are going to want some juicy news, you know? You're going to have to open up here, or we're finished."

Ruben thought about that for a moment. This being his first chance at any kind of TV exposure in years, he couldn't let it flop on its face. He signaled the waiter to bring another round of drinks.

THE MAN WHO looked like a washed-up tennis pro strode through the lobby and entered the elevator. Sam and J.T. watched the lights as the car stopped on the seventh floor, marked Penthouse, and took the other elevator to six. From there they ran up the stairs, and Sam peeked around the corner as someone yelled something unintelligible down the hall. Tennis Pro came out a door about fifty feet away and hurried toward the elevator, another man trailing him.

"I don't see how you could let him get away, Morris," Tennis Pro said. "It was pretty simple. You just had to sit there and watch him."

"It wasn't my fault. Baxter came in with a gun and took Reston with him."

"Baxter? I fired him after he let Reston get the jump on him." Tennis Pro jabbed his finger at the down arrow on the elevator.

"Yeah, but it was him. His arm was in a sling and all wrapped up like he'd been to the hospital."

"When did this happen?"

"Just a few minutes ago."

"You know where Baxter lives?"

"He didn't have a place. He stayed in a motel a couple blocks off US-1."

The elevator door opened and they got on.

Sam and J.T. raced down the stairs, beating them to the lobby, and walked outside to Sam's car.

"Why do you think this Baxter rescued him?" J.T. asked.

"He probably wants the money Reston took from those guys. Either that, or he's unhappy about Reston breaking his arm."

The two men came out of the hotel, got into a luxury

SUV, and rode out of the parking lot with Morris at the wheel. Sam followed, staying several car lengths behind them as they made their way down Duval toward the other coast. A few minutes later, they turned left for a couple of blocks and pulled into the Breezy Palm Motel, a one-story building with about twenty units. Morris stopped in front of a door at the far end. Sam turned in a few moments later and parked a couple of spots from the SUV. He lowered the window.

"This is where I picked him up a few days ago when his car wouldn't start," Morris said.

Tennis Pro knocked on the door and waited. Nobody answered. He knocked again. After a minute or two, he asked Morris for a credit card.

"Why do you want a credit card?"

Tennis Pro rolled his eyes.

After a second, Morris grinned and said, "Oh, yeah, okay," and pulled a card from his wallet.

Tennis Pro stuck it into the doorjamb and worked it for a few seconds. Then he twisted the knob, pushed the door open, and handed the card back to Morris. They went inside, stayed less than a minute, and came back out.

"He might have been here, but he's gone now," Tennis Pro said.

"Did you check him out when you hired him?" Morris asked.

Tennis Pro went to the passenger door, stopped, and stared at him.

"Look, he had a gun and he looked like he knew how to use it, so shut up. You're the one who let Reston get away. You got until morning to find him or you're gonna hit the road, too."

They got into the vehicle and sped away.

JACK CRAFT DROVE the car, with Baxter holding a gun on him, to a seedy motel with a sign out front that advertised weekly rentals. Inside the room, Baxter instructed Jack to bind his own ankles to the legs of a wooden chair using nylon ties. With that done, he told him to make a large loop of another tie. Then he snugged it down on Jack's crisscrossed wrists behind the chair back, cutting into the flesh like a hot knife.

"Hey, that's too tight! Cut me some slack; I'm an old man."

"Yeah, right," Baxter said. "You didn't seem so old when you fractured my elbow." He went out to the car, came back with a bottle of whiskey, and caught Jack trying to twist free.

"Save your energy. There's no way you can get loose."

Baxter set the bottle on the table, twisted off the cap with his good hand, and poured a full glass. He pulled two pills from his shirt pocket and washed them down with the whiskey.

"Want a drink?"

"Sure, I could use one."

Baxter poured another glass and set it on the table next to Jack.

"How am I supposed to drink that with my hands tied behind me?"

"Oh, yeah." He pulled a plastic straw from a sweating soft-drink cup, probably from the day before, and put it into Jack's glass.

Baxter grinned. "There you go."

Jack looked at the straw and decided he didn't really want any whiskey after all.

The man with the injured arm sat down on the other

side of the table and took another drink. His eyes had a shine that hadn't been there a few minutes before.

"Let's talk about the money again," Baxter said.

"I don't know why everyone is so upset. We just closed on a perfectly legitimate real estate transaction. That resort is worth every penny they paid."

"Yeah, you said that already."

"That's because it's true."

"You might be the best liar I've ever seen. They just handed over their money like you had them under a spell or something." He stared at Jack for a few moments and took another drink.

"The money has already been deposited, and I don't have access to the account. I was only the broker."

"Then I guess I'll have to find your partner and see if he'll talk."

"What partner?"

"The guy with the silver hair and the accent who said he owned the place."

Dave. "He's probably back in New York by now."

"Yeah, I bet. I'll go find him, and then we'll get down to business. One of you will talk, I can guarantee that."

Jack's captor pulled a cigarette from a pack on the table, put one end in his mouth, and lit it with a disposable lighter. After a long draw, he blew a smoke ring across the table, and laid the cigarette in the ashtray.

"I'm getting pretty good at this one-handed stuff."

Standing, he stuck the cigarette into his mouth again and started for the door.

"How about letting me take off my coat? It's hot in here."

Baxter gave him a smirk, walked to the air conditioner and twisted a knob.

"You better think about things while I'm gone," he said with the cigarette in the corner of his mouth. Smoke drifted past his face and he coughed without opening his mouth.

"What if I could get you a share in the hotel?"

Baxter smirked and coughed again, then ambled out the door and locked it behind him.

THREE

MORRIS DROVE TO a small house on the Gulf and Tennis Pro got out. Sam went past them and turned into a driveway a few doors down. He waited for Morris to leave, drove by the mailbox so J.T. could get the address, then floored it and caught up with Morris.

J.T. clicked laptop keys and after a few moments said, "The guy's name is Ernie Brent."

They followed Morris back to the Outpost Mariner Hotel.

"Stay here and work the computer," Sam said.

Morris went into the lounge and took a table. Sam sauntered to the bar and ordered a beer.

A waiter brought Morris two drinks. He downed one of them, took out his cell phone, and made a call.

"Baxter came back with a gun and took Reston away," Morris said.

He lowered his voice and Sam couldn't hear his words for a minute or so. Then he sighed and Sam heard him say, "Okay, I'll go to my room and make some calls. See if I can find somebody who knows anything about the guy."

Morris put the phone away and poured down the second drink. He left a bill on the table and went out to the lobby, moving slower now after the drinks. Sam followed and saw him get onto the elevator.

Back in the car, Sam said, "Morris has a room here, but he doesn't have a clue where Jack is."

Sam told J.T. about the phone call and asked if he'd found anything on Ernie.

"Here's a news story from four years ago about a police investigation in California. They suspected him of peddling stolen goods, but the charges were dropped due to lack of evidence."

Sam peered at the computer screen. A picture of a man who resembled Tennis Pro, with more hair and no mustache, smiled back at him.

"Yeah, I think that's him."

He started the car and drove out of the hotel parking lot.

"Did the article mention Morris?" Sam asked.

"No, but it did talk about an interview with Ruben Vale, who told the cops that Brent's a model citizen."

"Who?"

"Ruben Vale. You know, the actor who had the TV show a few years ago. He played a private detective. I liked it, but it didn't last long."

Sam shook his head. "Doesn't ring a bell."

He drove to the Breezy Palm Motel and went into the office while J.T. stayed in the car. An air conditioner in the wall blew warm air across the counter. It smelled like nicotine. A sleepy-eyed woman sat behind the counter reading a romance novel. She put the book down and asked if she could help him.

"I'm looking for my friend Baxter," Sam said. "He told me he's staying here."

"Joe Baxter?" Her voice sounded like a file rubbing against a wooden board.

"Yeah… Joe."

"He was here, but not anymore."

"You sure? He said he'd meet me here tonight."

"Yeah, I'm sure. He came in here today with his arm in a sling. Said he'd been in some kind of accident and had to leave."

"That's too bad. Do you know where he went?"

"I didn't ask. He didn't seem too happy about not getting a refund for the rest of the week." The desk clerk glanced at her book and said, "Anything else?"

"Do you know what kind of car he drove?" Sam asked.

She shrugged and lit a cigarette. "I think it was blue."

"Could you check the registration card? It's really important that I find him."

The woman blew smoke at him, stuck the cigarette in the corner of her mouth and reached into a plastic file box. She thumbed through several cards, then pulled one out and laid it on the counter.

The card indicated that Joe Baxter had a Ford Taurus, and Sam wrote down the Florida tag number on a motel brochure lying on the counter. He thanked the woman, went back to the car, and relayed the information to J.T.

Handing him the brochure, he said, "Check out the tag."

Sam heard the computer keys rattle for a couple of minutes, and J.T. said, "This might be the guy."

He read two separate newspaper notices about arrests of a Joseph Baxter in Miami, one for possession of a firearm without a license and the other for assault with a deadly weapon. Both incidents had happened within the last three months.

"Sounds right. See if you can find a Miami address."

Sam started the car, drove out of the Breezy Palm parking lot and headed toward Duval.

A few minutes later, J.T. said, "I found a video of that guy."

"What guy?"

"Ruben Vale. You know, the actor I mentioned, from the article on Ernie Brent."

Sam glanced at the guy on the screen and remembered watching his TV show a couple of times. He also remembered hearing his voice in the room when Jack had called.

BAXTER HAD BEEN gone a few minutes when Jack thought up a way to get loose. He couldn't move much with his feet tied to the chair, but it was enough to feel the rickety looseness in the wooden chair. Maybe enough for it to break. Pressing the tips of his shoes to the carpet, he thrust his body backward and then forward several times, the chair loosening a little each time, until something cracked, and he toppled to the floor on his back.

He slammed into the tiled floor and lay there, dazed and dreaming about being on a boat, the water smooth as glass, and the sun's rays warming his face. Nothing moved, including him. Didn't even need to breathe. Everything felt wonderful, but on some level it occurred to him that he might be dying. Finally, he gasped, drawing what seemed like gallons of air into his aching lungs. He opened his eyes to a blur, but after a few moments, the jaundiced light of the lamp brought the motel room back into seedy focus. His head pounded, and his numb arms tingled.

The chair underneath him seemed loose, maybe broken. He kicked his feet back and forth a few times, feeling the chair legs pull away from his bindings, then rolled onto his side and squirmed until the wounded chair back pulled free from his wrists. His hands hurt, and he hoped he hadn't broken any bones in the fall.

A car pulled into a parking space outside. Baxter? Breathing hard, Jack struggled to his feet and crept to the door. The eyehole had been painted over and he couldn't see anything through it. He dared not pull the curtain for fear that Baxter might see it. The car engine turned off, the door slammed, and after a few seconds, a key disengaged the lock next door.

The old air conditioner made a lot of noise, and the sheet metal covering it looked as if it just lay atop the unit, without being attached. He kicked it and it fell to the floor with a *clank*, its sharp edges facing upward. Turning around, he leaned down, but couldn't reach the metal cover, so he sat on the bed, lowered himself to the floor, and scooted backward until he could touch the metal. A couple minutes of rubbing his nylon ties against the sharp edge cut them loose and his hands were free.

Jack took the cap off the whiskey. He drank from the bottle, then took it into the bathroom and poured some over the cuts on his wrists. After another drink, he set the bottle on the table and picked up one of the broken chair legs, which looked a lot like the large end of a cue stick. He sat down, had another drink and waited.

Baxter returned about twenty minutes later. He came in the door, looked down at the wounded chair, and reached for his gun. Jack stepped from behind the door and swung the chair leg, striking Baxter about an inch above his right ear. It sounded like a coconut hitting a concrete floor.

FOUR

AFTER DRIVING THROUGH at least a dozen motel and hotel parking lots, Sam and J.T. gave up their search for Baxter's car. They checked into a small motel close to Duval about midnight and left again around 9:00 a.m. for breakfast at the Outpost Mariner.

Sam stirred cream and sugar into his coffee as he asked, "Did you find out where Ruben Vale lives?"

"Why?"

"I heard him talking in the room when Jack called me."

"No kidding. You sure?"

"I'm pretty sure."

Their bacon and eggs arrived, and they waited until the server left the table before speaking again.

"You think he's involved in this?" J.T. asked.

"Yes. He was there while Ernie Brent gave Jack the third degree about the money, and from your research, it sounds like they could have some kind of an association. It seems unlikely that a successful actor would get involved with someone like Brent, but we have to consider that possibility."

They ate their breakfast and left the restaurant a few minutes later. Back in the car, J.T. turned on his computer, found Ruben Vale's address in an online telephone directory, and entered it into the navigation system.

Sam started the engine and flipped on the air conditioner. Though only 10:00 a.m., it already felt like ninety degrees.

They found Vale's house within a few minutes. He lived in an oceanfront villa, a two-story stucco with a tile roof that might have cost more than a million dollars in Miami.

"Looks like Ruben is doing okay," J.T. said.

"I'd say."

An Acura sat in the driveway, a truck bearing the logo of a TV news station parked directly behind it. Sam pulled up next to the curb a couple of doors down where they had a clear view of the house and driveway.

"I guess he's done something to get his name in the news," Sam said.

They waited an hour before a pretty blonde woman came out the front door and went to the Acura. She got inside and started the engine, then pulled out a cell phone and made a call while sitting there in the driveway.

"That's Mona Miles," Sam said.

"You know her?"

Sam glanced at J.T. and then looked back at Mona Miles.

"She does the morning news."

"Hmm…she's a looker."

"I DON'T KNOW if this is going to work out," Mona said to the station manager on the phone.

"What do you mean?"

"It's like pulling teeth. All he wants to talk about is his home and what a great life he has. I asked him what kind of business he's in these days, and he just grinned at the camera and said, 'Oh, you know, the usual. What about the pool, you want to see the pool?'"

"Well, give it another hour or so. If it doesn't get better, tell him to find somebody else. I'm not so sure the viewers will be interested, anyway."

"Uh-oh, here he comes." Mona sighed. "I guess I'd better go."

"Okay, just keep me posted."

"Will do, but you're going to owe me big-time for this."

SAM WATCHED RUBEN VALE come out and stare at Mona Miles through the windshield. She had been out there for a while. After talking a few seconds longer, she got out and went back into the house with him.

"Do you suppose Morris was talking to Vale on the phone last night when you overheard him?" J.T. asked.

"That's my guess, and from Morris' side of the conversation, it sounded like neither of them knew where Jack might be."

"Yeah, so what are we doing here?"

"I'm not sure, but if Mona Miles leaves pretty soon, we'll have a talk with Ruben."

They waited two hours before a man came out carrying a camera. A couple of minutes later, Mona and Ruben came out and Ruben followed her to the car. She got inside and he leaned with his forearms on the roof of the car, looking through the window and talking for another minute or so. The van stayed there until Mona started the car and Ruben stepped away, then it backed out of the driveway and she did the same.

A dark green Mercedes came down the street and stopped a couple of car lengths from Vale's driveway. It waited until the van and the Acura drove away, then turned in and slammed on the brakes, screeching the tires. Ernie Brent got out and hurried toward Ruben, his face red, arms flying.

Ruben glanced up and down the street, and his eyes lingered on Sam's car for a split-second, then he said something to Ernie and motioned toward the house. They went inside and closed the door.

"OKAY," RUBEN SAID, "What was that all about?"

Ernie tried to contain himself, but his face felt like it was on fire and his head ached. "What are you doing talking to TV people?"

"Just hold on," Ruben said. "I told you about them coming for an interview."

"Yeah, and I said you couldn't do it. What did you tell them?"

"Nothing…well, nothing important. They mainly just wanted to know about my TV career."

"You don't have a TV career. That ended a long time ago."

"No, it isn't over. I'm going to make a comeback. I told them I'm looking for a good crime drama; maybe play a cop or a lawyer, something like that."

Ruben took a comb from his pocket and ran it through his hair a couple of times. Ernie grabbed it and threw it on the floor.

"Hey…"

"What else did you talk about?" Ernie asked.

"That pretty much covered it."

Ernie took a deep breath and felt the tension sliding away.

"You didn't mention my name, did you?"

"Oh, no! I don't think so."

"What do you mean, you don't *think* so? You either did or you didn't."

Ruben tilted his head and squinted his eyes, then said, "No, I'm pretty sure I didn't."

Ernie raised an eyebrow. "What about our business? You say anything about that?"

"No, not much."

Ernie thought his head might burst. "What, exactly, does 'not much' mean?"

"I just mentioned that you and I deal in high quality jewelry from time to time."

"Are you crazy?" His voice rose with each word. "You know they arrested me that time for selling stolen jewelry. And you just said you didn't mention my name."

"Well, just that one time. I just mentioned that you're the master at buying the merchandise and I'm the master marketer."

Ruben grinned as if he thought he'd just said something funny and complimentary that would settle Ernie down.

"You idiot!"

Ernie slammed his fist into Ruben's face, and the former actor's head snapped back. Though obviously stunned, he still had a silly grin on his face, probably wondering what had just happened. Ernie hit him again, harder this time, and the grin drained away. Ruben's eyes rolled up and he dropped to the floor.

Ernie leaned down, about to hit him again, when he noticed blood leaking out of Ruben's head onto the floor. Then he saw more blood on the corner of the table next to the sofa. He stood up, took a deep breath and rubbed his aching knuckles.

"Serves you right for being so stupid," Ernie said, but he knew Ruben didn't hear him. In fact, he was pretty sure that Ruben would never hear anything again.

He had to get rid of the body, but not in broad daylight. He'd have to come back later, after dark, and roll him up in a rug or something. There were lots of places to ditch a body in the Keys.

Right now, he had more important things to do, like chasing down that pair from the TV station. They couldn't be far away. Probably on their way back to Miami.

ABOUT TEN MINUTES passed before the door opened and Ernie came out. He hurried to his car, backed out and sped away. Sam U-turned and drove into Ruben's driveway. He and J.T. got out and strode to the front door.

Sam pressed the doorbell and waited. No answer. After a minute or so, he pressed it again with the same result. He tried the door, found it unlocked, and pushed it open. Stepping inside, Sam called Vale's name. Silence.

He glanced at J.T. They entered and searched the house until they found Vale lying on the floor in the den. Blood had puddled on the floor next to his head and spattered the corner of a table next to the sofa.

"We'd better get out of here," J.T. said.

Sam touched Vale's neck and felt a pulse.

"He's alive," Sam said.

"So? We'll get blamed for this if we hang around."

"We can't just leave him here."

"Sure we can," J.T. said. When Sam didn't say anything, he threw up his hands and sighed.

The phone on an end table had a speaker button.

Sam took out his pocketknife and punched the button with one end of the closed knife. When the dial tone sounded off, he punched 911.

"Emergency Assistance," an operator said, "how can we help you?"

Sam leaned down to the phone and said, "I hit my head and I'm bleeding," his voice slightly above a whisper.

"Do you need an ambulance, sir?"

Sam flipped the phone off the table with the knife and it clattered to the floor. After wiping the door for prints, they strode to the car and drove away. Within a few minutes, an ambulance and a police car passed them.

"They must've had an argument," Sam said, speeding toward US-1.

"Yeah, and Ernie didn't waste any time getting out of there, either."

"Maybe he went after the news team, thinking they filmed whatever he and Ruben had argued about."

"You're going to try to warn them?"

Sam nodded. "He left Ruben for dead, and might do the same with them. Besides, all this might be connected to what happened with Jack."

"You sure that's it, or did you just want to meet Mona Miles?"

Sam glanced at him. "That crossed my mind, too."

THE ACURA SAT outside a restaurant at the edge of town. Ernie waited in his own car a couple of spaces away, his engine running. Sam pulled in several spots beyond Ernie.

"How about watching him while I go inside?" Sam asked. "Call me if he leaves before I come back out."

"What if I wanted to meet her, too?"

"I'll introduce you later."

J.T. snorted a laugh. "Yeah, sure."

Sam got out of the car and took out his knife. He unfolded the blade and eased toward Ernie's car. Ernie watched the entrance of the restaurant as Sam leaned down at the left rear tire and sliced off the stem even with the alloy wheel. The air hissed out and smelled like pencil lead. Crouching, he duck-walked to the other tire, did the same to it, then stood and ambled inside to find Mona Miles.

The two sat next to a window overlooking the Atlantic, and appeared to be almost finished with their meal. Sam stepped over to their table.

"I need to talk to you about Ruben Vale."

Mona looked up at him and raised an eyebrow. She looked tired, but her long blonde hair and eyes the color of the ocean were still beautiful.

"Who are you?"

Sam shrugged. "Someone who knows something about Ruben."

"If this is about the shoot, I can't talk about that."

Sam glanced at the table next to them and noticed a man and woman listening. He looked out the window and saw outside tables unoccupied, probably because of the heat.

"Can we talk out on the deck?"

Mona shook her head. "Sorry, I told you—"

"I don't expect you to do anything except listen. It won't take five minutes."

The cameraman pushed back his chair and started

to stand up. "Listen, buddy, she said she doesn't want to talk to you."

Mona held up her hand. "No, wait, I'll listen to what he has to say." She stood and said, "Lead the way," then turned to the cameraman. "If I'm not back in a couple of minutes, come get me."

She and Sam went outside and sat at a table with a large umbrella.

"This had better be good," Mona said.

A waiter came out and asked if they would like to order a drink. They both declined and he frowned and left.

"A man came to Ruben's house as you drove away," Sam said.

"Yes, I saw someone drive in. Who was it?"

"I think his name is Ernie Brent."

Mona thought for a second and said, "Ruben's partner?"

"Maybe, I don't know."

"So, what about it?"

"I think he and Ruben had an argument, probably over something to do with you and the cameraman being there."

"Why do you think that?"

"He left Ruben inside with his head pouring blood on the floor."

Mona's eyes grew large. "I don't believe you."

Sam shrugged. "You can check with the hospital."

Mona took a deep breath and looked out at the ocean. Then she turned back and said, "You saw him? Ruben, I mean."

"Yes. The ambulance came and took him away."

She looked Sam up and down and narrowed her eyes.

"What were *you* doing there?"

"I wanted to talk to Ruben, and I guess I waited too long."

She took a tissue from her pocket and dabbed perspiration from her forehead.

"Did you tell the police what happened?"

"No."

"Why not?"

"I can't get involved in an investigation."

She stared for a moment. "I don't understand. Why are you telling *me* this?"

"I just wanted to warn you. Ernie is waiting outside, and I think he wants the video you shot."

She glanced through the window toward the front of the building, her eyes large.

"He's out there now?"

Sam nodded. "Don't worry, he won't bother you here. It's too visible and busy. He probably intends to follow you up the Overseas Highway, but he won't be able to."

"Why not?"

"I cut his tire stems."

Mona looked at Sam's hands, then at his face, and pushed back in her chair.

"How do I know you aren't the one who hurt Ruben?"

Sam shrugged. "Why would I warn you about Ernie?"

She glanced out over the ocean again, as if she might find the truth there.

"Gotta go," Sam said, and stood to leave.

"Wait." Getting to her feet, she grabbed his arm.

He glanced at her hand and she pulled it away.

"You can at least tell me your name."

Sam shook his head. "Sorry, I can't be part of your story."

"Okay, I think I understand. How about a phone number?"

"Sure, if you give me yours."

They exchanged numbers, and he turned and went through the door.

FIVE

Sam left mona Miles and the cameraman in the restaurant and ambled outside. Ernie, still in his car, glanced at his watch as Sam went by, probably wondering how much longer the news people would be having lunch.

Sam got into his car and J.T. asked him about Mona.

"She was pretty nice, considering the circumstances."

"What did she say about Ruben Vale?"

"She said very little, but I bet she's going to the hospital to see him. This is probably a bigger story than the one she had before."

Mona and the cameraman came out of the restaurant a minute later and hurried to their vehicles. She backed her car out and headed back toward Key West, and the cameraman pulled out behind her. Ernie followed, but a few seconds later, he pulled over to the side of the road. He got out, saw the flat tire on the driver's side, and turned to watch the van go south on US-1. Rubbing his forehead with the palm of his hand, he stepped around to the trunk of the car.

Sam pulled out and caught up with Mona and the cameraman. They went straight to the hospital, and she hurried to the entrance. She took out a compact and fingered a strand or two of hair, then put it away. The cameraman arrived with his equipment on his shoulder. He gave her a signal, and she started talking to the camera, concern on her face. Sam couldn't hear her voice, but she spoke for about a minute. When she finished, the technician stopped the action, and they entered the hospital.

Sam and J.T. waited almost half an hour before the two came out. They stopped and talked briefly, while Mona scanned the parking lot, probably looking for Ernie. Then they got into their vehicles and drove away. Sam followed them until they turned into a local television station.

"We'll probably see the story on the news tonight," Sam said.

ERNIE CHANGED THE TIRE, got back into the car and started it. Sweating, he turned the air conditioner on full blast. Before today, he hadn't had a flat in years, and hoped he didn't have another one any time soon. It looked like the stem might have rotted and broke off. The spare, one of those little temporary ones, looked as if it would work until he got the other tire fixed.

The news people had gone, and he didn't have any idea where they went. No big deal; he'd track them down. He eased out into traffic and felt the same drag on the wheels as before. Pulling over to the side of the road again, he got out and noticed that the other side of the car sagged. Further investigation revealed a second flat, the stem gone on that one, too. How could that happen? Maybe some kids did it while he waited at the restaurant. The kind of prank he might have done as a kid. He wished he'd seen them; he would've made them wish they'd picked another car. Pain throbbed behind his eyes as he felt his blood pressure rise.

There had been only one spare, so he called his auto

service and asked for a tow. This was going to put him out of commission for a couple of hours, but surely he'd have the car fixed before nightfall, so he could go back and dispose of Ruben.

It seemed like everything was crashing in on him at once. He couldn't have Ruben's big mouth splashing his name all over the news. There'd be FBI agents at his door within hours. Even worse, now they'd lost millions on a worthless resort purchase.

Ruben had said he'd checked it all out. A sure thing. They'd double their money in a few weeks. Now they find out Reston is a fake, and the money is gone, along with Reston. Hard to believe someone could put one over on them like that. Ruben! He caused all this grief. Ernie took a deep breath. At least Ruben wouldn't be causing any more problems, and Ernie had to see the bright side: if he did recover the money through some miracle, he'd keep Ruben's share, too. Ruben probably owed at least that much the way he lived, and the creditors could fight over his stuff. With the latest turn of events, Ernie thought he might go somewhere far away, maybe South America. He could run his part of the NewMood business from anywhere in the world. Ernie's head pounded, and he grabbed a plastic bottle from the glove box and took out three of the NewMood pills. That should do it. He chewed them up and swallowed, but couldn't stand the taste they left in his mouth, and walked back to the restaurant for a beer while he waited.

A half hour passed before the truck showed up, and Ernie ended up having three beers. He paid his bill and left. His headache was gone, but now he felt dizzy. While the driver hooked up his car, he climbed into the cab of the truck and fell asleep.

SAM AND J.T. went back to the Outpost Mariner on the chance that the man with the broken arm might show up. Though it was a pretty lame plan, they didn't know what else to do. They parked and waited for an hour. Even though the air conditioner ran constantly, the car remained warm, and Sam felt perspiration beading inside his shirt.

At 4:00, they decided to take a break and go for some Cuban sandwiches. Before Sam put the car into gear, a stretch Mercedes pulled up to the hotel entrance and stopped. A chauffeur got out, opened the passenger door in the rear, and a man stepped out. He wore a dark blazer, cream-colored trousers and an ascot, which seemed excessive with the summer heat. His hair, thick and silver, looked as if it had been recently styled. The man looked like someone with a billion dollars in the bank, and he hadn't aged a day since he worked a scam with Jack Craft ten years ago. Rutger Longstreet, aka "Uncle Dave."

Sam turned off the engine and he and J.T. ambled into the hotel. Dave lounged in one of the wicker chairs under a palm, reading a document of some kind. They took seats a few feet away and Sam picked up a newspaper from a stack on a nearby table. He looked over at Uncle Dave, who glanced at them and went back to his reading. His expression didn't change, and the casual observer might think them perfect strangers.

Sam looked at his watch and said to J.T., "It's been a long time since breakfast. You want to get something to eat?"

"Sure, I'm getting hungry."

"How about that place we stopped at yesterday, The Mean Manatee?"

"Yeah, that's fine."

They got up and went back to the car. Uncle Dave sauntered out of the hotel a couple minutes later and got into the Mercedes.

The restaurant, only a few blocks away, took just minutes to reach. The crowd had thinned and they asked for a table in the corner. A mural of a larger-than-life manatee covered the entire wall next to their table, its mouth open in a snarl and baring ten-inch teeth. Sam had to admit, this manatee did look pretty mean. The waiter brought menus, and they ordered two beers and a gin and tonic.

Uncle Dave entered the restaurant as the waiter set the drinks on the table. Spotting Sam and J.T., he stepped over and took a seat at their table. Glancing at the gin glass, he said, "Ah, you remembered," and he drank half of it down in one swallow.

"You're looking good, Dave," Sam said.

Dave smiled. "One does what one can."

His accent came out slightly British, and J.T. grinned.

"Where's Jack?" Sam asked.

Dave raised an eyebrow. "I wish I knew."

"When was the last time you heard from him?"

"Yesterday. He said he had been invited to a meeting, but didn't know why."

Sam nodded. "The meeting didn't end well for Jack." He recounted the phone call and then the conversation between Ernie Brent and Morris, about how Baxter had taken Jack away at gunpoint.

"Baxter did that?"

"That's what they said. Why are you surprised?"

"Oh, he just seemed like a hired gun that might not have too much upstairs." He drained his glass and caught the waiter's eye across the room. Dave was the kind of person who could do that, even in a busy restaurant. He touched the empty glass with his index finger and the waiter nodded.

"What are you guys into down here?" Sam asked.

"Yeah," J.T. said, "what happened to all that money Brent mentioned?"

Sam shot J.T. a glance that said, *Let me do the talking.*

Dave looked at J.T. and smiled. He said to Sam, "I'll let Jack tell you about all that."

"Jack can't tell us much if we don't know where to find him," Sam said.

"That is true," Dave said. The drink arrived and after the waiter left, the old guy took another healthy swallow. "But I assume you will find him. You are very good at that sort of thing. Otherwise, Jack would have called someone else."

"We need some help here, Dave. We've been looking all over the island since yesterday, and haven't seen any sign of him. And by the way, you can drop the accent."

Dave smiled at the remark, and seemed to consider Sam's plea for a couple of seconds. Either that or the fast consumption of gin had slowed his brain activity.

"I understand your dilemma," Dave said, now sounding more like someone from the Midwest, maybe Chicago. "I just don't see that knowing about our project will help you find him."

Sam took a drink of the beer and said, "Maybe not. But Jack's been gone for almost a day now. I'd say the longer it goes on, the slimmer the chance we'll ever find him."

Dave drew a deep breath and let it out. He reached into the inside pocket of his blazer, took out a business card and laid it on the table. Sam picked it up and looked at it. Large, fancy letters advertised *Sonja Lazar, Psychic*. Smaller type at the bottom indicated a phone number and a Key West address.

"What can a fortuneteller tell me about Jack?" Sam asked.

Dave shrugged. "Madame Sonja sees all." His accent back, he dragged out the words, his upper lip wrinkling as he spoke, possibly giving away something about the woman that he didn't intend to give. Then he downed his second gin and tonic, stood, and left the restaurant.

SIX

JACK SLEPT VERY little after slugging Baxter with the chair leg, afraid the man might die if left alone. An hour or so after dawn, the wounded man awoke and mumbled something about the money. After taking Baxter's car keys and gun, then retrieving his Outpost Mariner room key that Baxter had confiscated, he went out the door. The sun peeked over the crumbling tile roof of the motel as he drove the old blue Taurus onto the street.

Ernie would be looking for Baxter's car, so Jack rode around until he found a cab in front of a hotel. Leaving the Taurus in a parking space, he took the cab to the Outpost Mariner. A group got off a charter bus at the entrance as his cab arrived. He mingled into the crowd going into the lobby and went up on the elevator to his room.

Someone had taken the suitcase—probably Baxter— but Jack didn't care about that. Finding the place next to the closet where he had cut a one-inch slit in the wallpaper, he stuck his fingernail underneath, and dug out the tiny piece of paper with the numbers written on it. He left the room, went down the stairwell and out the side door to where his rented Mercedes had been parked for a couple of days.

Jack drove to US-1 and headed north, debating on whether to go back to Miami or stay and find out what went wrong. His stomach growled, reminding him that his last meal had been about twenty hours before, so he stopped at a Denny's for breakfast. After eggs, bacon and several cups of coffee, he returned to the car and drove toward Sonja's house.

He turned into the driveway and went around the garage to the back so he wouldn't be visible from the street. Sonja opened the back door when he got out of the car, and Jack went inside, sat down at the kitchen table and told her what had happened.

"I knew something had gone wrong when you didn't call last night," Sonja said. "Why don't you go upstairs and get some sleep? I'll make some calls and try to assess the damage."

"I need a drink," Jack said. "You have anything handy?"

Sonja smiled, squeezed his arm and kissed him on the cheek. Her lips felt warm and soft on his skin, and when he looked into her eyes, he wondered for a split second how he could have ever let her go.

SAM AND J.T. climbed the steps to the porch of Sonja Lazar's place. A two-story frame house, it stood on a side street near the bridge to Stock Island. Sam had expected a neon sign over the front porch that advertised "Sonja the Psychic," but saw none.

He pressed the doorbell, and it either didn't work or wasn't loud enough to be heard from the outside. Before he could try again, a woman opened the door. At least fifty, she might have been the most striking woman Sam had ever seen, with full lips and long hair the color of ripe blackberries.

"Yes, can I help you?" Her eyes seemed empty, and

she had an accent that Sam couldn't place. He wondered if it might be as fake as Uncle Dave's might be.

Sam held up the card and said a friend had given it to him.

"I am sorry, but I work by appointment only." She started to close the door.

"Please, this is really important," Sam said.

She studied them for a couple of seconds, glanced at her watch, and asked them to come inside. The living room, furnished with antiques, seemed too elegant for a fortuneteller.

"Who gave you the card?" she asked.

"He didn't tell me his name."

"I thought you said he was your friend."

"Well, we did have a friendly conversation."

She seemed to consider that and shrugged. "All right, my fee is five hundred dollars for a half-hour session."

Expensive. "Sure, that's fine."

Sonja smiled and led them into a parlor where they sat at a small table with polished leather in the center. No crystal ball.

"Is there someone you are trying to contact?"

Not bad.

"Yes, I know a man who might be in trouble."

"What is his name?"

"Does that matter?" Sam asked.

Sonja stared for a moment. "Do you have anything that belongs to him?"

"No, I'm afraid not."

She sighed. "All right then, tell me something about him."

"He's from Miami, and he lives on a boat."

"You will have to be more specific. Tell me about

his appearance." She closed her eyes and pressed her fingertips to her temples.

Sam described Jack Craft and watched Sonja's face. It remained the same, as beautiful with her eyes closed as with them open.

"Please let me concentrate." She massaged her temples for several seconds, and then opened her eyes. "I'm sorry, but I don't seem to be getting any connection with this person." She stood up. "Of course, there will be no charge."

"That's it?" Sam said. "You're giving up?"

"It happens this way sometimes."

She glanced at her watch and said her next appointment would be arriving soon.

"His name is Jack Craft." Sam thought he saw something change in her eyes but she looked away.

"Well, as I said, there is no connection, so we're wasting our time."

She stepped to the front door and opened it for them to leave. Sam looked at her one last time, searching her face for what he had seen before, but it had drained away. Her eyes were now as vacant as when he first saw them.

Sam and J.T. stepped out, and Sonja closed the door behind them.

JACK ENTERED THE living room rubbing sleep from his eyes. The sound of a car driving away had awakened him, and he had come down from the bedroom.

"Was someone here a few minutes ago?"

Sonja touched his cheek with the back of her hand and smiled. "Just two men looking for you."

"You think she was lying?" J.T. asked.

"Sure. Dave didn't send us there for nothing."

"Then why didn't you tell her he gave you the card?"

"She already knew. I could see that from the way she asked me."

J.T. chuckled. "Oh, so now you can read minds?"

Sam shrugged and turned into a shopping center. He parked close to the street so he could see Sonja's house in the distance.

"We're just going to sit here?" J.T. said.

"Yeah, for a little while. She wanted us out of her house for some reason. Maybe we'll find out why."

J.T. sighed, leaned back in the seat and said, "Aw, man."

Nothing happened for almost an hour. Then, about six o'clock, a dark car came from behind the house and turned out of the driveway onto the street. It got closer and they saw a man inside.

Sam started the engine. "That's Jack."

"It's about time," J.T. said. "This was looking like a wild goose chase. I guess I'll start calling you The Great Mackenzie, since you know so much."

Sam grinned. "Yeah, that's good. I'm glad you're finally learning something."

J.T. shot him a sidelong glance that said he could do without the comedy.

They followed Jack for several miles until he turned into a neighborhood. He pulled over to the side of the street, and Sam stopped behind him. Jack got out and walked back to the car.

Jack put his hands on the door and said through the open window, "What are you two doing here?" He looked as if he had just showered and shaved, but his eyes were hollow, with bags underneath.

"You're asking me?" Sam said.

Jack nodded with recognition. "Oh, yeah, you got the call I made."

"I got it, all right."

Jack looked up and down the street and said, "Let's go someplace where we can talk."

Sam followed Jack's car to a bar along the highway and pulled in behind him. The sign out front said "Jonesey's." They went inside and took a table in the corner. A fifty-year-old song played on the jukebox, the record scratched, clicking on every revolution. Two guys sat on stools at the bar. Both looked as if they might have been there all day, and the scratched record probably sounded just fine to them.

A white-haired bartender sauntered over to the table. He wore a stained tee shirt and his arms were covered with tattooed images of tigers and dragons, and slogans about "fighting 'til the death." The ink looked older than the song on the jukebox.

"You Jonesey?" J.T. asked.

The bartender shook his head. "Nah, that's my daddy. You want a drink or you just here to shoot the breeze?"

J.T. huffed a chuckle.

"I'll have the usual, Junior," Jack said.

The man said, "Okay, gin and tonic."

Sam and J.T. ordered beer, and Jonesey's son nodded and stepped away.

"Sounds like you've been here before," Sam said.

"Sure, a few times."

"Huh." Sam leaned back in his chair.

"Why are you surprised?" Jack asked.

"Just doesn't seem like a place you would go."

"Yes, well, maybe other people will think the same thing."

A silence dragged on for a few moments. "So," Sam said, "where have you been?"

Jack shook his head. "It's a long story. Let's have that drink first."

Normally, Jack looked pretty fit for a guy in his fifties: salt and pepper hair, a few pounds overweight, but enough muscle to carry it well. Right now, he had dark circles under his eyes.

"That bad, huh?"

"Yeah, but you know what they say. It could always get worse."

The bartender came back with the drinks. Jack took a long swallow and set the glass down. "You came to Sonja's, didn't you?"

"Yes. Where were you?"

"Upstairs asleep. I didn't wake up until about the time you left."

"She told you about us?"

Jack drained his glass and motioned for the bartender to bring another round. His eyes shone from the infusion of alcohol. The drinks arrived and Jack took another big slug before he told them the story.

Sonja Lazar had been guiding Ruben Vale in financial matters for a while, and she knew he took her advice without question. She also knew he had a lot of money, and she wanted to run a game on him and his partners.

"You knew Sonja before this?" Sam asked.

"I met her a long time ago in Singapore when she helped me and Dave with a scam on a gun runner. We stripped his bank accounts clean and put him out of business, at least for a while. We worked several other jobs together, but then she disappeared. That was almost thirty years ago, and I didn't hear from her again until she called from Key West."

Jack paused, took a drink and continued. "She said she didn't mind Dave being involved, as long as I did the front work with Ruben and Ernie. I didn't like the idea, but she talked me into it."

"How did she do that?" Sam asked.

Jack shrugged. "She can be persuasive."

Sam could understand how that might happen with a woman like Sonja, but it still surprised him a little about Jack. Apparently, they had done more than just work some jobs together.

"I sold them the Outpost Mariner and the property surrounding it, including enough land for a golf course. Do you know what a golf course might be worth in Key West?"

"A lot, I guess," Sam said.

"Yes, quite a lot."

"Who owns those properties?"

"A group in Canada. The hotel hadn't done very well, and I cut a deal with them for a three-month lease. We represented Dave as the owner, and I played the role of the broker. Sonja said Ruben wanted to get into a legitimate enterprise and start his acting career again. So after we got set up, she looked into her crystal ball and told Ruben she saw him buying a hotel on the beach and selling it a couple of months later, doubling his money."

"I didn't see a crystal ball," J.T. said.

Jack flashed him an impatient smile. "Just a figure of speech."

"So that's all it took?" Sam asked.

"That's all it took. I sent him a classy-looking e-mail advertisement the next day about properties for sale in Key West, all of which were bogus. Sonja called and told him she had a vision and described the property to him, even the address. He pulled out the brochure and, lo and behold, there it was, so he called the telephone number on the ad. I gave him a tour of the property that day, and he talked Ernie into going along. Ernie didn't seem too interested at first, but made a couple of phone calls and said he thought he could swing it. After all, it was a steal. I was offering them a 30 million dollar resort for a third of that."

"Why so cheap?" Sam asked.

"I told them it was a distress sale; owner needed money fast to take advantage of another investment."

"Okay, so what went wrong?"

Jack downed his drink and motioned for the bartender to bring another round.

"That's the funny part."

"What do you mean?"

"Nothing went wrong. I had papers drawn up by one of the best guys in the country. A work of art. Ernie even had a lawyer look them over and he passed on them."

The drinks came. Sam and J.T. still had glasses of beer from the previous round that remained half-full.

Jack took a sip of gin and tonic and said, "It looked like a go, so I let them move their offices into the penthouse. Then we consummated the sale a couple of weeks later, and they transferred the money to an account in the Caymans. Everything seemed fine until Baxter called and said they wanted to meet."

"They knew you were a phony by then?"

Jack grimaced. "Samuel, please. I like to think of myself as an artist."

"Okay, so they knew you were an artist by then?"

Jack nodded.

"What happened to the money?" J.T. asked.

Jack swirled ice in his glass, ignoring the question.

After a few seconds, Sam said, "How do you think they found out?"

"I don't know, but after the meeting they kept me in a room for a couple hours, and then Baxter came in with a gun and took me away. At first, I thought he might still be working for Ernie, but he told me later he'd been fired because I broke his arm."

"Baxter wanted the money?" Sam asked.

"Yes."

"Where is he now?"

"I left him in a motel room with a knot on his head."

It all seemed to fit. Sam knew anything Jack told him would fit, even if not completely true. Especially if not completely true.

Sam told Jack what happened to Ruben Vale and about him being in the hospital.

Jack's eyes grew large. "I don't think Sonja knows about that."

Sam shrugged. "Does it make a difference?"

"I suppose not. Ernie and Ruben being at odds doesn't hurt anything. By the way, how did you two end up at Sonja's house?"

"We ran into Dave. He wouldn't tell us anything about you, but he gave us her card."

Jack nodded and smiled.

"Did those two have something going?" Sam asked.

Jack's smile leaked away.

"Long ago, Dave and Sonja thought they were in love, but it didn't last long."

"Did you have something to do with them breaking up?"

A wistful look on his face, he said, "Maybe." Jack picked up his glass and finished his third drink. He looked at his watch. "Dave should be here by now. I called him on the way over."

"What are you going to do?" Sam asked.

"We're going to Grand Cayman."

SEVEN

Ernie awoke disoriented, slumped in the seat of the tow truck. Then he remembered what had happened to his car. The afternoon sun bore down on him through the windshield. Sitting up and wincing at his now-stiff neck, he wiped perspiration from his face with the tail of his shirt, rubbed his neck, and wondered how long he'd been there. His Mercedes sat on the edge of the lot, the tires repaired. He opened the door, got down from the cab and ambled on unsteady legs into the office.

A man sat behind the counter, punching numbers into a calculator, the machine clicking away as it printed a paper tape. He didn't seem to notice Ernie standing there. A TV played on the end of the counter with the sound turned off. On the screen, a talking head stood in front of a car wreck, his mouth moving silently. Ernie saw a bell on the counter and slapped it with the palm of his hand. The man at the calculator stopped his work and swiveled his chair around. He had "Gus" embroidered above his shirt pocket.

"Help you?"

"That's my Mercedes over there."

"Oh, yeah, we finished it a couple of hours ago. You had a lot of problems."

"I had a flat tire," Ernie said.

"Yeah, you had that, but your brakes and rotors were worn out, too. I knew you'd want them replaced."

Gus pulled a bill from under the counter and handed it to Ernie. The total amounted to eight hundred dollars. A ripoff. Ernie felt his blood pressure rising.

"You're crazy if you think I'm going to pay eight hundred dollars for a flat tire."

"Hey, buddy, I said your brakes were gone. You'll have to pay it if you want your car back."

The man reached to the counter where the TV played, picked up Ernie's car keys, and dangled them in front of him. A still image of Ruben appeared on the TV screen and caught Ernie's eye. An old picture, but Ruben just the same. It disappeared and the pretty blonde reporter he'd seen at Ruben's house stood talking in front of the hospital. She had probably gone back and found his body. Not good. He couldn't remember what he had touched while there, thinking he would come back later and clean up. He would have, too, if his tires hadn't been sabotaged, and he hadn't gone to sleep in the truck. Just bad luck, all around. Now this clown was trying to rip him off.

Ernie looked back at Gus, his head throbbing again. He turned and went out to his car, found the door unlocked, and popped the trunk lid. Reaching deep into the trunk, he pulled out a gun with a noise suppressor he'd hidden there in case he had to do something with Ruben. Of course, he didn't need it for that anymore, but he could still put it to use. He stuck it into his waistband and pulled his shirttail over it, then closed the trunk and went back into the office.

Ernie pulled out the gun, worked the slide, and fired two rounds at the calculator. *Pffttt pffttt.* The machine exploded and the paper tape flew out, dropped to the floor and rolled out the length of the little office.

"Looks like you've got a problem with your calculator. You probably need to get that fixed before adding up any more bills."

He pointed the gun at Gus's head. "Give me the keys."

"Oh, yeah, sure, take 'em," the man said, his eyes wide.

Ernie grabbed the keys with his free hand.

"You didn't repair anything but the tire, did you?"

"Well…"

Ernie shook the tip of the gun at him. "You better not lie to me."

"No, no we didn't."

"Okay, for trying to cheat me, you have to pay a penalty."

He stepped around the counter and saw a cash drawer pulled open part of the way. He jerked it out, took the money and stuffed it into his pocket.

"Hey, that's all I collected today."

Ernie pointed the gun toward his face and fired. A crimson spatter the size of a garbage can lid appeared on the wall behind Gus as a piece of his ear disappeared. Blood oozed from the side of his head. He screamed and clapped his hand over the wound.

"Okay," Ernie said, "you call the cops about this and I'll come back and put a hole in your head. You understand?"

"Yeah, yeah, no cops." Gus sat down, taking quick breaths. He looked as if he might cry.

Ernie flipped the safety, put the gun back in his waistband, and went out the door. He had to figure out what to do. The law might already be looking for him for killing Ruben. Maybe he would drive home to get a few things, and clean out the bank account in case he had to run. Ruben had talked him into investing a lot of money. Money he didn't have to invest. He could disappear permanently, if he could get that back, but first, he would have to find Reston.

He started the car and pulled into the street, then took out his phone and saw he'd missed a call, probably while sleeping in the truck. He called the number and Morris answered. Ernie asked if he'd found Reston yet.

"I sure did."

"Where is he?"

"Right now, he's inside Jonesey's Bar with two other guys. I went by the psychic's place, in case he might be in cahoots with her, and sure enough, he came driving out a few minutes later."

"Okay, stay there, I'm on my way."

So the psychic had been involved. Maybe Morris had more sense than Ernie had thought. Well, maybe a little, but not much. Ernie had told him a week or so ago he didn't trust her. Morris must have remembered that and gone by her place. Big deal. Still, Ernie thought his luck might be changing.

DAVE HAD BEEN there about ten minutes when Sam said, "It looks like you guys have everything under control. I think I'll head back to Miami."

He stood up to leave.

Jack frowned. "We might need you if Ernie goes berserk on us."

Sam shook his head. He didn't want to get any more involved in Jack's scam than he had already. "I've got some things to do."

Jack leaned back in his chair and sighed. "Are you sure, I'll make it worth your while."

Sam laid some bills on the table to cover his drinks. "Yeah, I'm sure."

"You could have a free trip to Grand Cayman."

"No, thanks."

"I'll stay," J.T. said.

Jack looked at Dave and Dave nodded.

"Okay," Jack said to J.T. He turned to Sam. "If you have to go, give me your phone number again, in case we need you. I had it on my speed dial, but Ernie took my phone."

Sam told him the number and Jack wrote it down.

Jack said J.T. could ride with him, so Sam left them there and went to his car. He headed north on US-1 and thought he would stop in Key Largo for dinner.

ERNIE ARRIVED AT Jonesey's and parked next to Morris' car. He lowered his window and Morris told him one of the men with Reston had just left.

"Okay, go see if you can catch up with him. I'll wait on the other guys."

Reston and two other men came out of the bar about ten minutes later. Reston had called one of them Stanford, and represented him as the seller of the hotel. Now, Ernie knew that had to have been a sham. He didn't think someone who owned the Outpost Mariner would hang out at Jonesey's. Ernie knew the other guy, a tall man with a ponytail, from someplace before, but he couldn't remember where. Then he recalled seeing him in the hotel bar. He and another guy. Probably the one Morris followed.

Stanford got into a car by himself and Ponytail rode with Reston. Both cars went in the same direction, and Ernie followed. A few minutes later, they turned onto

Government Road and headed toward Key West International Airport. They probably planned to fly away with the money, but that wasn't going to happen.

SAM APPROACHED THE Stock Island Bridge when his phone chirped. He thought it might be Jack calling to try to change his mind, but it wasn't. The number looked familiar, and then he remembered.

"Hello."

"Is this the good Samaritan?"

"I've been called worse," Sam said.

Mona Miles laughed. "I'll bet you have."

"How's Ruben Vale doing?"

"Unconscious, but the doctor in ER said he'll probably be okay. If Ruben hadn't called when he did, he'd be dead. That must have been you who called."

"I don't know what you're talking about."

"Yeah, okay. How about meeting me for a drink if you're still in town?"

A drink with Mona Miles, as opposed to driving the car for the next three hours or so. She would try to pick his brain about what happened to Ruben. That would be okay, because he didn't know much.

"Sure, I could use a drink."

HE ENTERED THE RESTAURANT, and spotted her waiting at a table overlooking the Gulf, talking on a cell phone. She wound up her conversation as Sam approached the table. A full drink sat in front of her, but judging by the wet coaster, it had been there a few minutes.

Sam sat down at her invitation, taking a chair across from her. A waiter appeared and Sam ordered a beer.

"Thanks for the tip on Ruben."

He shrugged. "I just wanted to make sure you weren't in danger."

"I saw the man you mentioned sitting in his car with the engine running when I left the restaurant. Ernie Brent?"

Nodding, Sam said, "You might want to do some research on him."

"You think he's dangerous?"

"Probably."

The waiter brought the beer and left. Mona took a drink from her glass and dabbed her lips with a napkin. She looked even more beautiful than she had earlier in the day.

"I really need to know more about what happened."

Sam smiled. "I saw you taping in the parking lot at the hospital."

She stared for a moment. "You followed me?"

"Yeah. I guess you'll be on the local news."

She checked her watch. "It aired a few minutes ago as a bulletin, and will be on the news in more detail tonight."

"Sounds like you got a pretty good story." Sam sampled the beer.

She shrugged. "The interviews with Ruben were worthless. But if Ernie tried to kill him, I might be able to use that."

Sam mentioned the article he'd seen about Ernie's brush with the law. "He probably wouldn't want Ruben talking about their business on a TV show."

"Well, he told me all about how they'd made a fortune selling things on the Internet. Said they were pioneers at doing that, and that's how they made it so big."

"Yeah, and the margin might be a little better if the merchandise is stolen."

She took a sip from her glass and sighed. "But it doesn't seem like Ernie would have tried to kill him over that."

"Maybe he had another reason."

"Oh, yeah?" She glanced out over the Gulf.

Though she was trying to look disinterested, Sam knew she was playing him. He might play her a little, too. "Just thinking out loud."

The waiter appeared at the table and asked if they wanted to order dinner. Sam said they might later, and the man left. Mona seemed different. Maybe she'd done something to her hair, or put on some new makeup. Then he noticed the earrings dangling from her lobes. They were gold and spiral-shaped, like seashells, and they glistened in the half-light. He wondered if she'd worn them because of the meeting with him.

"What do you mean?" She seemed more eager now.

Sam shrugged. "Maybe they lost a lot of money and Ernie blamed Ruben."

She nodded. "That might do it. How much money are you talking about?"

"Like I said, just thinking out loud."

"Oh, yeah, but if that were really the case, how much would it be?"

"Millions."

Her eyes went wide and Sam smiled. They talked another few minutes and he finished his beer.

"Gotta go." He put money on the table for the drinks and stood to leave.

She got up, too, and followed him outside.

"Aren't you going to tell me how they lost the millions?"

The sun sagged on the horizon, the air still hot and muggy. Sam heard a rock band nearby. He listened a couple of moments before pulling out his keys.

"That's only speculation," he said over his shoulder, heading for the car.

"Yes, but..." Her voice trailed off when a man stepped in front of them, blocking their path. It was the man Ernie had called Morris. He had a shiny sport jacket draped over his right hand. It was also draped over most of a gun barrel that was pointed at Sam.

Mona grabbed Sam's arm and squeezed.

"That's a gun!" Her voice was almost a whisper and laced with panic.

"Yeah, I see that."

Morris said to Sam, "Get in the car."

"Where're we going?"

"That's none of your business. Just get in." He pointed the gun at Mona. "You, too, lady."

Sam wondered why this might be happening and decided Morris must have seen him with Jack at the bar. That probably meant Jack had a tail, too.

Sam smiled. "You think you can hold that gun on me while you're driving?"

Morris looked as if he hadn't considered that. Then a light seemed to come on and he said, "No, you're going to drive."

"Okay."

Morris' eyelids drooped and his face sagged. Ernie had jumped on his case about letting Jack get away, and he'd probably been up all night worrying about it. However, that wasn't Sam's problem, and Morris shouldn't have pulled the gun on him.

Sam dropped his car keys at the guy's feet. They

made a jingle on the asphalt and Morris glanced down for a split second. Long enough. Sam struck the gun hand with the side of his left fist, knocking it away, and slammed him between the eyes with his other fist. Morris' head snapped back, and his eyes widened before rolling up behind the lids. He dropped to the asphalt like a fainting drunk.

Sam took the gun from his hand and flipped the safety. He looked around and saw a man and a woman at the restaurant entrance staring his way.

"Let's get out of here."

They went to his car and he opened the door. Mona stayed right behind him and had hold of his arm again, digging in with her fingernails.

"Shouldn't we call the police?"

"No, let's not do that."

"Why not? He planned to rob us, and no telling what else."

"He wouldn't have robbed us. He works for Ernie."

Mona took a second to digest that and glanced at the couple still standing at the doorway.

"Can I ride with you? I'll get my car later."

"Sure."

She got in his door and pushed over to the other side. Sam drove away from the restaurant and Mona said, "That happened so fast. One second, I had visions of him killing us, and the next he lay unconscious on the ground. How did you do that?" She sounded nervous, her voice at a higher pitch than before.

"Probably just got lucky."

EIGHT

SAM TOLD MONA he needed to make a call and pulled the car over. He got out, eased over to a palm tree next to the sidewalk, and punched in the number for J.T.'s cell phone.

"You in Miami yet?" J.T. asked.

"No, I decided to hang around here tonight and go back tomorrow."

Sam told him what had happened with Morris. "I figure Morris saw us go into Jonesey's bar, and probably the only reason he would've followed me when I left is if Ernie's watching you and Jack."

"Well, we haven't seen him. We're in a hangar at the airport. Jack chartered a plane to fly us to Grand Cayman, and we're supposed to leave in about thirty minutes."

"What for?"

"He was pretty tight-lipped about it, but he did say there might be some trouble, and wanted me to go along."

Sam glanced at the car and saw Mona staring at him, probably wondering who he had called. He had said they would go somewhere to dinner before heading back to the restaurant to get her car. That would give Morris enough time to wake up and leave.

"Well, you should be on the lookout for him," Sam said, "just in case."

"Yeah, okay, I'll tell Jack…" his voice trailed off, and then he said, "uh-oh."

"What is it?"

"Ernie just came in, and he's got a gun."

J.T. remained quiet for several seconds. Sam kept the phone to his ear and got back into the car. Mona gave him a questioning look, but didn't say anything. He started the engine, pulled into traffic, and pressed the accelerator.

Sam heard Ernie telling someone, probably J.T., to hand over his gun. Then Ernie said, "Gimme that." The connection died a couple of seconds later. Sam closed his phone and dropped it into his shirt pocket.

"Is everything okay?" Mona asked.

"I've got to go to the airport. I'll drop you at your car on the way."

"What's the problem?"

He glanced at her and could see the stress in her eyes. "It's nothing for you to worry about."

"Does it involve Ernie?"

"Yes."

"Okay, I want to go with you."

"Sorry, this could get dangerous."

"What do you call what happened back there at the restaurant?"

Sam sighed. "Okay, but Ernie has a gun and he's probably ticked off."

A silence stretched into a couple of seconds before she said, "That's fine; I'm going anyway."

Sam drove as fast as he could in the light traffic, exceeding the speed limit by twenty or more miles per hour and passing cars when they got in his way. He turned onto Government Road and a couple minutes later, the aircraft hangars rose in the distance. Passing by a couple of them, he spotted Ernie's Mercedes parked on the street next to a tall chain-link fence and pulled in behind it.

"Stay here," he said to Mona. "I'll be back in a few minutes."

"Forget it. I'm going in, too." She opened the door and got out of the car.

"Okay, your funeral."

She gave him a funny look as he pulled a Smith and Wesson 9mm from his pocket.

"Let's go."

Hurrying through an open gate in the fence, he saw the side door of the hangar standing ajar. He looked at Mona and held a finger to his lips. She nodded, and he leaned to the edge of the door so he could hear the voices inside.

"What makes you think you got scammed?" Jack.

"Hey, I don't care what you call it," Ernie said. "I want my money back."

"It was quite a fair deal," Dave said with his best accent.

"Shut up. I know a slime ball when I see one. You didn't own that hotel. I don't know how you made it look like you did, but I know you're all a bunch of crooks."

Ernie's voice sounded almost hurt. Probably no one had ever tried to cheat him, even though he had built his fortune on crime.

Sam peered around the edge of the doorway. Ernie held a gun on them. Turning back to Mona, Sam signaled for her to stay back, and then stepped into the hangar and pointed his gun at the back of Ernie's head.

"Lay the gun on the floor," Sam said.

Ernie jerked around, his face twisted into a grimace.

"Lay it down, now!" Sam said, louder this time.

"Okay, okay, already." Ernie sighed, bent down, and put the gun on the floor.

"Back away from it."

J.T. picked up the gun. Ernie smiled at something behind Sam, and he turned and saw Mona, her eyes large and full of terror. A man with a bandage on his head and his arm in a sling held a gun on her.

"Man, you couldn't have come at a better time," Ernie said.

The man pushed Mona into the hangar with his gun hand and said, "You're forgetting something, aren't you?"

"What's that, buddy?"

"You fired me, remember?"

"Just a misunderstanding. You're rehired, with a bonus for today."

The man with the bandage sneered. "Just like that, huh?"

"Baxter, be a sport. Things happen, you know. I'll make it right. Okay?"

Baxter took a deep breath and looked as if he might be thinking about it, then said, "Okay, but I'll be watching you. Get his gun."

Ernie took it and put it into his pocket, then looked at Mona.

"Well, if it ain't the news broad."

Jack glanced at Mona and smiled.

"You're Mona Miles," Jack said. "I watch you on TV all the time."

Mona looked at Jack as if he might be a leper.

"Shut up," Ernie said, his eyes narrow, his mouth pinched at one corner. "This ain't a fan club meeting."

Ernie stepped over to Mona and stood a few inches away, his face close to hers.

"What'd you do with the movie?"

"What movie?" Mona asked.

"The movie with Ruben telling you about our business."

Mona rolled her eyes. "You've got to be kidding. Interviewing Ruben is like talking to a four-year-old. He went on and on about his mansion on the beach and how wealthy he is. Nobody's going to air that."

"Really, you think so?" Ernie said.

"Trust me. It's garbage."

Ernie grinned, as if that might have made his day. He turned and looked at Jack.

"So, con man, where were you planning to go in this airplane?"

Jack smiled. The "con man" reference hadn't bothered him in the least.

"Grand Cayman."

"Grand Cayman? Sounds like you might be visiting a bank."

"Yes, we have some loose ends to tie up down there."

"Loose ends." Ernie chuckled. "That's pretty funny. You call cashing out my money, 'loose ends'?"

Jack shrugged.

Ernie turned and peered at the airplane waiting outside the hangar. A large turboprop. He said to Baxter, "Go get the pilot."

Baxter grimaced. "Hey, you can't order me around like you did before. We're partners now."

Ernie narrowed his eyes. "You ain't a partner unless I say so. You got that?"

Baxter sneered, his face red.

After a couple of beats, Ernie sighed and said to Jack, "Go get the pilot. Tell him we're all going along."

Jack strode to the office in the rear. He stayed inside a few seconds before coming back out with a man wearing a pilot's uniform and carrying a clipboard.

"You said there were only three passengers," the pilot said. "There are seven people here."

"Yes, well, our plans have changed. Can't you just add them?"

The man looked at his clipboard for a couple of seconds, as if he might need to do more paperwork. He gave Jack a stare. "Okay, but the price will be more. Extra weight and all that, you know."

"Sure, that's fine. Just charge it to the card I gave you."

Walking back toward the office, the pilot said over his shoulder, "We'll leave as soon as the plane is fueled."

Jack looked Sam's way and winked. What could he be up to?

Ernie told Baxter to watch the group, and he stepped to the front of the hangar with his cell phone in his hand. Sam saw him make a call and talk to someone, but couldn't hear his voice. A few minutes later, he stuck the phone into his pocket and came back. He had a smile on his face. Not a pleasant sight.

THE FLIGHT TO Grand Cayman smoothed out once they ascended above the clouds. Jack managed to sit next to Mona and kept her ear bent for the whole trip. Sam sat next to Dave, who didn't want to talk about anything.

When they landed in Grand Cayman, two cars sat waiting. When they deplaned, Ernie went over and spoke to one of the drivers, calling him Cal, as if he might know him. The other driver stood a couple of inches taller than Sam. His nose a lump of scar tissue, he looked like an ex-boxer about thirty years past his prime.

Ernie rode with Jack, J.T., and Dave, while Baxter rode with Sam and Mona. After they left the airport, Sam leaned forward and looked past Mona at Baxter.

"You know you can't trust that guy."

Baxter snorted. "Yeah, you're telling me. Who are *you*, anyway?"

"Mona and I just got caught in the middle of this. We don't have anything to do with it."

Baxter looked at Mona, his eyes lingering a few seconds before breaking away. "I guess you just decided to hold up Ernie and score a little extra cash, huh?"

"I thought he might do them like he did Ruben," Sam said, ignoring the remark.

"What'd he do to Ruben?"

"Put him in the hospital with a hole in his head." Sam didn't see the need to mention that it might have been an accident. "He would've died without medical attention."

"I didn't hear anything about that."

"On the news today. Mona did the story. You'll never see any of that money."

"What makes you so sure?"

"I've known a lot of guys like Ernie. In the end, they always want it all."

Baxter remained silent for a while, gazing out his window at the silhouettes of palms against the moonlit sky. Then he said to the window, "Yeah, well, just keep your opinion to yourself."

They arrived at a house a few minutes before midnight. The driveway curved by a palatial front entrance and led to a four-car garage. The other car had already arrived.

Mona leaned over and whispered into Sam's ear, "Your friend Daniel is quite a guy. He told funny stories on the plane to keep me from getting upset."

Sam had been trying to decide what his next move might be, and it took him a second to figure out that Jack had introduced himself to Mona as Daniel Reston, preserving his cover.

"Yeah… Daniel, he's a laugh a minute."

She gave him a quizzical look.

Baxter scooted over on the seat and got out of the car behind them. He nudged Sam in the back with his gun, pushing him toward the door.

One of the drivers led them to a large living room. A patio door overlooked a lighted backyard with a pool surrounded by palms. Lights also shone from underneath the water, casting everything in a warm aqua tint. A man with bushy red hair sat at a table by the pool, facing the other way. Next to the table stood a muscle-bound man wearing a T-shirt with the sleeves cut out, red and blue tattoos running down his arms from his shoulders to his fingers.

The man who looked like a boxer pointed toward the patio door and said to Ernie, "He wants you to come out and see him by the pool." His words wheezed out like notes from a leaky accordion.

Sam watched through the glass as the man with red hair turned to look inside. A shiver of recognition ran up his neck.

NINE

DELRAY JINKS AND Sam had worked for the same company several years before, doing contract jobs for the government, most of which were illegal. Though Delray had said he came from California, Sam suspected he had emigrated from somewhere in Europe, judging from his lingering accent. He frequently boasted about his kills on previous jobs. The guys in the unit pegged him as a bigmouth, but Sam guessed he had done everything he'd said he had, if not more, and he might have enjoyed it. His eyes looked empty, except for a feral flash when he smiled.

They had partnered once on a mission to shut down a factory that made assault weapons known to be used by criminals around the world. Their intelligence said the place had closed that day and all the workers were gone. Sam and Delray were assigned to sweep the area before the demolition team set the charges. If they encountered any security personnel, their instructions were to bring them in. There were to be no casualties. Delray didn't return as scheduled, and then a couple of shots were fired. He showed up a few minutes later, and said a sentry on the south end of the perimeter tried to fire on him and had to be eliminated.

The company overlooked that incident, but Delray became involved with several other similar shootings within a few months, and earned a reputation for being trigger-happy. Then one day, he didn't show up for work, and the unit leader said he'd quit. Sam wondered if he'd left on his own, or got fired.

Sam heard later that Delray, definitely alive, had come into possession of a truckload of prescription painkillers and had set up channels for distribution. He targeted celebrities and professional athletes with a steady appetite for the drugs and the money to pay.

From the looks of the place on Grand Cayman, Sam guessed his former colleague had found more trucks. Knocking over pharmaceutical companies probably proved to be a lot easier than stealing from drug lords. Given Ernie's background in stolen property, he might have helped arrange some of Delray's procurements.

Ernie went out the patio door and walked over to the table. The redheaded man pointed to an empty chair and Ernie sat down. Tattoo Man poured drinks from a cart next to the table and headed inside.

Sam and the others waited in the living room. The Boxer served drinks, and they had a couple before Ernie and Delray finished their talk and came in the door. Delray scanned the crowd and his eyes settled on Sam. He ambled over to him.

"Mackenzie, how's it going, man?"

Sam gave him a questioning look. "You tell me."

Delray turned to Ernie, who stood a few feet away. "Me and Mackenzie used to work together." He eyed Mona and whistled. "Who's the babe?"

"She's the TV broad that did the interview with Ruben," Ernie said.

Delray moved closer and introduced himself. Mona pushed back in her seat, her fingers digging into Sam's arm. The redheaded man held her gaze for a couple of seconds, like a cat preparing to pounce. He stepped back and spoke to The Boxer. "Joe, take everybody but Mackenzie and the babe back to the big guest room. Give 'em a sandwich and some booze, and make sure nobody leaves."

"Hey, wait a minute," Baxter said. "I'm with Ernie."

"That true?"

Ernie nodded. "Yeah, he is."

"Okay, you can stay, too."

Joe herded Jack, J.T. and Dave down the hallway, and Delray took a seat in a chair across from Mona.

"So, Mackenzie, I thought you might be dead by now."

Sam smiled. "Funny, I thought the same about you."

"No, dude. I been living the life."

"Yeah, I heard about the truck full of drugs you knocked off."

Delray looked at Mona, then back at Sam. A tic snapped at the corner of his eye for a couple of beats.

"You must've heard wrong. I didn't steal nothing. My business is strictly legit."

They remained silent for a few moments before Delray said, "Whatever happened to Raker, the unit leader?"

They had found Raker's body a few days after Delray's departure. Shot in the face with his own 9mm handgun. Deemed a freak accident at the time, Sam now realized Delray had probably killed the man.

"He died, about the time you left."

"Huh. That's too bad." Delray smiled, the scaly creature slithering in his eyes. "What's this business about taking our money?"

So he had been in on the deal, too. Was it a coincidence that Jack wanted to come to Grand Cayman for the money, or had there been another reason? Sam didn't believe in coincidences. Besides, he remembered Jack's wink at the airport when Ernie had forced his way into the trip.

"Got me. Mona and I just happened to be in the wrong place."

"That's a load of crap!" Ernie said. "He pulled a gun on me. He would've gotten the drop if the man here with the broken arm hadn't come along."

"Huh," Delray said. He looked back at Sam for a few seconds, and then turned to Ernie. "So, what do you want me to do?"

"Just watch these Bozos while I go with Reston to get the money."

"Reston's the old guy?" Delray asked.

Ernie nodded. "Yeah, he's the ringleader."

"Okay, but we got to get that money back, like yesterday, and I know a few people around here that could grease the skids if you need it."

Ernie shook his head.

"That won't be necessary. I overheard Reston say he's meeting a woman tomorrow morning at the bank to complete the transaction. I figure it's the fortune-teller, and they'd planned to split the money and go their separate ways. Of course, they didn't know I would be there to take it. If everything works like it ought to, we'll have everything back before noon."

Delray talked another few minutes, telling Mona about a newspaper reporter he'd known a few years earlier in Miami.

"I gave the guy all his stories and helped him get

on his feet." He told her the man's name and asked if she knew him.

She shook her head. "Doesn't ring a bell."

"Huh. I figured he's the head guy by now."

Mona shrugged. "Sorry."

By then, Joe had returned. Delray told him to put Mona in a separate bedroom.

"I want to be in the room with him," Mona said, pointing at Sam.

"You sure?" Delray said. "Mackenzie's a dangerous man."

She squeezed Sam's arm. "I'll take my chances."

Joe came in a few minutes later and told them the food was ready. They ate in the dining room and listened to Delray talk some more.

"You ever have lobster like this, Mona?" Delray asked.

"Yeah. These are pretty good."

"I get 'em fresh off the boat, dirt cheap. Shrimp and crab, too. Eat all you want. I got more in the kitchen."

Mona patted her lips with a napkin and said she'd had enough. Delray looked disappointed and poured more wine.

Ernie's face turned red and he kept rubbing his temples. Finally, he reached into his pocket, pulled out a small plastic container and took two pills from it. He washed them down with another glass of wine.

"Doctor's orders," he said. "I got a condition."

Sam wondered what the pills were. Ernie's words began to slur. After a few minutes, he laid his head on the table and snored.

"That's where he's sleeping tonight," Delray said,

a note of resentment in his tone. "*I* ain't carrying him anywhere."

Joe took Sam and Mona to a guest room toward the rear of the house and left them there. Sam wondered if someone would stay outside all night. It really didn't matter, because he didn't plan to go anywhere. Locking the door, he turned and saw Mona peering at the king-sized bed.

"I hope you didn't get the wrong idea about me being in the room with you. I just thought that would be the safest alternative."

Sam had guessed that might be the only reason, but it disappointed him to have her confirm it so quickly.

"Sure, I'll take the floor. I think I could sleep anywhere right now."

Mona gave him a pained smile. "That's not necessary. This is a big bed. Just stay on your side."

"Okay, fine with me."

They agreed to turn off the lights before undressing and getting into bed.

About a minute later Mona said, "So, what's your first name, Mackenzie?"

"Sam."

"Hmm, Sam. I guess that fits you pretty well. You really do know what's going on here, don't you?"

"Part of it."

"Is Daniel some sort of con man?"

Sam sighed. He didn't see any reason to lie to her.

"You might say that."

"He's your friend?"

"I guess."

"You don't seem too sure."

"I've known him a long time, and he's caused me a

lot of trouble over the years. But he's a pretty good guy, and occasionally he does something that surprises me."

"What about Delray? Is he a pretty good guy, too?"

"No, the less you have to do with Delray the better."

"Why is that?"

"People die when he's around."

SAM WOKE TO light coming through the window and the shower running. He got up, put on his pants and opened the door to the hallway. A tray lay on the floor with two plates of eggs and bacon and two cups of coffee. He took it inside, set it on a small table with two chairs alongside, and closed and relocked the door.

Mona came out of the bathroom dressed in the clothes she'd worn the day before, but looking as fresh as a flower. The sight of the tray brought a smile and she said, "Good morning." The rays from the window shone through her golden hair like a halo.

"Cream or sugar?"

"Yes, both. Thanks."

He felt as though he'd been dragged through a swamp, and probably looked the same way.

Mona took a sip of the coffee, set it down and grimaced. "I hope I didn't keep you awake last night. I usually turn and twist in my sleep."

Sam shrugged. "No, you were fine."

"So Daniel is going to meet this woman at the bank, and they'll…what?"

"I suppose they planned to show IDs to the banker and give him two account numbers where they want the money sent. Ernie probably has a different idea about what they'll do now, though."

Mona nodded. "Ernie said the woman is a fortune-teller. Do you know her?"

"I met her. The name she's using is Sonja Lazar. She has a place near the bridge to Stock Island."

"What does she have to do with anything?"

"I really don't know, but I think she and Ja-a-a…uh, Daniel, share some history."

Mona looked at him and smiled, as if she thought he might be keeping something from her. "You think they'll let us go free after that?"

Sam shrugged. "I hope so. But I'm sure Ernie has darker plans for the people who took his money."

"You mean Daniel and this Sonja Lazar?"

"Yep."

"What about the other guy, the one who looks like a duke or something, and the big guy with the ponytail?"

"Dave is the duke. Ernie might have a problem with letting him go, too, because he probably played a big part in the deal. J.T. came to Key West with me, so there's no reason for anyone to be angry with him, except for him being with them when Ernie got to the airport."

Mona remained quiet for several moments. Sam watched her looking down at her plate, absently stirring her food.

"Everybody should be safe until Ernie gets his money."

She looked up from her plate. "He said he'll get it back this morning."

Sam smiled and shook his head. "He's dreaming."

"Why do you say that?"

"I know Daniel pretty well, and I'd be willing to bet he's already got a new plan."

She paused for a second or two. "Daniel isn't his real name, is it?"

So she *had* caught his misstep earlier. He didn't feel like lying to her about it.

"No. His name is Jack Craft, and I hope you know you'll never be able to use any of this on TV. He wouldn't let you do that."

"What do you mean? Last night you said he's a pretty good guy."

"Yeah, he is, but he didn't live as long as he has by letting things like that happen."

"You're saying he can get mean if he needs to?"

"Yes, he can."

She nodded and said, "That's fine, because all I want to do is get out of this mess."

"Don't worry, we're going to get out of it."

She reached across the table and touched his hand. "You promise?"

Her blue eyes had acquired a moist sheen, and he felt his breath catch, as if deep sea diving with an empty air tank.

"I promise," he said.

Sam wondered if he really believed it, or if he just said what the beautiful woman wanted to hear. Attachments usually made situations like this more dangerous. On the positive side, though, he made few promises, and knew he would do everything he could to keep from breaking one.

He got up. "I think I'll check out that shower myself."

He used a fresh razor and toothbrush from the cabinet, showered, and came out fifteen minutes later.

TEN

JOE ESCORTED SAM and Mona to the living room about 8:00 a.m. Jack, Dave and J.T. were already there, having cups of coffee on the sofa. Ernie and Baxter sat in chairs nearby. Ernie's eyes were bloodshot. Sam and Mona took the loveseat, and she laced her arm inside his.

Delray stood looking out the sliding glass doors. A yacht lazed in the sound a hundred feet or so beyond the pool. Sam wondered if it belonged to him. The Caribbean glistened in the distance, like a raw emerald awaiting the jeweler's chisel.

Ernie leaned forward in his chair and put his elbows on his knees. "Okay, this is the plan. Me and Baxter'll go to the bank with Reston and meet the fortuneteller. She's supposed to be there at 11:00, so what we're gonna do is catch her in the parking lot and let her know the jig is up. Then we'll all go into the bank, and Reston and the fortuneteller will give the bank guy some kind of identification." Ernie glanced at Jack. "That's what you're supposed to do, right?"

Jack nodded. "Something like that."

"What do you mean? Either it is or it's not. Which is it?"

"We each have the same account number, but a different PIN, and neither of us knows the other's PIN. We have to enter the numbers into a computer and show the banker the result. Then he'll let us do whatever we want with the money."

Ernie pulled a piece of paper out of his pocket and handed it to Jack. "Tell him to send the money to this account number."

Jack took it and looked it over.

"You clear on that?" Ernie asked.

Smiling, Jack said, "Sure, but what if I won't do it?"

"It's pretty simple. If you don't do it, I call Delray here, and he takes all your friends on a little pleasure cruise. Only they won't be on the boat for the return trip."

Jack glanced at Sam, and then looked back at Ernie. "Okay, I guess you've got me."

Baxter cleared his throat and said, "Yeah, but what about the fortuneteller?"

"What about her?" Ernie asked.

"What if she balks at the idea? She probably couldn't care less about these people."

Ernie grimaced. "Yeah, that's a good point." He thought for a few seconds and smiled. "Okay, change of plan. We meet her in the parking lot, like I said before, only we put a gun to her head and get her PIN number. Then we tie her up and leave her in the car. The news broad can go with us and put on a wig and do her part in the bank."

Mona gasped. "I can't do that."

Ernie grinned. "Sure you can, unless you want Lover Boy and the rest of these guys to take that cruise I mentioned."

Mona made a face and squeezed down close to Sam. Sam didn't like the idea, but knew Delray would have no problem doing what Ernie had said, and Mona might be safer going along with Jack.

JACK AND MONA rode in the back seat of Delray's stretch limousine. Ernie and Baxter rode in the seat facing them and Joe drove the car. Joe had gone out and brought back a wig for Mona, and she looked good as a brunette. No surprise to Jack. She would look good with a dust mop on her head. Though Delray didn't seem to know anything about computers, Cal had an elaborate system in the house, and he used it to produce a good facsimile of a Florida driver's license, with a picture of Mona wearing the wig and Sonja Lazar's name on it.

They got to the bank at 10:30 and waited for Sonja to arrive. At 10:50, Ernie began to fidget in his seat.

"Okay, where is she?"

"Maybe her flight got delayed leaving Miami, or she's stuck in traffic," Jack said.

Ernie looked at his watch. "You said she would be here by now."

"That was the plan. Something must have happened to her."

Ernie fumed for a couple of minutes. He took some pills. "Okay, smart guy, how are we going to get that money if she don't show?"

Jack shook his head. "We have to have Sonja's PIN."

"That's pretty stupid. What if she got killed or something? You didn't think of that?"

Jack smiled. "Actually, we chose to have separate PINs to lessen the chance of that happening."

Ernie shrugged. "Yeah, well, we're going in anyway. You can tell them she lost her PIN. She's a pretty girl. They'll give it to her."

"That isn't going to work," Jack said.

"We'll see about that." Ernie raised his gun and pointed it at them. "Get out of the car."

Jack and Mona went into the bank, with Ernie following close behind, and strode to the manager's office. A short man with gray hair, whose nameplate identified him as Henry Wells, stood up when they appeared at his door.

"Is there something I can do for you?" Wells asked with the hint of an English accent.

"My name is Daniel Reston," Jack said, "and this is Sonja Lazar. We need to complete a banking transaction."

The manager's eyes widened. "What sort of transaction?"

"A funds transfer to another bank."

After studying Jack's face for a moment, he said, "Please have a seat. I'll need to see some identification."

The three of them sat, leaving Ernie standing just inside the door. Jack and Mona pulled out their Florida licenses and showed them to the manager. Wells examined the laminated documents, then removed his glasses and stared, alarm pinching at his eyes.

Putting his license away, Jack said, "Is there a problem?"

"Yes, I'm afraid there is. A Daniel Reston and a Sonja Lazar were already here this morning. They transferred a very large sum of money and left an hour ago. If they were not the real depositors, a crime has been committed. Please give me your identification. I'll have to call the police."

He held out one hand for the IDs and picked up the phone with the other.

Jack glanced at Mona, who looked as if she might

cry, then at Ernie, who narrowed his eyes and ran his hand into his pocket to his gun.

Jack stood. "This is an outrage! You've given our money to impostors, and now you're treating us as if we've done something wrong. I'll see what the Prime Minister has to say about this." He took his cell phone from his pocket, pressed a couple of buttons and held it to his ear.

Wells looked as if he might have a coronary and dropped the phone into its cradle. "Mr. Reston, wait!"

Jack closed his eyes for a moment, sighed, and hung up his phone.

"I don't understand how this could happen," Jack said. "Didn't you check their identification?"

"Yes, they had all the proper credentials."

"Very well, I suppose there's nothing else we can do here now. My attorney will be in touch within the hour."

Mona stood, and they turned to leave.

"But…the police will want to talk with you."

"I'll be at the Ritz-Carlton." They strode from the office and through the sumptuous lobby. By the time they stepped out of the bank, Ernie had already reached the limo.

As they drove away, Ernie popped a small handful of pills into his mouth, swallowed, and pinched his face into a sneer. "Looks like the fortuneteller double-crossed you."

Jack sighed. "Yes, it certainly looks that way."

Ernie pulled the gun from his pocket and rested it on his knee, his finger on the trigger.

"You better tell me you know how to find her."

ELEVEN

THE HOSPITAL PATIENT opened his eyes and looked around the room. An IV tube hung from his arm. He sat up a bit, but his head spun, so he lay back, then touched two fingers to his temple and felt a thick layer of gauze above his ear.

The sun beamed through the window at the foot of the bed, so it must be daytime, but that didn't tell him much. There seemed to be nothing but blank space in his head.

Although he wanted to go home, he wondered why he couldn't picture it in his mind or remember how to get there. A phone book for the Key West area lay on the bedside table. He picked it up to look for his name, and discovered he couldn't remember that, either.

For several minutes, he lay there, looking at the ceiling, trying to focus his aching mind.

A nurse stepped into the room with a chart in her hand. "Well, you're finally awake. I'll bet you're hungry." She raised the head of his bed. No dizziness.

"How long have I been here?"

"Since yesterday. You had a pretty hard knock on the head, but you were lucky. Just a slight concussion. A few days of bed rest and you'll be fine."

He started to ask her if she knew his name, but decided that might not be a good idea. Besides, it would come to him. Lunch arrived a few minutes later and he ate. When he finished, he decided to try sitting up on the side of the bed. It worked okay this time, and he got to his feet.

The IV tube tugged at his arm, so he peeled off the tape and pulled out the needle. Unsteady legs took him to a closet that contained some clothes and a pair of shoes. His pockets were empty except for a money clip with several bills in it. Not much help there. A flower arrangement sat on the window ledge. The card said it came from the staff at The Outpost Mariner Resort, whatever that might be. He wondered for a second why they would send him flowers, then staggered into the bathroom and flipped on the light.

The person peering out of the mirror looked like a complete stranger with a pile of gauze on his head. Stripping off a piece of adhesive tape loosened the gauze and several feet of it peeled off to reveal a nasty looking place over his ear about an inch long with stitches in it.

The man still seemed to be a stranger. Not a bad looking guy, though. He'd had an accident, or somebody had hit him in the head with something. Though he didn't know why, the latter seemed the right answer. Maybe he could find out who had hit him if he could get out of this place.

For a second, a name formed on the tip of his tongue, but then it leaked away. His teeth felt grimy, so he brushed them with a complimentary toothbrush he found on a shelf above the sink. After washing and drying his face, he smoothed his hair with his fingers, eased to the closet and put on the clothes.

He found the hall empty when he stepped out of the room, and made his way to the elevator. A couple of minutes later he got into the back seat of a cab and told the driver to take him to the Outpost Mariner Resort.

The trip took only a few minutes. He paid the fare and walked inside to the desk. A pretty blonde woman about thirty years old greeted him with a smile and asked if she could help him.

"Do you know me?"

"I don't think so, sir. This is my first day, and I hardly know anybody."

"Well, that's all right. I just thought you might."

She cocked her head to one side.

"Are you trying to play a trick on me or something?"

He shook his head and opened his mouth to say, "No, I don't even know my own name," but stopped when he saw a sparkle of recognition in her eyes.

Her face lit up with a smile. "Wait a minute. Don't tell me. Don't tell me. I know it, just give me a second." She shook her finger at him, still smiling. "You're Mason Vogue, the famous private detective."

Mason Vogue, private detective. And famous, even. She could be right. He felt like he might be famous, and nodded his head.

"I guess you have a pretty good memory."

"Oh, I couldn't forget you. I was about twenty then. What happened to you, anyway?"

Was she talking about his injured head or where he'd been since she was twenty? He probably should keep his comments to a minimum, since he didn't remember anything about a relationship with this woman.

"Oh, you know...."

She stared at him for a second. "Well, I hope you come back. I really liked Mason Vogue."

"You did?"

"Oh, yeah. You were terrific." She blushed and reached across the counter to touch his hand.

He felt his own skin flush.

"Okay, well, thanks. I've got some things I need to investigate."

She laughed and said, "Of course you do. Can you give me an autograph before you go?" She found a piece of paper and pen and laid them in front of him.

"Sure, why not?" He signed the paper as Mason Vogue. Writing the name felt familiar to him, as if he'd done it before.

The woman picked it up and kissed it.

"Wow. I'll keep this forever."

"You do that." He pointed his index finger at her, his thumb standing upright like the hammer of a gun, and clicked his tongue. "And I'll see you…later."

He turned and strode out the door with a skip in his step, because the man with no memory now had a name.

TWELVE

SAM, J.T., AND Dave sat on the patio under the shade of the royal palms. A gentle breeze smelled of the sea and rattled the fronds. Jack and Mona stepped outside the house, took a seat and relayed what had happened.

"So the money's gone?" Sam said.

Jack glanced back at the glass patio door. Ernie stood just inside, his face intense, as if straining to hear.

"It's a minor snag," Jack said.

"Did she have a reason to double-cross you?"

Jack smiled. "Maybe."

Mona tossed the wig on the patio floor and fluffed her hair. Jack poured iced tea in a glass and set it in front of her. He smiled, his eyes lingering on her face for a couple seconds. "Mona was a real trooper. I don't think anyone would have guessed she wasn't Sonja Lazar."

"What are you going to do now?" Sam asked.

"I have some ideas." He scanned the property. "Where's Delray?"

"He told Cal and Baxter to keep an eye on us while he went down to his yacht." Sam pointed toward the water. A boathouse stood next to the dock and the moored yacht.

Jack seemed to mull that over for a few moments. "Ernie's inside right now, probably telling Baxter what happened. Might be a good time to take them while Delray's away. And I'd like to take a look around inside the house before we leave."

"For what?"

"Nothing in particular. I just thought I might get a better fix on Delray's set-up here."

Something didn't sound right. Jack wouldn't be looking around the house unless he thought he might find something specific. Maybe valuable. Anyway, it didn't matter, as long as it didn't get in the way of their plans for leaving this place.

"The big guy with the tattoos left a few minutes ago," Sam said, "to pick up some things for Delray. He should be gone for a while. I don't think Cal and the old boxer will be any trouble, and Baxter has a bad arm. Ernie would be a pushover if he didn't have a gun. Delray is the only dangerous one. He could shoot all of us and then sit down for lunch."

Sam turned to J.T. "You game?"

"Sure. Better than sitting around here."

"Okay, I'll go in and ask to go to the bathroom. One of them will follow me. You wait a minute and come in. By then, I should have the gun from the one following me, and that'll make it easier. If that doesn't work, we'll improvise."

J.T. smiled. "Yeah, improvise. That sounds like a good way to describe it."

Sam looked at the others. "This shouldn't take more than five minutes, if we're successful. Get ready to leave." He turned to Jack. "You better be quick with your search."

Jack nodded. "Ten minutes, max."

Mona's eyes widened, her face flush. "Your plan sounds pretty iffy. Are you sure it'll work?"

"Yeah, it'll work."

Jack took a long drink of his iced tea. "What about Delray?"

"I'll take care of him," Sam said.

They all looked at each other for a couple of beats, and Sam went inside. Three of the four men sat there. Ernie had taken a seat on one end of the sofa, the butt of his handgun protruding from the pocket of his pants. Baxter sat at the other end, his gun lying on a table next to him. Cal sat in a chair, his gun on a table next to his chair. No Joe. That might be a problem.

"Hey," Cal said, "you gotta stay out there 'til Delray gets back."

Sam asked about going to the bathroom. Cal looked at him for a second and glanced toward the dock.

"Okay, but make it quick."

Sam went down the hall. Cal walked behind him with his gun hanging from one hand. They passed the door to the kitchen on the left, and Sam saw the bathroom door further down on the opposite side. He walked to it, started to go in and spun.

Cal's eyes widened. Sam hit him on the jaw with his fist. Cal's head snapped to one side, his eyes rolled up, and he slid down the wall with a thud. Sam hoped the noise wouldn't bring the others. He grabbed the gun, dragged the unconscious man inside the room and started back up the hall.

Joe appeared from the kitchen, wiping his hands on a towel, and Sam pointed the gun at him.

"Be good and you won't get hurt."

Joe grinned and dropped the towel. He clenched his fists and stepped forward, like he might have done a thousand times when he boxed in the ring.

Sam thumbed the hammer back on the gun.

"I'm not kidding, pal. One more step and I'll put a bullet in your skull."

The big man stopped and his grin leaked away.

"That's better. Give me the keys to the limo."

Joe handed them over and Sam told him to go back the way he'd come.

They reached the kitchen and Sam hit him behind the ear with the butt of the gun. Joe dropped, and Sam grabbed him and laid him on the floor without as much as a whisper.

Hearing J.T.'s voice, he eased back to the living room. Ernie saw him with the gun and lurched for his own. Sam pointed the barrel at Ernie's head and he froze. Baxter reached for his weapon with his good arm. J.T. picked up a plate from a table and threw it like a Frisbee. A piece of sandwich flew into the air, and the plate shattered as it struck the top of the table next to where Baxter's 9mm lay. Baxter jerked his hand back and J.T. hurried over and retrieved the gun.

"Go find some tape," Sam said to J.T.

Ernie rolled his eyes. "Delray's going to kill all of you."

Sam grinned. "You think so?"

"You can count on it. Especially if you hurt his people."

"Yeah, well, we'll see about that." Delray had never cared about anyone but himself.

J.T. came back with a roll of duct tape, bound their feet and hands, and put a piece of tape over their mouths.

Sam told him to do the same thing with the men in the kitchen and bathroom, and tossed him the keys. "Then go to the limo. I'll check on Delray."

Sam went out the patio door. "You have ten minutes," he said to Jack, and told the others to get into the car.

"Where are you going?" Mona asked.

"I need to see Delray."

"Can't we just leave?"

"Don't worry, it'll be okay."

She tried a smile. "It better be. You promised, remember?"

Sam looked at her face and knew he would do whatever it took to get them out of there.

"Get going," Jack said to her. "He can take care of himself."

She narrowed her eyes. "That's a lousy thing to say."

When they had gone, Sam strode toward the dock with Cal's gun in his hand. He had seen cameras on the rear deck and there probably were more down close to the water, so he knew Delray might be waiting for him. As he approached the boathouse, he peered around the corner. The yacht swayed in the breeze, tugging at its lines, scrubbing the rubber dock bumpers.

His gun led the way as he eased around the corner. Something flashed to his side, a reflection of sunlight on metal. He dropped to the deck and felt the wind from an object passing over his head. It made a smacking sound, like that of an ax striking a log. Rolling over, he pointed the gun at Delray, who held the handle of a gaff, its hooked point lodged in the wall of the boathouse. Delray grinned and kicked Sam's hand. A shock wave ran up his arm. The gun clattered to the deck and slid away.

Sam rolled to the side, got to his feet, and grabbed a boat cushion that hung on the wall. Delray worked the gaff out of the wall and swung it again. It sank into the flotation device with a thump and came out the other side, just inches from Sam's throat.

Letting go, Sam stepped back. Delray tried to swing his weapon again, but realized its ineffectiveness with the cushion stuck on the end and tossed it to the deck.

The redheaded man smirked, hate in his eyes. "You tried to embarrass me in front of the chick last night."

That's what he's worried about? Sam shook his hand, still numb from the kick. Delray swung a haymaker and he stepped back, feeling the wind on his chin.

Delray glanced toward the house, probably wondering if Mona might be watching. "You're a guest in my home. You should have better manners."

Sam kicked him in the stomach and he doubled over. "You never were any good without a gun."

Delray staggered backward, reached down and retrieved the gun from the deck. He pointed it at Sam. His face glowed crimson.

"Maybe you're right about that, but I happen to have a gun now." He thumbed the hammer and Sam saw his finger tighten on the trigger.

"Hey, loudmouth!" J.T. called from the backyard.

Delray turned for a split second, and Sam slammed his fist into the redhead's face. The man's nose spurted blood, and he gave Sam a dazed look and dropped straight down like an imploded building. Sam twisted the gun from his hand and wiped his bloodied knuckles on Delray's shirtsleeve.

J.T. sauntered over and gazed down at the unconscious man. "You okay?"

"Yeah, I'm fine."

Sam took a couple of deep breaths and looked around, wondering if the neighbors had heard the disturbance. He didn't see anyone.

"Help me move him."

They dragged Delray into the boathouse, found some rope, and tied his hands with it.

As Sam turned around, J.T. said, "You're leaving him alive?"

Sam stared for a moment, his breathing labored. "Yes."

J.T. shook his head. "Man, you'll never learn. He would have killed you, and now he'll do it for sure."

Sam mopped sweat from his forehead with his shirt-tail. "Yeah, maybe."

If Delray showed up again, Sam would have to deal with him then. He already had enough baggage upstairs and didn't need another killing to add to the stack, especially when they could just walk away.

"Let's go, our limo's waiting."

JACK CAME OUT of the house a few minutes later, shaking his head. Probably hadn't found what he'd hoped for. Sam wondered what it might be, but knew asking about it would be fruitless. Besides, he didn't really care. He just wanted to get out of Grand Cayman and leave any thoughts of Delray Jinks behind.

Dave drove them to the airport while Jack called the pilot. The man complained about not finishing his vacation, and said he couldn't fly them back before the next day. Jack doubled the price they'd originally agreed upon and he relented.

They boarded the plane and flew back to Key West in about two hours. At their cars, Mona asked Sam to take her back to the restaurant, and Jack, Dave and J.T. headed toward town.

"Are you going back to Miami tonight?" Sam asked when he turned into the restaurant lot and parked next to her Acura.

Mona smiled. "Actually, that's what I wanted to talk to you about. Jack said he needs me to help."

Jack had persuaded Mona to sit by him on the plane again, and Sam had noticed him bending her ear.

"What about your job?"

Mona shrugged. "I have some vacation coming. They might not like it, but there isn't much they can do about it."

Sam shook his head.

"What is it?" she asked.

"The guy just doesn't quit. The money's gone, but he wants to keep mixing it up until somebody gets hurt. Now he wants you involved, too."

"That isn't all."

"Oh, yeah? What else?"

"He wants you to stay because he says he can't trust your friend, J.T. I told him I'd try to talk you into it."

Sam wanted to say no, but Mona didn't realize the kind of danger she could face, and she could get hurt, if not worse. Jack the manipulator had won again.

Mona broke the silence. "He said he'd get rooms at the Hilton and wanted us all to have dinner there."

Sam looked out the window. A lot had happened since the evening before. He really didn't want to do this, but even more, he didn't want Mona to do it. And something about the way she looked at him made his heart skip. He didn't like that, either. Well…he liked it, but knew it could only lead to trouble in a situation like this.

"You told him you'd meet him there?" Sam said.

"I said I wouldn't be there unless you agreed to come along."

She gave him that look.

THIRTEEN

THE MAN WHO might be Mason Vogue thought about flagging a taxi. He wondered where he would go, and couldn't think of a place. The girl at the desk had told him his name, but now what?

The side entrance to the hotel bar looked inviting. Maybe a drink would help him think. He went in and sat on a stool. The bartender ambled over and placed a coaster in front of him.

"Mr. V. I heard about the accident. How you doing?"

"Oh, I'm doing okay, considering."

"The TV didn't say much about what happened. They didn't seem to know."

That's too bad, because he didn't know, either. He also didn't know what to say. His head began to ache, and he thought his medicine might be giving out.

"You know how news people are. They're always afraid they'll get sued."

"Oh, yeah, that's for sure." The bartender looked at him for a couple of seconds. "The usual?"

"Yep, the usual."

The bartender stepped away to make the drink and the detective wondered if his voice sounded as tinny as it did to his own ears. He recalled a once-popular movie detective who had a really distinctive voice, and wondered if a real detective should sound like that.

"There you go." The man behind the bar set what

looked like a martini in front of him and went to serve another customer.

He ate the olive and took a sip of the drink. Pretty strong, almost all gin. That must be the way he liked it. He sipped again. It actually tasted pretty good, and his headache seemed to be sliding away. Another customer sat a few seats down and the bartender went to fetch a drink for him. He came back a minute or so later when the martini had disappeared.

"Wow. You must have needed that. How about another?"

He thought he would try the detective voice and watch the bartender's reaction.

"Yeah, play it again, Sam."

The bartender just stared for a second, then broke into a grin and pointed a finger at him. "Hey, that was pretty good." He stepped away for a minute and returned with a new drink. "How's Mr. Brent? I haven't seen him today."

Mr. Brent? He couldn't remember ever knowing anyone by that name. Maybe he should know him, though.

"Oh yeah?" he said, using the detective voice again. "I was looking for him myself."

The bartender gave him the same blank look as before. "Is he supposed to meet you here?"

"Uh…yes, he said he would be here." He looked at the clock on the wall, which indicated 7:15. "At seven."

"Might still be in the penthouse."

"The penthouse?"

"Yeah, you know, the office."

"Oh, I guess I could check there."

He drained the second drink and got down from the stool. "Thanks. How about putting this on my tab?"

"Sure thing."

"And add in a good tip for yourself."

The man behind the bar beamed and said, "You got it, Mr. V."

Mr. V. left the bar on wobbly legs. In the elevator, he punched the top button labeled "P." The car ascended for several seconds before the doors opened. An office entrance lay straight ahead, and he stepped over and tried the knob. Locked. A picture window next to it ran about twelve feet down the hall. No lights shone behind it. He pressed his face to the glass, but blinds on the other side obscured the view. Wondering how he might get inside, his eyes fell upon a phone sitting on an elegant table next to the elevator. It had a button on it for the bar, so he picked up the receiver and rang his new friend.

"Mr. Brent isn't here. Could someone come let me in?"

After an uncomfortable silence, the bartender said, "Forgot your key, huh, Mr. V.?"

"Yes, I forgot it."

"That's okay; I can get you a pass key."

"Hey, that would be great."

A few minutes later, a bellman emerged from the elevator and handed him a card key.

When the man had left, he unlocked the door and turned on the light. The lobby contained a reception area and some chairs, and a closed door on each side. Using the card key, he went inside the one on the right, flipped the light switch, and closed the door. A clean desk sat in the middle of the room, with a nameplate labeled "Ernest Brent" at its edge. He sat down and opened the top drawer. Empty. Another yielded the same thing. This guy Brent must not be doing much.

He sat there another minute, and started to leave, but decided to try the pen drawer in the middle of the desk before getting up. A large envelope inside contained a small stack of papers, and on top lay what looked like an agreement for the sale of the Outpost Mariner Resort to Ruben Vale, Ernie Brent, and Delray Jinks, dated just a couple of weeks before. Ruben Vale. "Mr. V."? Could the bartender have confused him, the famous detective, with this Vale person? Maybe they looked alike. Flipping through the rest of the papers, he just saw a lot of legal mumbo-jumbo about the sale.

With everything back in the envelope, he shoved it into the drawer. Something rattled in the corner. Pulling the drawer out all the way, he saw several plastic bottles that looked like medicine. One of them had the name "NewMood" on it. Sounded like a feel-good drug, and the guy certainly had stocked up: he had ten bottles containing sixty pills each.

Unsure what else to do, he sat there for another minute as his mind went blank. This investigator stuff was pretty tough. He thought the answers would just flow into his brain, but that hadn't happened. Though he'd learned a little bit about Ernie Brent, he still didn't know anything more about himself than he had before.

A man strode through the door, stopped and stared, his eyes wide in surprise. "What're you doing here?"

The detective dropped the pills in the drawer, closed it, and stood.

Must be Brent, his face really red, like somebody who'd been in the sun too long. More likely something else, though, judging from all those happy pills in the desk.

"The bartender gave me a key." He used the detective voice, and thought he did a pretty good job of it.

Brent cocked his head slightly. "I thought you, uh, might be in the hospital or something." His voice trembled, his eyes squinted. Probably classic symptoms of some kind of guilt.

"How did you know about the hospital?" He wondered if Brent might be the perpetrator who had put him there.

"Uh, I don't know, I guess somebody must've told me." Brent frowned. "Why are you talking like that?"

"Like what?"

"You sound like Bogart," Brent said.

"This is the way I talk."

ERNIE'S BLOOD PRESSURE felt sky high. He'd been sure Ruben was dead when he left him lying there, his head leaking blood all over the floor. Funny thing, though: Ruben didn't seem to be mad about it. Too bad he hadn't stayed dead, because now Ernie would have to figure out how to kill him all over again. One thing for sure, he didn't plan to share any of that money, that is, if he ever got his hands on it again.

Ernie's head throbbed, and he thought about his pills. He took out the bottle and swallowed a couple of them.

"Is that NewMood?" Ruben asked.

"What do you know about NewMood?"

Ruben shrugged, his eyelids fluttering. "I don't know. Just saw something about it somewhere."

So, he'd found the stash in the desk. Ernie had tried to keep the pill business from him, knowing he wouldn't go along with it. Delray had come up with the idea and pitched it to Ernie, who thought it sheer genius. Delray had all kinds of painkillers that he'd hijacked. Billed as "mood drugs," they had sold like hotcakes. And their bonanza probably wouldn't draw attention from the Feds, as long as the DEA didn't think they were selling narcotics.

Now, with the truck full of NewMood, they'd actually begun to sell the real thing. Ernie might have felt like a real businessman, had it not been for the fact that Delray had stolen the pills and killed an armed guard in the process. He still wasn't too sure why the guard would have been riding along on a truck transporting medicine.

Catching Ruben going through his desk drawer had made up his mind. He could take care of him tonight. This actually would be better than Ruben dying in his own home. That would've caused a big investigation, cops everywhere. This way he'd just disappear, with nobody ever the wiser.

"Let's take a ride," Ernie said. "I need to update you on a few things."

Ruben seemed to consider that and nodded. "Sure, an update. That would be good."

AFTER DINNER, MONA said she was tired and went to her room. The rest of the group went to Jack's suite for a nightcap. He had a full bar and a large sitting area. J.T. had already drunk several beers in the restaurant, and had begun to slur his words. Sam, tired himself, stood to leave. Jack's cell phone rang and he pulled it from his pocket and looked at the number, then motioned for Sam to wait.

Jack got up, walked into his bedroom, and returned less than a minute later. "I need to go downstairs," he said to the group. "I won't be long if you want to hang around." He turned to Sam. "How about joining me?"

Sam shrugged and followed him out the door.

Silent in the elevator, Jack looked as if he had something on his mind. They walked through the lobby and out the hotel entrance, where a black limo sat waiting. Jack opened the door and asked Sam to get inside. Sam gave him a sidelong glance.

"It's okay," Jack said.

Two men sat on the back seat, both wearing suits. One looked like an aging executive, probably Jack's client. The other looked like a steroid freak with a buzz cut and silver rivets the size of dimes in his earlobes. Sam got in, slid across the seat to the other side, and Jack followed and closed the door.

"I said to come alone," the old man said.

Jack smiled. "He works with me."

"How much does he know?" The man looked nervous.

"Don't worry, you can trust him."

The client sighed, pulled a plastic antacid bottle from his pocket, and popped several tablets into his mouth. "Well, I hope your friend here can keep his mouth shut," he said between chews. "Otherwise, we might all go to jail."

Jack chuckled. "That should be the least of your worries."

"What do you mean?"

"These are dangerous people. You knew that going in."

"Yes, so they are. Let's get down to business. Now that your plan has flopped, what brilliant moves do you *now* have in mind?"

"Continue as planned," Jack said. "The next phase is almost ready."

The old man crossed his leg and bumped Sam's knee with his shoe, but didn't seem to notice or care. "What are the odds that this new phase might work?"

Jack remained silent for a few beats, then said, "About fifty-fifty."

"That doesn't sound good. What if we just call it quits and cut our losses?"

Jack shrugged. "Your call, but you still don't have what you want."

The client took a deep breath and let it out slowly.

Rivets turned to his boss and spoke for the first time. "I can solve the problem. Just say the word."

"No, no. I told you I don't want to talk about that. At least not yet."

"Suit yourself," Rivets said, "but this guy is just leading us on. How do we know he'll do anything he says he will?"

The client looked at Jack. "Yes, how do we know that?"

Jack smiled. "I suppose you'll just have to trust me."

"Sure, we'll trust you," Rivets said. He made a show of curling his hands into fists, his knuckles cracking.

The old guy looked at him. "That won't be necessary. I'll go along for now. If we find out he's double-crossed us, you can do what you want with him." He remained quiet for a moment and glanced at Sam, as if considering what to say, then turned back to Jack. "So, have you established the location of the…ah…article in question?"

"We think we know where it is, but we'll need more intel before making a move."

"You were supposed to have that information by now. What happened?"

Jack smiled. "I've had my hands full the last couple of days."

"And whose fault is that?" Rivets asked.

Glaring at him, the old man said, "Please let me do the talking."

Rivets puffed up and crossed his arms.

The client leaned forward and looked at Jack. "He does have a point, though. Whose fault was it that you got kidnapped?"

"I'm looking into that," Jack said, his head cocked to one side, a chill in his voice, "but the plan is on track. You just need to let me do my job."

The executive settled back into his seat, an odd look on his face. After a few moments of silence, he spoke again, his voice more gentle and polite than before. "Please keep me apprised of any developments."

Jack smiled. "Sure, but I'll need more money in the meantime."

FOURTEEN

"Who was that in the limo?" Sam asked.

They stood waiting for the elevator. A couple passed by, whispering and giggling, as if they'd had a few drinks in the bar.

"Let's talk about it in the room."

Back in Jack's suite, everybody had gone. He mixed two drinks for them, using the last of the gin, and called downstairs for another bottle.

Jack took off his suit coat, hung it up, and sat in one of the large chairs. Sam took a seat on the sofa.

"The older guy was Grant Seams, the major stockholder of Seams and Perch Pharmaceuticals. I think you already know that Delray made his fortune by stealing from pharmaceutical companies."

Sam said he'd heard that rumor.

"Well, it's true. He'd been selling the drugs on the black market, but while he had plenty of product, his distribution network was never very good. Then along came Ernie with his Internet marketing scheme. All of a sudden, Delray's customer base expanded from a few hundred users who required hands-on treatment, to the vast millions who order drugs online."

"He sells painkillers online?"

Jack loosened his tie and took a long drink of his gin and tonic. "He sells whatever he steals, but the vast majority of the population is not inclined to take narcotics on a regular basis, so he markets the pills as the newest mood drug on the market: NewMood."

"And people don't see anything wrong with taking mood enhancers," Sam said.

"That's right." Jack nodded. "Delray fills the bottles with whatever he has, and some of their customers get a much bigger rush than they expected. And they just order more and more. About a month ago, Seams and Perch lost a semi headed from their manufacturing plant in New Jersey to their distribution facility in Miami. It was loaded with NewMood."

"Aren't you required to have a prescription for mood drugs?"

Jack swirled the ice in his glass and glanced at his watch. "Most of their customers do. Ernie's website instructs them to type in their doctor's name and the prescription number. That way, the customers are satisfied they're buying a drug through a legitimate process, and everything is cool."

"Don't customers want to be reimbursed from their insurance companies?"

Shrugging, Jack said, "They probably make the price so attractive that most customers don't worry about the little they would get from insurance reimbursement."

"What about the law? You'd think they'd be all over these guys."

"They try, but Ernie's slippery. He has computer people who can close down a website and open another in the blink of an eye. And another thing: the law already has its hands full with what they think are more dangerous drugs, like heroin and cocaine."

Sam sipped his drink. It sounded like a smarter operation than he would have thought Ernie and Delray capable of, but they probably had some smart people help set it up, and paid them well to keep their mouths shut.

The bottle arrived, and Jack tipped the waiter and made a fresh drink.

"You just mentioned Ernie and Delray," Sam said. "Is Ruben involved, too?"

Jack hesitated. "I don't think he's a player in this part of the business."

Sam wondered why he thought that, but decided it didn't really matter. Jack usually knew his "clientele" very well. "So, what're you going to do?"

"Take down their operation. Seams wants what belongs to him, and he wants them out of business."

Closing down crooks usually meant putting out hits, but that wasn't Jack's style. He usually just made the mark wish he were dead. That probably wouldn't work on someone like Delray Jinks, and Sam now understood why Jack had been so insistent on him staying in Key West. He knew Delray would be coming for him when he finished whatever he had in mind, and he needed someone good with a gun.

"Why didn't Seams just ask Mr. Rivets to kill them?" Sam asked.

Jack chuckled. "Seams doesn't want his hands dirty with a murder. He'd like to think he's solved the problem without anyone getting hurt."

"He's in for a big surprise."

"I'm afraid so." Jack gave his eyes a long blink and nodded.

"How did you get involved?"

"One of my contacts told me about Delray hijacking the truck, and I went to Seams with a plan."

"Just like that, huh? You had a contact who knew about it."

A grin blossomed on Jack's face. "What can I say? A man in my business needs a network."

Sam considered that for a moment and nodded. "Does Seams own the Outpost Mariner?"

Jack smiled. "Good guess. At least one of his companies does. It would be difficult to trace back to him."

Sam had wondered how Jack had taken control of the resort without the true owner getting wise to his scam.

"So, what's your next move?" Sam asked.

"I've got some people working on it."

Sam waited for him to say more, but the old con man just reached for his glass and downed his second drink.

"Working on what, destroying their facilities?"

"No. That would be like trying to wash away an anthill; they'd be back in operation in a week or two. This has to be something more…fundamental, more permanent. We have to take all their money and product, so they have no means to continue."

"They'll die before letting you do that."

"I suppose it could work out that way."

"Then Seams will have blood on his hands, anyway."

"I'll convince him we had no choice, and that he had nothing to do with that part." Jack got up and ambled to the bar. "Another drink?"

Sam looked at his glass: still half full. "Nah, I'm okay."

"Yeah, guess I've had enough, too." He sat back down.

"What if Seams gets a case of guilty conscience and wants to blab to someone?" Sam asked.

Jack smiled. "We'll cross that bridge when we come to it."

The bridge he meant connected the Low Road over a river of blood. Intimately familiar with this particular bridge, Jack would have no trouble crossing it when the time came. Sam remembered the conversation in the limo and the look on Seams' face right before they got out. He wondered if the old guy knew what could happen to him before all this ended.

Sam recalled something Seams had asked that seemed significant: *So, have you established the location of the...ah...article in question?* He obviously hadn't wanted to say much about it around Sam.

Someone knocked on the door. Jack walked over, peered through the peephole. He looked back at Sam with a grimace and opened the door.

J.T. came in. "Hey, I wondered what happened to you two. Is the bar still open?"

"Sure, help yourself," Jack said.

J.T. went over, made a drink and took a seat.

A few minutes later, Jack yawned and said he needed to get to sleep. Heading for the bedroom, he said, "Stay as long as you like. I'll see you in the restaurant for breakfast at eight-thirty."

They remained a while longer, and Sam asked if J.T. wanted to go for a ride.

J.T. shrugged. "Sure, not my bedtime yet."

In the hall, Sam said, "Get your computer. I want you to research something."

A few minutes later, Sam drove them down Duval and stopped at a red traffic light. A familiar car sat waiting to go in the other direction.

"That's Ernie," Sam said as the light changed. "I wonder where he's going at this time of night."

"Somebody was riding with him. Did you see who it was?"

"No, it was too dark."

After making a U-turn, he followed the car over to US-1, where it headed north over the Stock Island Bridge and continued up the Overseas Highway. There wasn't much traffic, and Sam feared Ernie would notice his car, even though he stayed as far behind them as possible without losing sight of the taillights.

He told J.T. about his conversation with Jack as they rode.

"So that's what this is about, huh?"

"Yeah, it seems so. But you know Jack. There's no telling what he left out."

"I don't think he trusts me."

Sam wondered if J.T. might be trying his hand at humor, but a glance at the side of his face in the glow of the dash lights told him that wasn't the case. There were reasons why Jack might not trust J.T., and Sam didn't see the need to bring them up. Though he'd earned Sam's trust a number of times, Sam always tried to avoid situations where something of great value might enter into the equation.

"Turn on your computer and see what you can find on this Seams guy."

Ernie's car finally turned off the highway at Cudjoe Key and traveled inland. There didn't seem to be anything on the highway except for an occasional house.

Sam cut his headlights and slowed until he could see by moonlight. The lead car went another mile or so before turning into a short driveway and stopping. Sam slowed to a crawl and saw Ernie's car outside a gate surrounded by dim lights. A fence stood about ten feet high around the property with razor wire on top. He pulled over to the side of the road and turned off his engine.

"I think I'll slip in and try to see what they're up to," Sam said. "How about staying with the car and calling me if there's a problem?"

"You got it."

"WHAT'S IN HERE?" Ruben asked.

"Just something I wanted to show you. It'll take just a few minutes."

Ruben had been acting kind of funny, Ernie thought, not his usual talkative self, and he seemed to be suspicious of something. Probably still mad about Ernie knocking him out. When he did speak, he continued with the poor Bogart impression. Anyway, it didn't matter. In a few minutes, Ruben would be dead.

Ernie punched in the code and the gate opened. He drove inside the compound, down the long drive, and parked beside the entrance. They got out of the car, and he used his key to unlock the door.

THE GATE, LONG and slow, took a while to open completely. As Ernie drove through, Sam got a gun and a flashlight from his glove box and ran to the gate, reaching it just in time to slide through before it closed. Staying in the shadows, he raced along the drive until he saw the car turn into the parking lot of a large, one-story building. Ernie and the other man, who Sam now recognized as Ruben Vale, got out and went inside. Since he didn't see any cameras, Sam decided to check out the grounds until they came back out.

He walked around the building, which had no outside lights or windows, and saw a couple of large trucks parked in back. They looked as if they had been recently painted. Scratching the surface of one of the doors with his fingernail confirmed fresh paint that covered a sign underneath.

A backhoe sat nearby. Dirt clung to the teeth on the bucket. Moving toward the woods behind the building, he saw tracks the machine had made and followed them into the trees. There were several places where the leaves had been cleared. Mounds of dark, sandy earth covered those spots, like graves in the old days when all the dirt from the holes got piled on top of the wooden caskets to settle in when everything underneath turned to mush. But these didn't look like graves. Using a stick, he dug down a few inches and touched something. Gripping the edge of the object with his fingers, he pulled it up and shone the light on it. It looked like a piece of a corrugated paper box. They'd been burying trash. Probably doing something illegal, and didn't want to risk taking the trash to a public landfill. After pulling out several pieces, he found one with a name on it: Seams and Perch Pharmaceuticals. This had to be Ernie and Delray's distribution facility. But what business would Ruben have here in the middle of the night? He'd been in the hospital only the day before with a bad head injury, and Jack had said he didn't think Ruben was involved in this part of the business.

Sam went to the rear of the truck closest to the building, shone the light on its cargo doors, and found a padlock. He found the cab door unlocked, so he climbed up and peered around inside. Above the visor on the driver's side, he found a bill of lading from Seams and Perch, indicating that the truck had been fully loaded with NewMood. Seeing nothing else of interest, he replaced the papers, went to the back of the truck, and took out his pick to work on the padlock. A relatively simple mechanism, he had it open in a matter of seconds.

The big doors opened with a squeak, and he stopped and listened in case he'd alerted anyone. Hearing nothing but crickets chirping in the underbrush, he climbed up into the bed of the truck. It looked as if only twenty or thirty boxes had been removed, leaving a few feet of space at the rear. A chair sat in the corner next to the door, along with a portable radio. Someone had ridden back there instead of in the cab. As he turned to climb down, he saw something lying atop a box behind the chair. Closer inspection revealed it to be a metal case, like the ones used to transport valuable or classified assets. One side of a set of handcuffs was attached to the handle. The other side was locked together and covered with blood.

Several dents surrounded the latches, which were sprung open, and a piece of the latch on one side had been broken out completely. The courier probably didn't have the key for the case. It might have been sent to the destination separately as a safeguard against theft, so the robber had used gunshots to open it. Sam lifted the lid with his shirttail and found nothing inside but a foam liner. A space the size and shape of a Rubik's Cube had been formed in the center, and now it had nothing in it.

This looked like a bigger crime than a simple truck hijacking. The person with the case locked to his wrist might have been killed. Maybe one of the holes in the woods contained a body after all. Delray would have no compunctions about hacking off a man's hand to get what he wanted. Sam wondered if Delray had known what was inside before he ambushed the truck.

A check on his watch indicated that he'd been inside the compound about fifteen minutes. Remembering the razor wire on the fence, and not wanting to have to climb over it to get out, he decided he'd better go back to the front of the building in case the two men came out. He closed the case and got down from the truck, replacing the lock on the doors.

THE AMNESIAC WONDERED what this place could be, and why they were visiting in the middle of the night with nobody around. Brent had said almost nothing since leaving the hotel, and the detective still wondered if this might be the man who had put him in the hospital. They walked down a hall, and Brent used a key to open a steel door. He flipped on the overhead light, illuminating a production room of some kind. It contained several machines assembled in a straight line, connected by conveyor belts. The equipment looked as if it had seen better days. A hopper at the head of the line of equipment contained little white pills. They looked a lot like the ones Brent had taken in the office. He glanced around and sighed.

"Don't worry," Brent said, "we're almost there."

They went to the rear of the room and through a door. Brent turned on the light and told him to go inside. A large machine stood a few feet away, next to a pile of pasteboard boxes. Inside the machine lay more boxes that had been flattened.

"This is what you wanted me to see?"

He turned, and Brent had a gun pointed at his chest.

"That's right. Move over a couple of feet and stand in front of it."

Brent planned to shoot him and put him into the machine.

"Why do you want to kill *me*? I haven't done anything to you."

That brought a chuckle.

"Yeah, nothing but cause me aggravation for the last five years."

"Aggravation?"

"That's right, and talking to Mona Miles just put the icing on the cake. Do like I said and move over."

"What if I don't? You're going to shoot me anyway."

Brent smiled. "You got it, smart guy."

This could be the kind of situation in which Mason Vogue found himself on any given day. If only he could remember things, he would know what to do. He had a stirring of memory about fighting bad people. It slid away before he could get a lock on it. Still, he must be good at it. Why else would he be a famous detective? Brent obviously did not know with whom he was dealing.

Rather than stepping closer to the machine, he spun and kicked Brent in the stomach. The man bent forward, his eyes bulging with surprise, and grabbed his stomach with his free hand. Then the detective kicked him in the face, the heel of his shoe striking Brent's mouth with a smacking sound. His head snapped back and he dropped to the floor, the gun falling free and clattering on the tile.

The detective picked up the gun and looked at it, then flipped the safety and put it into his pocket. Brent lay there in a pile, as if he might be dead. Blood leaked from his mouth, but not much. Leaning over, he touched Brent's neck and found a pulse. Just sleeping. He searched the man's pockets, took out his wallet and keys, and looked at the name and address on the auto license. After replacing the wallet, he turned off the lights and walked out of the building.

SAM HEARD THE door slam shut as he neared the corner of the facility. He stepped back into the shadows and watched Ruben Vale get into the car and start the engine. What had happened to Ernie?

Following in the shadows, he neared the vehicle at the gate and watched Ruben punch buttons on the keypad. After a couple minutes of that, Ruben got out and fired two shots at the chain that opened and closed the gate. It fell to the ground, and he pushed the gate open, got back behind the wheel and drove through.

Sam ran to his car, turned it around in the road, and left his lights off as he followed the gate shooter.

"What'd you find?" J.T. asked, punching keys on his computer.

Sam told him about the truck and the case that had been blown open with a gun.

"What do you think was inside?"

Shrugging, Sam said, "Beats me. But it had to be something valuable. More valuable than the drugs."

He glanced at his rider. The computer illuminated J.T.'s face as he gazed with smiling eyes at the taillights a quarter-mile ahead.

"What'd you learn about Seams?" Sam asked.

"He's ranked as the tenth richest man in America, with a home in New Jersey close to the pharmaceutical company's headquarters, another in Miami, and a third in L.A. Also has a yacht in Miami. According to his profile, he collects anything rare: paintings, books, stamps, gems, things like that. He bought a rare emerald a couple years ago that's worth $20 million. I'd like to get inside his vault, or wherever he keeps his things, and take a look around."

"I'm guessing you'd take some of the things, too."

J.T. chuckled. "I might, at that."

Sam asked him to look up stories about thefts within the last couple of months.

After a few minutes, J.T. said, "Let's see...some jewels worth $10 million got stolen from a store in New York...a painting by Manet was heisted from an art gallery...somebody lifted a bronze sculpture dating to the middle ages from a collector's home in New Mexico... robbers stole a blue diamond worth $30 million from a guy in New Jersey. There was a—"

"Did the robbers steal the diamond from Grant Seams?" A big diamond would fit in the padded case.

J.T. read more of the story on the screen and shook his head. "Nah. It belonged to some other rich dude."

After reaching US-1, Sam thought it safe to turn on his headlights.

Just over the bridge from Marathon, Ruben stopped at a store and stayed inside for a couple of minutes, looking as if he might be asking directions from the store clerk. When he returned, he drove toward Ernie's neighborhood, and turned onto the street where Ernie lived. He reached the house and stopped for a minute before pulling into the driveway. Sam parked next to the curb several houses away and killed the engine.

Ruben ambled to the front door, tried a couple of keys in the lock before it opened, and went inside. Sam wasn't sure why he had followed the man, but decided to stay a few more minutes to see what happened. He turned on the radio and tuned it to a local station, keeping the volume low. When he looked up again, he saw a man, whose bushy red hair gleamed in the streetlights, get out of a car parked up the street and walk to Ernie's door with a gun in his hand.

"Delray," J.T. said.

The redheaded man opened the door, which Ruben had left unlocked, and went inside.

Sam pulled his gun. "Yeah, we'd better see what this is about." They got out and strode to the front door, which stood ajar. Easing it open, Sam heard Delray and Ruben's voices from deeper inside the house. He took a chance and stepped into the foyer, his 9mm leading the way. J.T. followed. The voices grew louder, sounding like they came from the living room. Peering around the corner to his right, Sam saw Delray with his back to him holding the gun on Ruben. He ducked back into the foyer and listened.

"Where's Ernie?" Delray asked.

"He tried to kill me." Ruben's voice seemed different from the one Sam remembered on TV. It sounded a little like Bogart's.

"Is that so? He must've had a good reason."

"Maybe good for him."

"You didn't answer my question. Where is he now?" Delray asked.

"I left him lying on the floor in some kind of factory up in Cudjoe Key."

"Alive or dead?"

"I just knocked him out," Ruben said.

"Let me get this straight: Ernie tried to kill you, but you knocked him out?"

"That's right."

Delray huffed a laugh. "Well, Mr. Movie Star, this ain't your day, 'cause I'm gonna shoot you myself, and you ain't knocking anybody else out."

Upon hearing Delray thumb the hammer on his weapon, Sam stepped around the corner. Delray tried to turn when he heard the footsteps, but Sam slammed the butt of his gun into the mass of red hair, felt it smack against a hard scalp, and the would-be assassin dropped to the floor.

Ruben peered down at him, then at Sam and J.T.

"Who're you guys?"

"It doesn't matter," Sam said. "You probably need to get out of here before he wakes up."

Ruben glanced at Delray again. "I vote for that."

"What are you doing here, anyway?" Sam asked.

"I just want to find out why people are trying to kill me. First, I got knocked on the head and woke up in the hospital. Then that man tried to shoot me."

"You mean Ernie, your business partner?"

"He's my business partner?"

Sam nodded. Up close, this guy looked familiar. He had seen the TV show a couple of times. That had to be it.

Ruben's brow furrowed. "Is he a detective, too?"

"Not that I know of," Sam said. "Why would you ask that?"

"Because I'm a detective. Mason Vogue, at your service." He reached out his hand to Sam.

Sam smiled. In the TV series, Ruben had played that part, but he had forgotten the detective's name until now. "Okay, but like I said, you need to leave. And don't go home. That's the first place these guys will look."

Ruben gave him a blank stare. "I don't know where that is."

"Where what is?" Sam asked.

"Home."

"He has amnesia," J.T. said.

"I know I'm Mason Vogue the detective. Beyond that, I'm pretty fuzzy about everything."

"Go to the car and we'll take you somewhere safe." Sam turned to J.T. "I'm going to look around."

J.T. nodded and pointed a finger at Ruben. "Let's go."

When they were out the door, Sam knelt on one knee, rolled Delray onto his back, and checked his pockets. He found nothing but a wallet and a set of keys for a rental car. The wallet yielded only some cash—a thousand dollars in hundreds—and a Florida driver's license. No credit cards. No pictures. He replaced the wallet and stood up, putting the car keys into his pocket.

Ernie's living room looked like no one ever used it. No TV, no pictures or paintings on the wall, no magazines. A thin layer of dust coated the furniture. Lifting the cushions on the sofa, he just found more dust.

He eased down the hall and entered the den. Ernie probably stayed in that room when he wasn't sleeping. A recliner sat in front of a large-screen TV. Next to the chair sat a table with a lamp and an ashtray that overflowed with cigarette butts. Three empty beer cans lined the table's edge. Next to the lamp lay bills for electricity and water, and for three charge cards. Both of the utilities were past due. The charge bills indicated balances of $22,000, $19,000, and $33,000. Only a couple of recent charges showed up on the bills, both for Las Vegas casinos.

An 8"X10" frame containing a picture of a middle-aged woman and a little boy sat on the table next to the TV, their clothes and hairstyles from another era. Maybe Ernie and his mother. There didn't seem to be any place in the den to hide something.

One of the bedrooms had nothing in it, not even a bed. Sam checked the closet anyway. Nothing there. In the other bedroom, he found an unmade bed and clothes strewn on the floor. The closet contained a couple pairs of pants, three shirts, and a gold sport coat. Apparently, Ernie spent most of his money on gambling, and little on anything else.

A box sat in the bottom of the closet. It contained a high school diploma, some pictures of the same woman in the picture in the den, and one of a man who hammed it up for the camera with a tall can of beer in his hand. Maybe Ernie's dad. Everybody has a mother and a father. Even a scumbag like Ernie. Nothing in the box looked as if it would be transported in the ruined metal case.

Crossing the lawn to the street, he spotted a small, late model car parked against the curb a couple of doors down. The key from Delray's pocket fit the door. He searched the glove box and under the seats, then the trunk. Everything came up clean. If Delray had taken something of value from the metal case, he had left it somewhere else. The guy probably hadn't been in town long enough this trip to get a hotel room. Maybe he'd left it at his house in Grand Cayman. Probably had his goons guarding the place while he traveled. Could he also have a home in Florida? Leaving the keys on the front seat, he headed for his car.

Ruben insisted on going home, so they took him there. On the way, Sam told him what had happened the day the ambulance had taken him to the hospital. Ruben didn't say much at first, but finally said, "You mean… I'm just some sort of actor? Not a real detective?"

"I'm afraid so," Sam said.

After a couple of beats, he sighed and said, "I liked it better being a famous detective."

Sam noticed he had dropped the Bogart voice.

They reached Ruben's house, and someone had left floodlights on outside. The place looked like a palace.

"This is where I live?" He sounded surprised.

"Yes. Pretty nice, huh?"

"I suppose, but it doesn't look like any place I would want."

Ruben didn't have a key, so Sam used his lock pick to open the front door. He turned to leave and said, "I'd go to a hotel until this blows over."

Back in the car, Sam told J.T. what he'd found in Ernie's house. "I don't see how he came up with the money to invest in a resort. He owed $74,000 on credit cards, and with his gambling he probably had some other big debts."

"Maybe he borrowed his share from Delray."

"You're probably right. Except I can't imagine Delray coming up with $5 million, either. If he borrowed it, he probably had to go to an underground source."

"A shylock?"

Sam nodded. "That much money would've cost them a million dollars for a couple of months, but if they thought they would make $20 million, it would have been a good deal."

"And now Madame Sonja has it all."

They remained silent for a few moments.

"See if you can find a Florida address for Delray," Sam said.

DELRAY AWOKE WITH a throbbing headache and his cell phone chiming in his pocket. What had happened to him after the conversation with the actor, when the lights went out? Pulling out the cell phone, he saw Ernie's number. He answered it, feeling for his car keys, wondering if he'd left them in the ignition.

Less than an hour later, he drove through the open gate at the Cudjoe Key facility. The chain lay broken on the ground and he figured Ruben had done it. Almost daylight, the small crew would arrive soon. Somebody would fix it.

Ernie opened the door as the car reached the parking area and came outside. He didn't look too good as he walked across to the car and got in, rubbing the back of his neck.

"So, you let the actor get the drop on you, huh?" Delray wasn't about to tell him he'd been slugged, too.

"Yeah, well, his days are numbered. He runs his mouth too much." Ernie shook a cigarette from a pack, stuck it between his lips, and lit up.

Delray drove through the gate. "Hey, put that cigarette out. You ain't smoking in the car. Don't you know that's bad for your health?"

He tossed the burning cigarette out the window. "You giving health advice now?"

"I like to think of myself as a responsible citizen."

"Responsible citizen? How many people have you killed?"

"I'd say that ain't none of your business." Who did he think he was, asking that? And maybe trying to make fun. In that case, it probably wouldn't be bad for him to know. Might keep him in line, and keep his stupid mouth shut. "But I don't mind telling you; somewhere between twenty and thirty."

Ernie glanced at him, his mouth open. "Twenty or thirty. You mean you don't know how many?"

Delray shrugged. "You lose track. Anyway, back on the subject. You were talking about Ruben. Does he know about the pill business?"

"I don't think so, but he might, and it's just a matter of time before he says the wrong thing to the TV people. He's also the one who came up with the idiotic idea to buy the resort."

"I thought you came up with that. You acted like you found the property yourself. That's the only reason I agreed."

Ernie looked at him and grimaced. "Yeah, well, Ruben came up with it."

They got on the highway and Delray backhanded him across the nose. "Are you crazy? I gave you $5 million. You're saying that was all based on Ruben's idea?"

Ernie squirmed in his seat, and Delray knew he wanted to hit him back, but he didn't. Delray glanced at him and saw him wipe his bloody nose on his shirtsleeve.

After a long silence, Delray said, "Okay, so I got the picture now. What are you going to do about the money? The lender already asked me about it."

"You borrowed that money?"

"Yeah. You think I had that much cash laying around?"

"Who'd you borrow it from?"

"Somebody who wants it back pretty quick, with interest."

Ernie jerked his head toward him. "How quick you talking about? It might take a while to find the fortune-teller."

Delray chuckled, pretty sure he didn't sound amused.

"Better not take long, or we'll be pushing up daisies."

Ernie's face got red. "I told you we needed it for a real estate investment. Why would you borrow the money from a loan shark?"

"You said it would be a sure thing and we'd double our money."

"Maybe I did, but I told you it'd take a couple of months to get a good buyer. Nothing happens over-night in real estate."

Delray remained silent for a few moments, and then said, "Yeah, well, the shylock said something changed and they need the money back now. How much cash you got?"

"About a hundred thousand is all."

"That won't do much good, but they might hold off a couple of weeks if we can come up with a million of it."

After a long silence Ernie said, "Morris called yester-day and told me one of his contacts wants to buy a load of NewMood. I told him to forget it, because I thought things were going pretty well at the time."

"How much does he want to spend?"

"Morris said maybe two hundred, but if it works out, he'll want more in a few days."

"If it works out?" Delray said. "What did he mean by that?"

"I don't know."

"You sure the guy wants NewMood?"

"That's what Morris said."

Delray sighed. "Okay, get his number and call him."

"I DIDN'T FIND a Florida address for Delray," J.T. said. "He probably stays in hotels when he's here."

"Hmm, that's too bad. I thought we might take a look at his place."

"Yeah, we didn't exactly get a chance to do that while we were in Grand Cayman. Jack looked, but he didn't find anything."

"Yeah, we were in a hurry."

Sam had an idea and glanced at the time on the car dash: 11:15. He took out his cell phone and made a call to a man on his contact list, a pilot named Randy. Their paths had crossed a few months before on a job, and Sam had looked him up later when he needed an airplane. Randy had left his former employer and landed a job flying for a wealthy businessman on Key Largo.

He sounded as if he'd been asleep when he answered the phone.

"Randy, this is Sam Mackenzie."

He grumbled something, not sounding very happy to hear from him.

"I need a plane tonight, like right now. Can you help me out?"

A couple seconds passed before he answered. "Where to?"

Sam thought he might be rubbing sleep from his eyes.

"Grand Cayman."

"You in Miami?"

"No. Key West."

"I don't know… I've got to take the boss up north at ten tomorrow."

"We'll be back way before then. I need to stay less than an hour. You can fuel up during that time and we'll head back."

"Yeah, but… I don't know. That's cutting it close. If he found out I used his plane for other stuff, he'd probably fire me."

"Don't worry, he won't find out, and I'll pay you double the rate I gave you last time."

"Double?"

"Yes."

After a long pause, he said, "Okay, tell me where to pick you up."

FIFTEEN

THE SEAPLANE TAXIED on the water, slowed, and eased up next to the dock at the Hilton's marina. Clean and gleaming, the aircraft looked as if it had just been towed out of the showroom.

No one seemed to be around at this time of night. J.T. boarded first and Sam followed, shoving a bag he had taken from the trunk of his car into a storage compartment. They strapped themselves into seats directly behind the cockpit.

"How long do you think it'll take?" Sam asked. It had been about an hour since Sam had called.

Randy goosed the throttle, coaxing the aircraft away from the dock. "I can get at least 200 knots," Randy said, "so it should take less than three hours."

When they were clear of the dock, Randy taxied the plane away from the marina until he had a clear runway atop the Florida Straits. A crescent moon threw enough light to glisten their path. They had only a hundred yards or so, but that was enough. Randy opened the throttles and the engines revved, with no more noise than an outboard boat motor.

Pinned to his seat from the acceleration, Sam glanced at the time on his phone: 12:25 a.m. Once airborne, he said to the pilot, "If we get there by 3:30, we can start back about 4:30, and you can drop us off and be home by 8:00."

"That sounds good in theory, but I know how you guys operate. You're doing something bad, or you wouldn't need to go in the middle of the night. And I still remember the last time I flew you two down to that part of the world."

Sam recalled the trip, but quickly pushed it out of his mind. "Don't worry, nothing like that is going to happen."

"Yeah, okay. But if I didn't need the money, I wouldn't be here."

Sam actually didn't expect any problems, but that could change. Randy had been a nervous ninny since he had known him, and usually salved his tensions with alcohol. Nothing alcoholic seemed to be aboard the plane, and Sam hoped it stayed that way.

Having clear skies and a tailwind, they landed off the coast of Grand Cayman ahead of schedule at 3:10. Sam had been on the island several times, and thought he knew the area pretty well. He gave Randy directions to an inlet and a marina that would be close to Delray's house. The pilot eased the plane up next to the longest dock and slowed the engines to an idle.

"Okay," Sam said, "we'll be back in an hour."

Randy looked at his watch. "What if you're not?"

"We will be."

Randy stared for a couple of beats and nodded, probably worrying about getting his money if Sam didn't come back as expected.

"All right. I'll go get the fuel in the meantime. I hope the guy in my usual place is still there; otherwise, I'll have to gas up after I pick you up, when the marina's open. That might throw us behind a bit."

Sam slung his bag over his shoulder, and he and

J.T. stepped off the small craft. They strode away as Randy cut an arc and nosed the seaplane back toward open water.

The only lights burning in the marina were several outside floods. They walked quietly down the dock and past an office, and reached the street within a couple minutes. Delray's place should have been only a few doors up, but after walking for five minutes, they still hadn't reached it.

"I'm glad *you* know the way," J.T. said, "because I don't have a clue where we are."

Sam detected a hint of sarcasm in the remark.

Within another minute, they rounded a corner and the house came into view. A floodlight illuminated the front portico. The rest of the place lay in darkness.

They planned to search the yacht first, in case they ran into trouble inside the house. When they reached the backyard, Sam whispered, "So much for the plan." The boat slip where the yacht had been moored was empty. It may have been just as well; Delray would be less likely to leave something valuable on a boat that could be stolen, than in his home. Still, Sam wondered where they had gone with it.

"That means at least one of Delray's men is on the boat," J.T. said, also whispering. "Might make things easier inside."

They went back to the side of the house, past the closed garage bays. A door near the front corner stood slightly ajar.

Sam turned to J.T. "Somebody got here before us. Maybe they're still in there."

They pulled their guns, and Sam eased the door all the way open and stepped into a large garage. Another door in the corner, leading into the house, stood open, light spilling out. After crossing the thirty feet or so, they entered and stopped, listening for any sign of life. No noises except for the hum of the refrigerator. The alarm box on the wall to the left had a digital display indicating that the system had been disarmed. A lamp over the stove cast a dim light in the kitchen where they stood. They eased through to the hallway. The living room lay to the right, all lights off, the bedrooms farther down. They passed a bath on the right. Empty.

At the first bedroom on the left, where Sam and Mona had slept, the door stood open. Sam shone the light inside and saw a man lying on the floor, unconscious, hands and feet bound, mouth gagged. Tattoo man. Delray had left the muscled thug to guard the place, but apparently, he wasn't enough. He had probably gotten out of bed to check on a noise he'd heard and someone clobbered him at the door. Otherwise, the room looked undisturbed. Sam glanced at J.T. and he gave a thumbs-up sign that he had seen the man.

They went on to the next room on the right. The bed looked as if it hadn't been slept in, a comforter across its surface. Same with the next one. Then, farther down, the hall doglegged to the right and extended another twenty feet or so. About midway down on the left was a door. It stood half-open, a hint of light escaping into the hallway. They crept to the door and Sam heard faint clicking sounds.

Turning to J.T., he touched him on the arm, and pointed to the floor in front of him. *Stay here.* Sam stepped beyond the door, turned, and peered inside. He saw a man reaching into the headboard of the bed, a small flashlight in his mouth. As Sam leaned back against the wall, the bag over his shoulder scraped the doorway and he tensed. The noises inside the room stopped and the light went off. Moments passed, then a squeaking noise came from the bed. *He's standing up.* Then a different sound: *snick…snick.* What was that noise? The safety on a gun? Maybe fitting a noise suppressor?

They waited. Finally, hearing soft footsteps advancing slowly toward the door, Sam braced himself. The man eased through the doorway and glanced in J.T.'s direction, a silenced handgun and flashlight leading the way. J.T. jerked his gun up to eye level, ready to fire. Sam slammed the man's face against the doorjamb. *Whack!* His head bounced off the hard surface like a jai alai ball, and he dropped to the floor, unconscious.

Sam knelt and shone the light on his face. Buzz cut, rivets in the earlobes.

"Oh, man, I don't believe this."

"What?" J.T. asked.

"This is the guy who was in the limo with Seams."

"What's he doing *here*?"

"I'm guessing Seams' patience with Jack's scheme ran out, and he sent this guy to get whatever it is Delray stole from that truck."

J.T. checked the man's pants pockets. "Nothing here but some rental car keys and his wallet."

"Let's see the wallet."

According to his Florida driver's license, Rivets went by the name Earl Bates. He had several credit cards in the same name, three hundred dollars in cash, and a Coconut Grove address in Miami.

Sam handed the wallet back to J.T. and pulled an airline boarding pass from Bates' shirt pocket. It indicated that he'd flown in a couple of hours earlier.

They stepped into the room, which was much larger than the others were and had to be Delray's. Bates had gone straight to the bed. The mattress had been pulled away from the headboard, which served as a bookcase. Underneath, set into the concrete wall, was a safe, its door ajar.

"Wonder how he got that open," J.T. said.

"Must be more talented than I thought."

Sam sat on the bed and pulled the safe door open. Stacks of hundred-dollar bills lay inside.

They took the bundles of money out and counted.

"Looks like about fifty grand," Sam said. "Probably just a reserve, in case Delray had to run."

"Yeah, well, we're going to run with it."

Sam thought about the time. It seemed like a long time since Randy had left them at the dock. He pulled out his cell phone and saw that they'd been gone ten minutes past the one hour he'd promised. Randy might have already pulled out.

"Let's go. We're late."

They put the cash into Sam's bag, filling it almost to the top, and hurried out of the house, leaving Tattoo and Rivets asleep on the floor.

When they reached the marina, they saw no sign of Randy.

A dark man who might have been the dockmaster walked up behind them. "Are you waiting for a charter?" He spoke with a clipped English accent.

"Yeah," Sam said, pulling out his phone and glancing at the display. "The guy should have been here by now."

"You need any gear?"

Sam saw him looking at his bag. "No, we don't need any gear."

"Who's the captain? Some of them don't supply the gear."

"The captain?" Sam wished this guy would leave. If Randy had left them, they'd need to find another way home, and right now, he didn't know what that would be. If they had to take a commercial flight, they'd need passports. He had one, but didn't think to bring it. J.T. probably didn't have one with him, either. Maybe Randy had just gotten delayed and would show up.

"Yeah, the captain. The bloke that pilots the boat."

Sam turned to J.T. "You remember the captain's name?"

"Yeah, it was…" He closed one eye, as if concentrating. "It was George something."

"George, huh?" The man asked it as if he didn't believe them. "Would that be Captain George Cavanaugh?"

J.T. shook his head. "Hmmm…no, I don't think that's it."

"How about Captain George Little?"

J.T. pointed a finger at him. "That's it. Captain Little."

The man nodded. "Captain Little has the gear. But you should have called me. I could have set you up with a much better boat than Captain Little." He gave Sam a card that read, "Reginald Cork, Dockmaster."

Come on, Randy.

Sam looked at the card and said, "We'll call you on our next trip."

Cork smiled. "Yep, please do that. I'll get you a splendid deal."

He started back toward the office, and then Sam heard the buzz of the seaplane in the distance. It came into view, touched down on the water and taxied toward the dock. As soon as it bumped against the dock, Sam popped the door open and climbed in. J.T. followed and closed the door behind him. Randy goosed the throttle, pulled the craft away from the dock and turned back toward open water.

"Sorry I'm late," Randy said. "I had to call the guy on his cell to wake him up."

"That's okay," Sam said. "We'll take it out of your pay."

Randy turned and glared from the cockpit.

"Hey, I'm kidding. Believe me; we're glad you were late."

Randy seemed to relax. A half-smile on his face, he turned back to the controls and opened the throttle for takeoff.

Sam peered out the window at the man on the dock, who might have already guessed that they wouldn't be calling him for a charter. Less than a minute later, they were airborne, and a few minutes after that, Sam leaned back against the head rest and fell asleep.

He awoke on touchdown on the Florida Straits. Randy eased down on the throttle and taxied toward the Hilton's marina where they'd left the car. Sam checked the time: 8:15. When the plane came to a stop, he handed Randy two stacks of the cash.

"This cover it?"

Randy thumbed through the hundreds. "Oh, yeah, this is good. Forget everything I said about you."

Glancing at the floor of the cockpit, Sam spotted an empty half-pint rum bottle lying on its side. Randy probably had broken out the booze while sweating getting back in time to fly his boss to his meeting. That was probably an improvement; Sam remembered him drinking more than twice that much when he had flown with him in the past. Randy saw him looking, picked up the bottle and tossed it out the window into the water. He popped a handful of breath mints into his mouth as Sam and J.T. stepped down to the dock.

SIXTEEN

SAM AND J.T. went to their rooms and showered, shaved, and changed clothes. Mona had a table in the restaurant when they arrived about 8:45. She looked a little steamed. J.T. took a seat across from her and Sam sat to her right.

Mona looked at her watch. "I thought we were supposed to meet at 8:30."

"Yeah," Sam said. "I guess we're running late. Where's Jack?"

She shrugged. "I saw him go out the lobby door when I got off the elevator, and I thought he'd come right back, but he hasn't been in here."

The waiter poured coffee for Sam and J.T. and asked if they were ready to order.

"Give us a few more minutes," Sam said, and the waiter stepped away. "How long ago?"

"About thirty minutes."

"Order breakfast," Sam told them. "I'll go check on him."

At Jack's room, he found the door cracked, and knocked on it. When he didn't get an answer, he pushed through into the room. It appeared to be empty. The bathroom door stood open, the light off. He looked in and found the same thing. No luggage, and any personal articles Jack might have had were gone.

Unsure what name Jack had used, Sam called the

front desk with his cell phone and said he'd called Jack's room phone and no one answered.

The desk clerk went away for a minute or so, then came back and said the person in the room had checked out.

Sam went back to the restaurant and told them what the clerk had said. The food arrived and they ate, and then went to Sam's room.

Once inside and seated, J.T. said, "So, what do we do now?"

"Let's locate Jack. I don't think he would leave on his own like that. And let's see what we can do to bust up this pill business."

J.T. sighed. "Okay, but I better not find out he just left us here, or I'm going to be ticked off at Mr. Jackson Craft."

Sam asked him to try to find Ernie's websites on his computer.

"That'll be like looking for a needle in a haystack," Mona said.

"Yeah, but J.T.'s an expert at this kind of thing. Right, J.T.?"

J.T. smiled, and Sam thought he might have blushed. "I might be able to narrow them down. If Jack was right, Ernie probably has dozens of them, and they'll have to have some similarities for his programmer to be able to shut one down and start up a new one without losing much time."

"I'm going to look for Ruben and see what he knows," Sam said.

Seated next to him on the sofa, Mona linked her arm in his. "I'm coming with you."

"I'd rather you didn't."

"Why not?"

"It could be dangerous. I'm still not sure about Ruben. He could be as bad as the others."

Mona laughed. "He might be a self-absorbed jerk, but I don't think he's dangerous."

Sam thought about it for a moment. "Okay, I hope you're right." He told her about Ruben's adventure the night before.

"Sounds like they're gunning for him."

"Yep. I wish I knew why."

J.T. sighed. "Maybe they have hopes of getting back the money they invested and decided they'd just keep Ruben's part."

"He thought he was Mason Vogue?" Mona said.

"Yes, and he seemed disappointed when he found out he's just an actor, even a rich one."

Mona said, "That doesn't sound like Ruben. Maybe the knock on the head did him some good."

"Maybe you're right," Sam said. "He seemed like a pretty nice guy."

"Sounds like you saved his life."

She touched his hand. He looked into her smiling eyes, and something in his chest fluttered. Never one to overanalyze his feelings, he knew something might be there, but tried to push it out of his mind. J.T. stared, a grin on his face. Mona blushed and looked away.

"I think we should tell her the rest," Sam said.

J.T. nodded. "Fine with me."

He told about the limo, the truck, and the ruined metal case, and about their trip to Grand Cayman, leaving out the part about the money.

"So Jack is doing all this for a man named Grant

Seams, and you left his guy unconscious in Grand Cayman?"

"Yeah, he had a gun. I'd already seen what he did to the big tattooed guy."

"He's lucky he didn't get shot," J.T. said. "If you hadn't been standing right behind him, he'd be a dead man."

DELRAY AND ERNIE rode north on US-1 toward Miami, where they had an appointment with the man who wanted to buy a load of NewMood. After Ernie had talked with the prospective customer, they had gone back to the plant and taken one of the trucks that still had about a third of its load. They found the place on the outskirts of Miami.

"You sure this is it?" Delray asked. "This looks like some kind of factory."

"Yeah, it's the right address, and he said a black Jag would be parked out front. There's the Jag over there."

"He give you a name?"

"He said his name is Rime. Spelled R-i-m-e."

"Rime? What kind of name is that?"

"Hey, I didn't exactly get into a conversation about his family tree, okay?"

Delray eased the ten-wheeler through an open gate and parked next to a loading dock. They got out, walked up onto the dock, and knocked on the door. It opened and a man who looked seven feet tall stuck his head out. He had blond hair, almost white, pulled back in a ponytail, the skin on his face the palest Delray had ever seen on a living person. He wore round, rimless glasses with black lenses.

"You Rime?" Delray asked.

"You got it."

He came out to the edge of the dock, gave the truck a once-over, and spat a stream of what looked like tobacco juice into the parking lot. A smile revealed a mouthful of discolored teeth. They followed him down a hall to an office with a window overlooking some kind of factory where people were working.

He sat in a chair behind a metal desk and put his feet up.

"Sit down and we'll get to know each other."

"Hey, we didn't come here for coffee," Delray said. "You got the money or not?"

The man smiled and looked at Delray, then picked up a tin can from the floor and spat in it.

"Sure, I got the money. I just thought you'd want to know what I'm going to do with a truckload of mood drugs, especially since I might want about ten times that much more in a few days."

Delray stared at the people on the factory floor for a moment, then sat down. "Okay, it did occur to me what you're doing here, I mean, you probably can't peddle this stuff on the street."

Ernie sat down in the other chair and rubbed the back of his neck, a frown on his face.

Rime looked at Ernie. "You need something?"

Ernie shook his head. He pulled the plastic bottle from his pocket and chewed a couple of pills.

Rime looked back at Delray.

"See those people out there?" He pointed at the window behind him. "They're mixing up NewMood with a little ingredient I discovered when I was cooking meth. The result is a pill with a bigger kick than heroin. I call it Dead Man's Curve."

Delray frowned. "Why do you call it that?"

"You know much about baseball?"

Baseball? What did he care about baseball? He wanted to get on with the show.

"It's a stupid game. What's that got to do with these pills?"

The big man smiled, showing the dark teeth. He dropped his feet on the floor, took off the glasses and leaned forward on the desk. His eyes were two slits, and the look on his face caused Delray to push back in his chair.

"I knew a guy who used to pitch in the majors. A southpaw. He could throw a curve ball that would break two feet. It was fast, maybe a hundred miles an hour, and most batters wouldn't even swing, thinking it was way outside. Hit the strike zone right before it smacked the mitt. He struck out a lot of batters on that pitch. But he didn't see too well, and sometimes he'd pitch wild. Hit a few guys."

"So?"

"The last season he played, he hit two batters square in the middle of the chest. Stopped their hearts."

"They died?"

Rime closed his eyes and nodded.

"Dead as a ball-peen hammer."

Delray smiled. A pretty cool story after all.

"Dead Man's Curve. You saying some of the people that take this stuff could die?"

Rime grinned. "Maybe, if they get carried away. But they won't know 'til the umpire calls it."

"What do you mix the stuff with?" Ernie asked.

Rime spat in the can. "If I told you that, I'd be giving away the fortune I plan to make."

J.T. GOT UP to leave. "I'll go to the room and try to get a track on Ernie's websites."

When he had gone, Sam said, "This situation can get deadly with Delray involved."

Mona crossed her arms as if cold, or maybe afraid. "But he's been involved since the beginning, hasn't he?"

"Yes, but I didn't know about the other part, the metal case with blood on it. He has something Jack wants, other than the money. And if Delray killed somebody to get it, he won't hesitate killing people to keep it."

Sam sighed and leaned back on the sofa.

Mona shivered and sat silent for several seconds.

"I wanted you to know the potential danger," he said, "before it's too late to bail out."

Her eyes softened. "Are you staying?"

Although unsure exactly why, Sam knew he would. Helping Jack was only part of it, now. Jack had put off telling him the rest of the story, maybe because of J.T., but maybe he didn't trust Sam with the information, either. Regardless, whether Jack was in the picture or not, Sam now wanted to shut Delray down himself. And he wanted to find out what had been in that case, telling himself that he wouldn't want it if he got his hands on it…but who knows, maybe he would. He'd have to wait and see.

He nodded. "Guess so."

Mona seemed to consider that, then moved closer to him on the sofa and kissed him lightly on the lips. "Then I am, too."

Sam's heart moved into overdrive, and he could feel his face getting warm.

"I saw the way you looked at me in the restaurant," she said.

"Yeah?"

She looked at his lips and Sam pulled her to him. They kissed again, this time longer, and then she pulled away, went to the door, and put the Do Not Disturb sign outside.

SEVENTEEN

"EASY MONEY," Delray said. "Normally it would take us a couple of weeks to make that much."

Delray drove the truck back down US-1, the cab even hotter than the morning ride north.

Ernie lit up a cigarette. "That won't stall the shylock, though."

"Yeah, but the Rime guy said he'd turn this over tonight and wants ten times that much tomorrow."

"Do we have enough?"

"Yeah, we got it."

"Well, that's still a long shot," Ernie said, his voice edged with sarcasm. "Something's been bugging me, too. How come those guys let you have so much money? I never heard of them loaning that kind of cash to anybody."

"It ain't none of your business, but I had collateral, and that's all I'm gonna say about it."

"Collateral? You mean that estate in Grand Cayman."

"Hey, I said it ain't any of your business." Delray felt his pulse firing in his ears.

"Well, we still need a lot more cash."

"Yeah, and whose fault is that? Like I said, you should've told me we couldn't get that money right back."

Ernie took a deep breath. "Okay, I'm not arguing about this anymore."

Delray pulled the truck over to the side of the road. They were below Key Largo, with nothing in sight but open road and water.

"You got that right," Delray said. He jerked the cigarette from Ernie's mouth and stuck it in Ernie's shirt pocket. "Get out."

Ernie's eyes shot to his pocket, which was now smoking. He grasped the cigarette, threw it out the window, and rubbed his sooty fingers on his shirt. "What are you talking about?"

"Get out of the truck. I'm tired of your whining, and I'm tired of telling you about them cigarettes." He picked up a handgun from the seat and pointed it at Ernie.

Ernie threw up his hands. "Hey, hold on. I'm sorry, okay? My fault. I admit it."

Delray looked out the windshield. Several seconds ticked away. "All right, but you better not say any more about the shylock. And don't light any more cigarettes around me. You understand?"

"Yeah, I understand."

They started down the road again and were quiet for a few minutes.

Ernie said, "You know, I've been thinking. If Rime wants two million worth tomorrow, that probably means he's getting at least that much for the supply we already sold him."

"Yeah, so?"

"He's getting our pills cheap, that's all."

"We got as much as we would've got selling them to our regular customers, and we got it a lot quicker. So what's your point?"

"I thought there might be a better arrangement.

Maybe we could be partners. We supply the NewMood and he peps it up with his meth juice. He sells it, and we split the money fifty-fifty."

Delray laughed. "Why would he go along with that?"

"We put it to him; that's the only way we'll sell it."

Delray thought about it for a few miles. If Rime sold the two million dollars' worth of NewMood for ten times that much, he would have what? Twenty million? Half of that would be ten million. He whistled to himself, but it must have been louder than he thought, because Ernie turned and stared at him.

"What is it?" Ernie asked.

"Maybe you got something. We'd get ten million instead of two. And we don't ask him about the partnership, we tell him. Where else is he going to get that much product? Fifty percent is better than nothing. If he don't go along, we pop a cap on him and take over his operation. We'll pitch *him* the Dead Man's Curve."

"Maybe that's what we do anyway," Ernie said. "Wait'll he sells and take it all."

Delray smiled. "Yeah, the whole twenty million. Now you're talking."

SAM AND MONA drove to Ruben's house and knocked on the door. They waited a few moments and he opened it.

"What do you want?"

"After what happened last night," Sam said, "I thought I'd check on you."

"You were worried about me?"

"Sure."

Ruben looked at Mona. "Who're you?"

"Friend of mine," Sam said. Mona smiled and linked her arm inside Sam's.

Ruben glanced up and down the street. "Okay, come on in."

They went inside and sat in the living room.

"I thought you might've gone somewhere," Sam said.

"I had planned to, but the more I thought about those two trying to kill me the madder I got. I had Ernie's gun, so I decided I'd wait for them to come back and maybe give them a taste of their own medicine."

"Those guys are pretty dangerous," Sam said.

"Yeah? Well, so am I."

Sam asked if he'd gone anywhere since arriving the night before.

"Why?"

Sam told him about Jack.

Ruben gave him a confused look. "Why would *I* know anything about it?"

"He's the person who sold you the resort. I thought you might be bitter about it."

Ruben nodded. "I found some papers about that, and I also got a bank statement in the mail today. It didn't show any withdrawals, so I don't know where the money would have come from, if I invested in something like that."

Sam wondered about it, too. "Maybe you had another account."

"I suppose, but I searched the place well and didn't find any evidence of another account."

After a couple of beats, Ruben said, "Well, if there's nothing else, I need to try to figure out what I was doing in business with Ernie."

EIGHTEEN

"I HAD ANOTHER IDEA," Ernie said.

Delray drove the truck through the gate at their facility on Cudjoe Key and watched it close behind him in the rearview mirror. They'd fixed it, like he thought they would.

"Yeah? What's that?"

"Ruben has all these expensive things in his office. At least he says they're expensive. We could go over there tonight and load them up."

Delray looked at him. "What kind of things?"

"Paintings, vases, stuff like that. Ruben said they're rare. He calls it his retirement cache. He made a joke about it a couple of times; he laughs and says, 'Get it? Cache, like C-A-S-H?' Pretty stupid joke, I thought. I know how to spell cash. Nothing funny about that."

Delray didn't understand the joke, and didn't particularly care. He drove up the driveway, behind the building, and turned off the engine.

"What would we do with this stuff? Be pretty hard to sell if it's rare."

Ernie grinned. "You forget what business I'm in. I know a couple of fences who could get rid of it, maybe give us about half the market value."

"Half? How much would that be?"

"I don't know. Maybe half a million or more. I know Ruben spent a lot of money on it. He used to go to these auctions, and he'd complain about being broke for weeks after."

"You're kidding me? Why didn't you say something about this sooner?"

"I guess I didn't think about it. Besides, like I said, I don't know what the stuff is really worth."

Delray looked at his watch. It would be dark in a couple of hours.

"You have a key to the office?"

"Course I got a key. It's my office, too."

"Would he go to the cops if we stole his stuff?"

"No way. I don't think he'd want to say how he could afford to buy it in the first place."

BACK IN THE car, Sam called J.T. on his cell phone.

"You make any progress on the websites?"

"I think I've found them, about twenty-five different sites. All of them have different page designs, but they all sell NewMood, and they all have the same ordering method. I've also traced them back to a single set of servers, so I'm pretty sure they belong to Ernie."

A car passed by, and Sam recognized the driver as Morris, the guy who'd tried to roust him and Mona outside the restaurant. He had a passenger in the car with him, a woman with dark hair. Sam pulled to the curb and waited. Morris turned into Ruben's driveway and parked. He got out of the car and walked to the door.

"You still there?" J.T. asked.

"Yeah…can you put them out of business?"

"Sure, just say the word. They'll probably be able to rebuild the sites, but it'll take a while."

"Okay, do it, and make it as permanent as you can."

"I'm on it. Where are you?"

"Mona and I just left Ruben's place. He still doesn't have a clue about what's going on, and I'm pretty sure he didn't have anything to do with Jack's disappearing act. I gotta go. Morris just stopped there and he's going in to see Ruben."

He closed the phone. Morris rang the doorbell and waited a couple of minutes before giving up and going back to the car.

"That's the man who pulled a gun on us outside the restaurant," Mona said.

"Yes, it is."

Morris backed out and Sam put his arm around Mona and pulled her to him for a kiss. She pressed her lips to his as if it were real. He wanted it to last longer, but Morris drove by and he broke away so he could see. This time he got a good look at the passenger, and waited until they got up the street a couple of blocks before following them.

"Do you think he has something to do with Jack disappearing?" Mona asked.

Sam kept his eye on the car.

"Maybe. That's Sonja Lazar riding with him."

RUBEN HAD GONE through all his personal records. Although he and Ernie were supposed to be business partners, he had found no evidence of that. Maybe he'd check out the offices again at the Outpost Mariner. Now that he knew more about the situation, something might make sense. Something that would tell him why people were trying to kill him.

He'd also watched some videos from a television show. In the videos, he played the detective Mason Vogue, a man good at what he did. Just watching the shows made Ruben want to find Ernie Brent and work him over. The redheaded fellow, too.

In the garage, he found a silver sports car that looked almost new. His key fit the ignition, so it had to belong to him. He drove to the resort, went up to his office, and used the card key the bartender had gotten him. This time, he went into the office with "Ruben Vale" on the door. At the desk he punched the power switch on the computer. It took a few seconds for it to boot up. The screen looked familiar, and he knew the purpose of the various program icons. Funny, how he could remember that, but not remember anything about himself. He ran the e-mail program and three unread messages popped up on the screen. They were all from someone named Raven. He opened the oldest one, from a couple of weeks before. It read, "We're all set for tomorrow."

Raven. It sounded female, but he supposed it might be a man or a woman. Hadn't there been a Raven in one of Poe's poems? A black bird, but he didn't remember anything about it being male or female. Anyway, he wondered what he and Raven had planned for that day.

The second message from the day before read: "It's been two days. Why haven't you called?" Then, the last one from later that day, read: "Where are you? Call me!"

Sounded like Raven might be getting a little upset.

Should he send a reply? What would he say? He wasn't sure he wanted anybody else knowing he couldn't remember anything, yet.

The word processor had no documents stored there, except the junk that comes with a computer. Seeing nothing else of any interest on the machine, he turned off the power and began a search of the desk drawers. It yielded a copy of the same papers he'd found in Ernie's desk, about their purchase of the hotel. It seemed pretty obvious from the lack of paper accumulation that he hadn't occupied the office very long.

Leaning back in the chair, he noticed the office furnishings for the first time. Pretty impressive. All antiques, in good condition. A painting on the wall looked like an original Picasso. Another appeared to be an original Dali, and some others looked as if they might have been painted hundreds of years ago, their colorful surfaces covered with intricate webs of fine cracks. They had to be worth a lot of money, if they were real. Ruben wondered how he might have acquired them… but, then, maybe he didn't want to know.

Deciding he hadn't learned much, he went back to Ernie's office for another look around. The pills and the hotel sale papers were still in the middle drawer, but there seemed to be nothing else of any value. What he noticed most was the difference in the office decor. Ernie's office had a couple of cheap hotel prints on the wall that looked as if they'd been there since the place got built. A lamp that looked like a lighthouse, probably purchased in a gift shop, sat on the corner of the desk. Otherwise, the place looked pretty drab. Now dark outside, he gave up and left.

Ruben went to his car and started it. Another car came down the hotel driveway with Ernie and the redheaded man inside. Ernie drove past the parking area to the far side of the lot and stopped. Ruben slid out of the car, duck-walked behind several other vehicles, and peeked over a hood to watch what the two men did. They got out, scanned the lot, as if making sure nobody was watching, and then went in the side entrance of the hotel.

After a few minutes, they came out, each carrying an armload of paintings. They put them in the car's trunk, closed it, and went back inside.

They were stealing his art collection!

The two men came out a few minutes later carrying two or three more paintings and a couple of vases. With those items stowed in the trunk, they got into the car and drove away.

SAM BRAKED AND watched Morris turn into the driveway of a house on a quiet street. The car disappeared around the house, and a minute later, he walked back to the front yard where he pulled a "For Rent" sign out of the dirt and tossed it under a palmetto. Sonja opened the front door from the inside and let him in.

The place looked as if it had been vacant for a while. Sam wondered why Sonja Lazar would be hanging around with Morris, and if Jack might be tied up inside the house. If so, why? Sonja already had the money. Maybe Jack had something else she wanted. He always seemed to have an extra card up his sleeve.

"Wait here," Sam said, turning off the car. "I'm going to talk to them."

He pulled a gun from under the seat and opened the door.

"Can't I go with you?" Mona asked.

Sam shook his head. "No way. This should be easy, but you never know."

"Okay, but you better be right back or I'm coming in."

He looked at her.

"Don't do that. If I'm not back in fifteen minutes, call J.T." He gave her J.T.'s number.

"You better come back, though."

Concern flashed in her eyes. She probably remembered the gun Morris had pointed at them.

"Don't worry. It'll be okay."

He closed the door, stuck the gun in the back pocket of his pants, and walked down the street toward the house where Morris had gone. A thicket of palmetto, elephant ears, and palms bordered it on either side. Stepping into the yard next door, he eased to the backyard and pushed his way through the cool shrubs to the other side. A yellow and black spider the size of a half-dollar dropped on his arm. Though he brushed it off, a shiver ran up his spine. The door on the screened back porch wouldn't budge, so he took out his pocketknife and cut the screen wire enough to get his hand through. Feeling a latch on the other side, he flipped it out of its eyelet. The hinge squeaked when he opened the door, and he winced.

The back door knob wouldn't turn. It didn't have a deadbolt, so he pushed a credit card into the crack next to the knob, released the locking mechanism, and opened the door. Pulling the gun from his pocket, he eased through the kitchen and could hear them talking in the front part of the house.

When he made it to the far side of the dining area, he hugged the wall and peered into the living room. Morris came through the door. The man's eyes widened and he grabbed for his gun, which didn't seem to be where he thought it should be. Sam stepped back and kicked him in the chin. Morris's head snapped back and his eyes rolled up like window shades. He fell back onto the floor. Sam stepped over him into the living room.

Sonja Lazar stood there, her eyes wide with surprise.

"Remember me?" Sam asked. "You were all out of fortunes the last time I saw you."

"What do you want?" Though she scowled at him, her face remained beautiful, like that of an aging movie star.

"Where's Jack?"

"How would I know?"

"You're the fortuneteller. Get out your crystal ball and see what's there. Otherwise, I'm going to hurt your friend in there."

Morris groaned from the other room and Sam reached in and dragged him through the doorway, keeping the gun trained on Sonja. He put his foot on Morris's neck. The man jerked for a couple of seconds, but stopped when Sam applied more pressure.

"All right, you've made your point. But I haven't seen Jack in a couple of days."

"Not good enough," Sam said and pressed harder with his foot.

Morris made a choking sound and grabbed for Sam's foot, but more pressure made him still again. "You're breaking my neck," he said, his words raspy, barely intelligible.

Sonja stepped toward Sam and held her hands up, palms out. "Please stop. I'll give you whatever you want." Then her eyes widened, she put her hand to her chest and gasped. "My heart... I need my medicine."

She grabbed her purse off a table about a foot from Sam and opened it.

"Careful," Sam said. "You better not have a gun in there."

Taking a deep breath, she pulled out a prescription container. She opened it, shook a capsule into her hand,

and broke it in her palm. Something that looked like white dust poured out.

A split second later, she blew it into Sam's face.

Sam tried to step back, but his feet felt heavy, as though encased in cement. Sonja smiled and said something, only it sounded a lot like Donald Duck doing a scat routine. Then he heard screeching sounds like those issued from a bad microphone, and the wood floor swung up and slapped him in the face.

NINETEEN

A STREET NOISE woke Ruben. He'd been sitting in his car down the street from Ernie's house for nearly an hour, waiting for the two men to make their move. They'd gone inside and left the stolen art in the car. Worrying about these two guys the night before had ruined his sleep, and now fatigue had caught up with him. In fact, a lot of things were catching up with him. The headache had returned, and he'd forgotten to bring any pain medication. Inside the glove compartment, he found a bottle of aspirin. Since he didn't have anything to wash them down with, he let them melt in his mouth and swallowed. The bitter taste nearly made him gag.

Ernie and the redheaded man came out a few minutes later, got into Ernie's car, and drove away. Ruben waited until they got down the block before following. After driving several miles up the highway, he thought he knew where they were going. They passed Stock Island and kept going north until they reached Cudjoe Key, then turned where Ernie had turned the night before, and rode inland. Unsure whether or not he wanted to go down that road, he eased up on the accelerator. What if they'd seen him follow them? This could be a trap. Maybe they just planned to ambush him and put him in the compactor.

Ruben took the turn at the convenience store and saw a clearing with a shell-and-sand road leading into the woods. He slowed, turned in, and parked behind a stand of palmetto. No one would be able to see him there, but he could view the road and the lighted parking lot of the store.

More than an hour passed before a set of headlights came back up the road. It turned out to be a truck instead of Ernie's car, and the redheaded man sat in the driver's seat. It pulled into the convenience store, and Ernie got out and went inside, returning with a twelve-pack of beer.

SAM WOKE UP in the trunk of a moving car. The confined space smelled like grease and tire rubber. He heard muffled voices, but he couldn't make out any of the words. Though he didn't feel bound, he lay in a twisted position, his feet and legs tingling. His face felt hot, his head spun, and nausea crept into his throat. He took a deep breath, drawing the foul air into his lungs. The sick feeling subsided after a few seconds, and he remembered the powder Sonja had blown into his face. Though he couldn't begin to guess what it was, it had been fast and effective.

The backside of one of the taillights glowed about a foot from his eyes. He wondered how long he had been unconscious, and if Mona had seen Morris put him into the trunk. Not likely, since the car had been parked in the backyard. Hopefully, she had called J.T.

Remembering the knife, he worked his hand into his pocket. Gone. Morris might be smarter than he seemed.

ALMOST TO MIAMI, Ruben trailed less than a mile behind the truck. Beethoven's Fifth broke the numbing drone of the highway, playing on the phone in his pocket. It startled him for a moment, because he hadn't heard it ring since finding it on his bedside table. Pulling the phone out of his pocket, he opened it and said, "Hello."

"Where have you been?" The voice of a woman.

"Who is this?"

"Stop playing. You know who this is."

Remembering the e-mails, he said, "Are you Raven?"

A sigh on the other end.

"Yes, I'm Raven. Tell me where you are."

Ruben wondered if Ernie had put her up to calling.

"Why do you want to know?"

Another sigh. "We need to talk about what happened."

"Do you work for Ernie?"

"Are you crazy?"

"Maybe I am." He told her his location.

AT LEAST AN hour had passed, the trunk getting hotter and hotter, the odor more nauseating than ever. Sam thought he might get dizzy again, but then something happened. A crashing impact sent him smashing into the wall between the trunk and back seat, and then the car sat deathly still and silent.

Seconds passed. He heard people yelling outside the car, and he reached up and tapped on the trunk lid. Nothing happened, so he tried again, this time louder. After a few seconds, the lid opened, and Porky Pig stood there with a gun in his hand. Sam wondered if he might say, "That's all, folks," and pull the trigger.

"What're you doing in there?" The man with the pig mask had an accent, maybe New York or Jersey.

A second Porky came into view and said, "We gotta go. Cops will be here any second." He looked into the trunk. "Who's this?"

Porky One said, "I don't know, but we're gonna take this car." He said to Sam, "Get out of the trunk."

Sam slid to the edge and struggled out. The air outside smelled fresh and clean, but then the sweet, chemical odor of automobile coolant drifted by his nostrils. He glanced at the car a few feet from the front end of Morris' car. It leaned to one side, the hood crumpled, and steam rose from underneath.

The Porkys looked inside Morris' car and Porky One said to Sam, "I guess these are not your friends."

The airbag had deployed on the driver's side where Morris sat. He lay against the seat, the bag on his lap, out cold. Sonja looked as if she might be taking a nap, still as a baby, her face pressed against the dash.

"Good guess," Sam said.

A siren screamed in the distance.

The guy giving the orders clutched a plastic store bag in one hand that looked as if it might be half-filled with money. He nodded toward the other masked man and told Sam to give him a hand with the two in the car.

They got Morris out and shoved him into the back seat, then did the same with Sonja. Sam felt a pulse under her arms when he picked her up, and wondered how bad she might be injured. He thought it curious that he would be interested in her health after she had blown knockout dust in his face. Still, compared to the rest of these guys, she probably wasn't that bad.

Porky Two jerked the airbag out of the way, got behind the wheel and started the car. He told Sam to sit in front, and Porky One sat in back with the gun trained on him.

"You do anything stupid, I'm going to shoot you."

RUBEN HAD WATCHED Delray and Ernie check into a motel in south Miami a few minutes after midnight. Sleepy, he thought he might get a room, too, but wanted to see Raven first.

He had waited nearly an hour when a car tore out of a convenience store lot next door, went through a red light, and crashed into another car. It sounded like a shotgun blast, followed by a sickening screech of grinding metal. After a couple seconds of silence, the car that ran the light started up and tried to back away from the other car, but the wheel was broken off and its axle dragged on the pavement. The front doors shot open and two men jumped out. They wore pig masks, and one of them had a gun in his hand. Sirens droned in the distance. The two masked men surveyed the broken wheel, then went over to the other car and looked inside. Ruben couldn't see the faces of anyone in that vehicle.

The men yelled at each other for a few seconds, then opened the trunk and a third man climbed out. Ruben recognized him as the guy who had saved him from the redheaded man. He looked like someone who could take care of himself, and Ruben wondered how he had gotten locked in the trunk of the car.

They moved some people around, then got in and rode away, leaving the crumpled vehicle steaming under the streetlights. Ruben glanced at his watch. Raven should have arrived already, and Ernie and Delray looked as if they might be finished for the night. He sighed, started the car, and followed the pigs.

SAM WONDERED WHERE they were going. They rode several minutes through neighborhoods where salsa music

blared, and young men sat on hoods of low riders yelling at the girls who passed.

They finally turned into a driveway, rode to a spot
behind a small block house, and stopped. The driver
ripped off his mask and tossed it on the floor. Sweat
dripped from his mustache. Sam could still hear the
music, but it seemed miles away.

The robber in the back seat said, "Well, well, Sleeping Beauty's awake."

Sam glanced at Sonja, who rubbed the side of her
face with her fingertips, then at the robber in back. He
had unmasked, too, and had only one distinguishing
feature, a nose that crooked to one side, as if broken
in a fight.

"Who are you?" Sonja asked, her eyes trying to
focus.

"You wrecked our car, lady."

She looked confused for a couple of seconds, and
then gave him a frown. "You ran the red light and hit
us."

"Just shut your face and get out of the car."

"I'm not getting out. This is my car."

Sam heard a click as the man with the crooked nose
thumbed the hammer on the gun.

"Yes you are, unless you want to die right here. And
wake up your friend. We're not gonna carry him."

Sonja shook Morris. He sat up in the seat and stared
at her, as if seeing her for the first time.

They got out of the car and went in the back door of
the house, Sonja holding onto Morris' arm. The man
with the mustache led the way to a cramped living room
and turned on a floor lamp at the far end of a thread-

bare sofa. He told them to sit down. Sam took a seat under the lamp.

"We gotta figure out what to do. We'd be in the Keys by now if it wasn't for you two."

Morris looked at him with the same blank stare he'd given Sonja. Mustache turned on an old TV in the corner and flipped the channels. Crooked Nose handed him his gun and told him to watch them while he got a drink from the kitchen. He walked out, still carrying the bag. Mustache laid the gun on the table next to the TV and went back to the channel selector.

Sam thought this might be as good a time as any. He grabbed the lamp, jerking the power cord from the wall, stood, and swung its base in the flickering light of the TV. Mustache seemed to realize something bad had happened and reached for the gun, but the heavy end of the lamp struck him on the side of the head before he got to it. He fell backward on the tile floor with a *whump*.

Sam picked up the gun, went looking for the other man, and met him coming back into the room with a drink in his hand. He shoved the gun barrel at the man's face.

"Put the glass on the table and get on the floor."

Crooked Nose looked down at his partner, hesitated, and tossed the drink at Sam's eyes. Sam sidestepped and struck him on the back of the head with the butt of the weapon. The man pitched forward and smacked the tile. The bite of cheap whiskey filled Sam's nostrils, and his eyes lost focus for a moment with a wave of dizziness like what he'd experienced in the trunk of the car.

Sam tried the light switch on the wall. Nothing happened, so he re-plugged the lamp. Though the shade looked mangled, the bulb still worked.

"Take off their belts," Sam said to Sonja, "and use them to tie their hands behind their backs." She did as instructed, her eyes large with surprise. Sam glanced at Morris: still no threat, nodding off every couple seconds.

The sound of footsteps came from the kitchen. He turned and pointed the gun at the doorway in time to see Ruben burst through with a gun in his hand.

"Freeze," Ruben said, "or I'll shoot."

He glanced at Sam standing there with the gun, and looked at the two men on the floor.

"What are you doing here?" Sam asked.

Ruben looked down at the men on the floor. "Are these the guys with the masks?"

Sam said they were. He wondered how Ruben knew anything about them.

"I wanted to rescue you," Ruben said, "like you did for me." He told him about seeing the masked men with guns ride away with Sam in the car. "But it looks like you have everything under control," he said, sticking the gun in the waistband of his pants.

"Okay, we're even," Sam said. "You probably should make sure the safety is set on that gun."

"Oh, yeah, good idea." He took the gun out, examined it, put it back. "It is."

Sonja stood up and grabbed Ruben's hand.

"Who are you?" Ruben asked.

She looked hurt, or it might have just been an act. "You don't remember?"

Ruben's face brightened. "You're Raven?"

"Yes, what's wrong with you?"

Ruben turned to Sam, as if he didn't know what to say.

"He had a head injury," Sam said to Sonja. He turned

to Ruben. "She's the fortuneteller who got you into this jam."

Ruben stared at her. "What'd you need to see me about?"

Sonja squeezed his hand and said, "I'll tell you later."

"Get the masks from the car," Sam said to Ruben.

After he left, Sam got the moneybag from the kitchen, went back to the living room, and dumped it on the floor at the feet of the robbers. Ruben came back and Sam told him to drop the masks next to the money. He found a cell phone in the shirt pocket of one of the men and dialed 911. When the emergency operator answered, Sam said, "We just robbed a store and want to give ourselves up." With a last look around, he dropped the phone next to one of the men and they hurried out the door.

TWENTY

SONJA DROVE, AND SAM sat in front with her while Morris lay on the back seat. Ruben followed in his car. They rode out of the neighborhood and saw two police cruisers speeding in the direction of the house they had just left.

"Okay," Sam said, "let's pick up where you blew the angel dust in my face."

Sonja glanced at him but said nothing.

"What have you done with Jack?"

She seemed to consider the question for a moment, then said, "Why do you want to know?"

Sam shrugged. "He's missing, and I thought you might be responsible. If he's dead, you're going to pay."

"That's funny; you look like a hired killer yourself."

"I'm working for him."

She glanced at Sam. "He never mentioned anybody like you."

"Well, if you know Jack, you know he doesn't tell everything."

She nodded. "I've been looking for him, myself."

"Why?" Sam asked. "You already have the money. Jack went to the bank in Grand Cayman where you were supposed to meet him to split it. You'd already been there with someone posing as Jack and took the money."

"Jack obviously didn't tell *you* everything, either."

Sonja turned into the motel where Ruben had suggested they meet. He parked in the spot next to them and got into the back seat.

"What's wrong with this guy back here?" Ruben asked.

Sam looked at Morris. "He might have a concussion."

"I plan to drop him off at the ER," Sonja said.

Several seconds passed before anyone spoke again. Finally, Sam said to Ruben, "Why'd you want to come *here*?"

Ruben told them about following Ernie and Delray to the motel after they'd stolen his things from his office and changed vehicles on Cudjoe Key. He pointed out the truck parked close to the street, taking up several spaces. "They stopped here about midnight and got rooms."

"They're probably on their way to sell that stuff," Sam said, "and they must have something else on the truck, too."

"Like what?" Ruben asked.

Sam remembered the meeting in the limo with the man from the drug company. "Like stolen pharmaceuticals." And maybe something else.

"You mean NewMood?"

"You know about that?" Sam asked.

"I know Ernie got real touchy when I mentioned it in the office, and that's when he decided to take me to the plant in Cudjoe Key and put me in the compactor."

Sonja turned around in her seat. "He tried to kill you?"

"Yep, but I was too fast for him."

"What did you do?"

"I kicked him in the mouth and took his gun." Ruben,

quiet for a moment, sighed and said, "That was when I thought I was a famous detective."

"You *were* a famous detective," Sonja said, "and you will be again."

"I will?"

"Yes, we just need to get all this sorted out."

Sam wondered about the relationship between Ruben and Sonja. She obviously liked the guy, but he couldn't see them as a romantic couple. Mona had, in so many words, described Ruben as a self-absorbed prima donna. Maybe too vain to date a woman her age, even with her beauty.

Sam needed to call Mona and let her know what had happened. Maybe after all the dust settled.

"I'd like to steal that truck and take all my stuff back," Ruben said to Sam. "Do you think you could hot wire it?"

"It might be better if we let them go wherever they're going and then take it."

"Why is that?"

"We'll know who they're dealing with, and we might be able to break up their drug business."

"I don't care about their drug business," Ruben said.

"Ernie's your partner, and sooner or later he's going to get you in trouble, or kill you."

"You think following them will help us bring them down?"

"Maybe."

Sonja put the car in gear. "You two can take all the time you want to figure this out, but do it in your car. I need to find a hospital before Morris dies on me."

They went to an all-night diner and ordered a couple of greasy burgers. Sam called Mona and told her about his misadventures. She said she'd been worried sick since going into the house and finding him gone.

"Did you call J.T.?" Sam asked.

"Well, I called you first, and when you didn't answer, I called him. He said he might be able to find you using the GPS signal from your cell phone."

"Okay, I'll give him a call. Try to get some sleep, and I'll see you tomorrow morning."

After hanging up, he called J.T., and told the story again. J.T. said he'd gotten a lock on his location right after Mona had called, and would be there in an hour or so.

"We're not far from a motel where Ernie and Delray are staying. I think they have a truck full of NewMood and will probably unload it in the morning."

"Wonder why they would go wholesale," J.T said. "I bet they were doing pretty well selling the stuff on their websites. I closed them down before Mona called, but they probably don't know it yet."

"They might need some fast cash. They put a lot of money into that resort. Hold on a minute."

Sam said to Ruben, "Do you remember anything about your investment in the resort?"

Ruben gave him a blank look and shook his head. "I saw the contract yesterday. It looked like Ernie and I put in about five million each, but I didn't have nearly that much money in the bank, and my records didn't show any large withdrawals."

Sam nodded, put the phone back to his ear and said to J.T., "You hear that?"

"Yeah. So Ernie had to come up with five million. You think he borrowed it from Delray?"

"I'd say, and Delray probably got it from a loan shark. Those guys aren't noted for long-term loans."

Sam wondered about Ruben's share of the investment. Maybe he'd cashed in some assets…or maybe he didn't put any of his money into the deal, and they just made it look that way. He remembered the conversation between Sonja and Ruben, and wondered if they were in the scam together. If so, Jack had left that part out.

Sam told J.T. he could use his help if he'd come to Miami. "Get the keys from Mona and drive my car."

"Okay, I can be there before those clowns get out of bed," J.T. said.

"Make sure you leave Mona there."

"She won't like that."

"Yeah, well, she'll get over it. She might get killed if she comes up here." He described the location where they would be waiting and hung up.

Back at the motel, Sam took the first shift, and Ruben leaned his seat back and dozed off behind the wheel. J.T. arrived a little while later and got into the car with them.

About an hour after daybreak, Ernie opened his motel door and stepped out looking as if he'd slept in his clothes, his thinning hair wild about his head. He lit a cigarette and waited until Delray showed up a few minutes later from the room next door. They got into the truck, Delray in the driver's seat.

"I'll follow in your car," J.T. said and got out.

The truck started, gears ground, and it rolled out of the lot into the morning traffic. Ruben waited until several cars had passed before pulling out, and J.T. followed behind him.

TWENTY-ONE

THEY RODE FOR fifteen minutes before the truck turned down a side street and into the parking lot of an old factory. A fence surrounded the property, obscuring visibility except through the gate. Passing the entrance, Sam saw the truck pull up to a loading dock.

"Keep going," he said to Ruben

They stopped about fifty yards away at an abandoned gas station and got out. J.T. pulled in next to them.

An old liquor store stood next door, a tire dealer on the other side, both with boards on the windows. No traffic at this time of the morning, maybe at any time. Perfect place for a drug transaction.

"You think it'll be okay to leave my car here?" Ruben asked.

"Stay here with it," Sam said. "We won't be gone long."

"No, that's okay. I'm going with you." Ruben checked the safety on his gun and stuck it in his waistband, flashing a nervous smile. Sam hoped he didn't get killed. Other than being connected with Ernie, he seemed like an okay guy.

Sam took out his gun, popped the clip, and found it still full, as it had been before Morris had taken it from him. He reinserted it and chambered a round.

J.T. had his gun out. "What's the plan?"

"I want you to drive the truck out of here."

J.T. frowned. "I wanted to be in on the action."

"Yeah, I know, but I really need you to get that truck. You know how to hotwire it if they don't leave the keys, and I might have trouble with that. Besides, if things go well, there won't be any action."

J.T. shrugged. "Okay, you're the boss." He handed Sam his car keys.

"Take the truck to Hector's Auto Shop. It's about five miles down the road."

Hector, a struggling immigrant from Cuba, had helped Sam before in cases like this, and Sam always paid him well. His auto repair business never seemed to thrive, probably because he spent a lot of time repairing junk cars for his friends without charging them. Sam threw some business his way when he could, and sometimes the business involved hiding something in one of his garages.

"Yeah, I've seen Hector's."

They eased to the edge of the factory entrance and Sam peered around the corner of the fence. Delray and Ernie stood on the loading dock, talking to a man who appeared to be in his mid-thirties, with white hair pulled back in a ponytail. Standing about four inches taller than Delray, the man's skin looked ghostly, as if covered with talc, and he wore glasses with lenses as black as ink. Sam thought he looked familiar. The three men stood talking on the dock for a few moments before going inside.

NO ONE WORKED in the room visible through the window behind Rime's desk. A muscle guy, who looked like he could lift a small car, sat in a chair directly on the other side of the glass, reading a magazine. A cheap suitcase lay on a table next to him.

"Where are the workers?" Delray asked.

"They're coming in tonight," Rime said. "You bring the amount of product we discussed on the phone?"

Delray had called Rime the night before and told him they were going to be partners, but he still wanted the two million up front that they had agreed on. Rime didn't like it at first, but warmed up to the idea when Delray told him he would kill him and his entire crew if he didn't go along.

"The truck is full, we brought everything we had," Delray said. "You got the two million?"

"Of course," Rime said, nodding toward the suitcase visible through the window behind him.

"Okay, let's see it."

Rime turned and tapped on the window. When the man on the other side of the glass turned around, Rime pointed at the suitcase. He opened the case so they could see stacks of money inside.

Delray nodded. "Okay, we'll take that with us now, plus we get half of what you make when you sell the stuff."

Rime took off his dark glasses, narrowed his eyes.

"Half? We didn't discuss the split."

"We're discussing it now," Delray said. "Half is fair."

Rime leaned back and put his glasses back on. Seconds passed.

This dude had his nerve. Delray thought he might go around the desk, kick him out of the chair, stomp his face, glasses and all. Or maybe shoot him. It would make a lot of noise, but there wasn't anybody in this part of town who would care. He'd have to shoot the guy behind the glass, too, but that would be okay.

Delray pulled out his gun, laid it across his stomach, his finger on the trigger.

"Hey, let's think about this," Ernie said.

Delray looked at him and frowned. "What do you mean?"

"I mean, we can work out the percentage later."

"We ain't giving in to this scumbag," Delray said. "It's half or nothing."

Rime smiled, showed his tobacco-stained teeth. "There's no need to get personal."

The guy really *didn't* need to agree, since they planned to take all the money, anyway.

As if Rime knew Delray's thoughts, he said, "You're right. Half is a fair percentage."

Delray relaxed his finger on the trigger. "Okay, when can you have the stuff sold?"

"Four days," Rime said. "We can meet here and split the proceeds, fifty-fifty."

The truck started up outside, the engine revving, and sounded as if it were driving away from the building.

Delray's eyes narrowed. "What's that?"

"Sounds like somebody driving off with our truck," Ernie said.

Delray jumped out of his chair. "Shoot these guys if they move." He ran into the hall.

J.T. STARTED THE TRUCK, steered it away from the dock, and headed for the gate.

Sam went to the entrance and waited. Within seconds, he heard someone running on the other side, the noise louder with each footfall. The sound stopped for a fraction of a second, and the knob turned. As the door cracked open, Sam slammed his heel into it and felt it hit something and stop. He pushed through into a hallway. Delray lay unconscious on the floor, his arms splayed. He had a gun in one hand. Blood streamed from his nose down both sides of his face.

Ernie came out a door several feet away, pulling a pistol from his pocket.

Sam stepped over Delray, took a couple of steps, and aimed his gun. "Don't do it."

Alarm distorting his eyes, Ernie got the weapon out and brought it up. Sam fired. The round caught Ernie in the shoulder, spinning him around. He stumbled, fell to the floor with a thump, and lay still, his eyes closed.

Sam took the gun from his hand and went to the office door. The pale man stood behind the desk. A muscle man stood a few feet to his left, pointing a handgun with a barrel the size of a flashlight. Visible through a window behind the desk, a suitcase filled with money lay open on a table.

The pale man sighed. "You going to shoot us, too?"

Pointing the gun at the man's chest, Sam said. "I might."

Up close, Sam recognized him. The guy had been thinner then, but the glasses and pale skin were the same. Lamar Hingle. Pitched for a couple of major league teams. Had a deadly curve ball…in more ways than one. He had hit a couple of guys at the beginning of his last season. They almost died, and he left baseball after that. An investment scandal exploded a few years later involving a company Lamar had founded. It went belly-up and his high-profile investors lost upwards to $100 million. He disappeared, and the FBI looked for a couple of years. People probably remembered the scandal more than the pitching.

"You used to play baseball," Sam said.

Lamar Hingle smiled, showing discolored teeth. "Were you a fan?"

"I thought you were the best in the league."

Lamar seemed to reminisce for a second. Then he looked down at the other man's gun and said, "Looks like we have a standoff."

Ruben stepped through the door behind the muscle man and stuck his gun to the back of the man's head.

"Not exactly," Ruben said. "Make a false move and I'll turn your brain into Swiss cheese." It sounded like something he might have said as a TV detective. "Put the gun on the desk."

The big man's eyes grew large and flashed toward Lamar, who nodded. He laid the gun on the desk and, in a blur of movement, dropped down and threw Ruben over his shoulder into Sam. They fell to the floor while Lamar and the muscle man ran out the back door.

Sam struggled to his feet and went after them through the deserted factory, reaching the back dock as they sped away in a black Jaguar. He made a mental note of the license plate.

Ruben came out a second later.

"They're gone," Sam said, watching the Jag shrink as it rounded the corner of the building. He wondered how a man like Lamar could go from professional baseball to dealing drugs.

They went back into the building and saw the suitcase full of money still on the table. Sam tore away the plastic wrap from one of the stacks and thumbed through it, finding a one hundred-dollar bill on top. The rest was plain paper.

TWENTY-TWO

THE CELL PHONE in Delray's pocket played its little jingle. His face throbbing to the tune of the phone, he opened his eyes and looked at the ceiling. What had happened? Touching his nose caused a pain to shoot through his head like a lightning bolt. After lying still for a minute or so, the phone noise stopped, and he sat up and looked around. It all came back to him: the noise from the truck outside, racing down the hall with his gun, a painful smack against the door.

Delray noticed he still had his gun, at least one good thing. Standing, he stuck the gun in his pocket, and saw Ernie lying behind him. Maybe dead. Looking for the money, he saw the suitcase. It contained nothing except stacks of white paper. The Rime guy had stolen the truck, had planned to stiff him all along. He thought about the two hundred thousand he had left in the truck, and realized that was gone, too. His head felt as if it would pop.

Wanting to kill somebody, Delray started toward the door, and then remembered that he didn't have a ride. He took a deep breath, glanced down at Ernie.

"This is all your fault!" He drew back his foot and kicked Ernie's face, splattering blood on his shoe and pant leg. Ernie jerked awake and looked at Delray as if he might be a complete stranger, a hurt look on his face.

Maybe he'd been a little premature, but he did feel better after the kick.

"What happened to you?" Delray asked.

"Mackenzie shot me. I thought I might be dead."

Mackenzie!

"Why didn't you shoot *him*?"

"He came through the door like a rocket, and stepped over you and popped me before I could get my gun out."

Delray felt like shooting Ernie, himself, but he did know how Mackenzie could be with a gun. Now, everybody had left, taking the money, the truck full of NewMood, and the paintings. Everything!

Delray wondered how they would pay back the money they'd borrowed from the shylock. He had his ace in the hole locked away on Grand Cayman, but he wasn't about to tell Ernie about that, and he didn't plan on giving it to the shylock, either. They had to get that money back somehow. The cell phone sounded off again. He pulled it out, looked at the number and grimaced. Shaking his head, he pressed the answer button.

"Yeah?"

"Where you been? I called you, like, ten times. You was supposed to meet me over an hour ago."

"Yeah, I had a little accident. I need to reschedule 'cause I'm kinda tied up right now."

Silence, then: "You better have that money. You don't, we're gonna drop you under the causeway."

A comedian. He could always meet the guy, say he had the money, and let his friends Smith and Wesson cancel the debt. Only thing, he might not be the only guy, and then there'd be a problem. He'd have to think about that. But not right now, his face hurt too bad.

"I got the money. I just have some loose ends to tie up, that's all. I need a couple of days."

Another silence, then, "You got 'til tomorrow, same time." The line went dead.

Delray closed the phone and said to Ernie, "You know who that was?"

"Sounded like the loan shark."

"We have until tomorrow, otherwise, we're gonna be dead."

Ernie's face looked slick with perspiration. "They wouldn't do that. We owe too much. They'd lose it all."

"They got ways. They know about my place on Grand Cayman. It's worth a lot more than $5 million."

"They couldn't do that. They wouldn't be able to get a deed."

"A deed? You think I got a deed?" Delray's voice rose in volume with each word. "You don't need anything like that if the last owner is at the bottom of the ocean."

Ernie's eyes bulged, and sweat and blood ran down the sides of his face. He gasped and said, "I need to go to a hospital."

SAM CALLED J.T. and asked his location. After taking the money stacks with hundreds on top, and fruitlessly searching Delray and Ernie, Sam and Ruben had left in their respective cars and had driven several blocks away from the defunct factory.

"I'm at the shop. Hector wasn't too friendly until I mentioned your name."

Sam asked J.T. to put Hector on the phone.

"So, my friend, Sam," Hector said, "will this truck cause me some trouble?"

"No, I hope to get it out of there by tonight. I just

need to have it off the street for now." Sam said he would make the job worth Hector's risk.

"You are always very generous, my friend."

Sam had looked for a tail since leaving the factory, and now he spotted the black Jag in traffic several cars back. Lamar was driving, probably hoping Sam would lead them to the truck.

When J.T. got back on the phone, Sam told him to search the truck.

"Look for something valuable, something smaller than a baseball. Then walk several blocks away and take a taxi back to the motel where we were this morning."

DELRAY AND ERNIE got into the back seat of the taxi and Delray told the driver the address. He leaned forward and caught his face in the rearview mirror. It shocked him, like looking at a sick raccoon. When he sat back, he noticed the driver staring at him in the mirror.

"What are you looking at?" Delray asked.

The driver jerked his head to the front and pulled out into traffic. They rode for fifteen minutes before pulling into the sand driveway of a small house that hadn't been painted in at least thirty years. Weeds and fast-food litter blanketed the front yard.

"I thought we were going to a hospital," Ernie said, his face pale, breaths short and quick.

"Shut up. This is better." Delray paid the driver and they got out.

The taxi backed into the street, spun its tires, and sped away. Delray dragged Ernie through the weeds to the front door, which opened before he could knock.

A man who seemed the size of the Goodyear Blimp filled the doorway, eclipsing everything behind him, his head like a coconut atop his blubbery body. Delray knew him only as Needleman.

"What do you want?"

"He's been shot."

Needleman leaned his coconut through the doorway—a considerable effort—peered up and down the street, and waddled aside to let them in. They went through the house, which smelled of chili peppers and dirty socks, to a room in the back with a cot in one corner and an old refrigerator in another. A roach crawled across the linoleum floor. Needleman stepped on it and mumbled something Delray didn't catch. Ernie stared at the dead roach and then at the big man, fear in his eyes.

"I'm in a lot of pain," Ernie said. "You got any pain-killers?"

Needleman held out his hand. "Five hundred dollars."

"For pain pills?" Delray asked.

"The whole deal."

"I've got the money," Ernie said. "Get it from my back pocket."

Delray pulled out Ernie's wallet and counted the cash for the waiting hand. Ernie sat down on the cot, his eyes wide and pinched by panic.

The big man went to the refrigerator, reached among bottles of beer and sandwich condiments, and pulled out a hypodermic syringe that looked as if it had been in service since the Vietnam War. A spot of something red glistened on the side of it. He stuck the needle into a bottle of something clear, filled it, and reached for Ernie's arm.

"Wait!" Ernie said. "Is that blood on that thing?"

The big man smiled, touched his finger to the spot

on the syringe and put it into his mouth. "Don't worry, just hot sauce."

He stuck the needle into Ernie's arm before he could ask any more questions, and within seconds, Ernie's eyelids drooped and he fell back on the cot.

Needleman took Ernie's shirt off and looked at the wound.

"Is this going to take long?" Delray asked.

"Why, you late for another shootout?"

Very funny. Maybe when he finished the medical work, Delray would put a bullet in his head and take Ernie's money back.

"I need to rent a car."

"I got a car you can have for another five hundred."

"Does it run?"

Needleman smiled. "Like new." Taking a key from his pocket, he said, "Mercedes, out behind the house."

Probably an old smoker, but maybe it would get him back to Cudjoe Key where they'd left the car.

"Why don't I just come back in a couple of hours and get him?" Delray said, pointing to Ernie.

"That'll cost extra. I'm not running a hospital here. If he dies, you got to take him with you."

"That's okay, I'll wait awhile."

Needleman pulled a small case from under the cot and opened it. There were several tools inside, and he selected a scalpel and a pair of pliers with long jaws that tapered to the size of toothpicks on the end. He stuck the scalpel into the wound and Delray turned away.

"I'll go look over the car."

Needleman stopped his work and said, "Better not skip out on me."

Delray sauntered through the kitchen toward the back door.

"Gimme a cracker."

It sounded like Needleman's voice, only a little higher pitched. He turned and glanced around the room. A black and brown bird with yellow spots behind its eyes sat on a perch atop the kitchen counter.

"Gimme a cracker."

The bird could talk. He'd heard of that, but never believed it. Walking over, he said, "What's your name, birdie?"

"What's your name, birdie?" The bird bobbed its head as it spoke.

"No, what's *your* name?"

"No, what's your name?"

Delray snorted a laugh. Just a dumb bird. He turned to leave.

"Rolly wants a cracker."

So, it did have a name. He liked that, Rolly.

"I don't see no crackers around here, Rolly."

"Crackers in the cabinet."

Pretty smart, for a bird. Opening the door of the cabinet above the counter, Delray spotted a box of saltines. He took out a cracker and held it out to the bird. Rolly took it, hopped down from the perch, pecked the cracker into pieces on the counter, and began whistling and bobbing its head as it ate.

Grinning, Delray shuffled out the door, through a screened porch, to the backyard.

TWENTY-THREE

IT TOOK ABOUT an hour for Needleman to finish with Ernie. Though he remained unconscious, the big man insisted that Delray get him out of the house.

Delray heaved Ernie over his shoulder and went through the back door to the car he'd bought, which was a Mercedes. He opened the passenger door and dropped Ernie into the seat. After getting into the driver's seat, he turned the ignition key, and the engine started right up. Ernie woke and looked around.

"Where are we?"

"We got us a new car. Stay here, I'll be right back."

He left the car running and went back into the house. Needleman stood at the kitchen sink eating a sandwich the size of a football. The room had only a small dinette table next to the wall and no chairs. Needleman probably wasn't able to sit at the table because of his size.

"Forget something?"

"Gimme some bread." Rolly talking again, bobbing his head. Delray liked that bird.

Needleman broke off a tiny piece of his sandwich and handed it to the bird.

"I asked you a question." A little edge in his tone.

Delray frowned. Who'd this guy think he was?

"Where'd you get that car?" Put a little edge in *his* tone, too.

The big man chewed for a few seconds.

"Last guy came in with bullets in him left it there."

"Is it hot?"

Needleman shrugged and went back to his sandwich.

It really didn't matter to Delray. He probably wouldn't get stopped on his way to the Keys. He took out his gun and thumbed the hammer.

"Gimme the money back."

"Gimme some bread."

Needleman coughed up a piece of sandwich and said, "Your friend die or something?"

"No, I just want the money back." He snapped his fingers and held out his open palm. "Hand it over before I lose my temper."

"Gimme some bread."

The big man turned, laid the sandwich on the counter, and then spun back around faster than Delray thought possible with a wide-bladed knife in his hand. He flung it at Delray's head, and it flew through the air.

"Duck, you moron."

Dropping down an inch or so, Delray felt it crease his hair. It clattered to the floor and he grinned.

"You got to do better than that."

He aimed the gun at the big man's head. Needleman stared at him and then at the floor, a look of surprise on his face.

Delray followed the big man's eyes down to where he saw what looked like a furry animal, about the size of a squirrel, lying next to the knife, the color...of his own hair. The top of his head felt as if someone had set it on fire. He reached his fingers to it, and instead of plush hair, he touched a slick, wet surface.

Aiming again at Needleman's head, he fired.

The big man lunged for Delray at the same time the

slug hit him below his left eye. He toppled forward and Delray jumped back, but not fast enough.

SAM WAITED IN the motel parking lot for more than an hour before J.T. arrived and got out of the taxi and into Sam's car.

"What did you find in the truck?" Sam asked.

"It was loaded with NewMood pills, like you said, and some paintings and vases. Probably Ruben's stuff."

"That's it?"

"Oh yeah, there was a briefcase full of money in the cab. I counted almost two hundred thousand."

The phone rang and Sam took it out of his pocket. Mona.

"My boss wants me to come into Miami to tape a special crime feature." She paused a beat. "It doesn't have anything to do with Delray or Ernie."

She told him she had already crossed the bridge to Stock Island. He agreed to meet her for dinner when she reached the outskirts of Miami.

They stopped at a coffee shop. Ruben stayed in his car to take a nap. Sam and J.T. went inside and got coffee, and J.T. started his research on Baxter again. After everything that had happened, Baxter seemed to be the only person they hadn't seen, other than Delray's flunkies, on Grand Cayman, so Sam thought he might be the one who had come after Jack.

He remembered from the last time J.T. had looked Baxter up that he'd had two separate arrests in Miami: possession of a firearm and assault. Both incidents were recent.

"Take a look at this," J.T. said, turning the computer screen so Sam could see. "It's an obituary for a Joseph

Baxter up in Jacksonville, dated about a week after the arrests."

They had been searching only the Miami area before and hadn't run across this item. Another story in the Jacksonville paper mentioned a small-time crook named Joseph Baxter being killed by a jealous husband. The writer described Baxter as having blond hair, and since there had been no formal identification at that time, the police had listed him as a John Doe.

"This happened before we even saw Baxter, so it isn't him," J.T. said. "I just thought it coincidental, it being so recent and him having the same name as another criminal."

"Yes," Sam said, "a little too coincidental. The Baxter in Jacksonville dies and another Baxter shows up down here within days."

"What are you thinking, undercover cop?"

"That's exactly what I'm thinking."

J.T. chuckled. "Well, good luck pinning anything on Jack."

"The guy might be just trying to run down the money. If that's the case, Sonja Lazar is the key."

J.T. leaned back in his chair. "Too bad we don't know where she went."

Sam remembered that Sonja had called Ruben before she'd wrecked the car. He went to the parking lot, woke Ruben up, and got the phone number.

She answered on the first ring.

"This is Mackenzie. You still in Miami?"

After a short hesitation, she said, "Yes, as a matter of fact. I thought I'd check on Morris. Why?"

Sam told her his theory about Baxter.

"You might be right. Jack called a few minutes ago

and said Baxter wants the money. He'll let Jack go if we turn it over."

Jack must have had her telephone number all along.

"What are you going to do?" Sam asked.

"I'm thinking about it."

A POPPING NOISE awakened Ernie in the car. It seemed like Delray had been gone a long time, so he struggled out of the seat and shuffled into the house on wobbly legs. The fat man lay on the floor, a pool of blood next to his head, his massive arm next to a red wig, Delray nowhere in sight. A bird sat atop a perch.

"Gimme some bread."

A myna. Ernie had known someone who had one. Amazing birds, can say anything, if you say it first.

Ambling through the house, he called Delray's name, but got no answer. Back in the kitchen, he noticed something pinned under the big man: a hand, holding a gun that looked like Delray's.

"Delray!" the bird said, repeating Ernie's call.

Ernie walked around to the other side and saw what looked like part of Delray, his head under a glob of armpit. He picked up the big man's hand and tugged on it using his good arm. Nothing seemed to budge. Ernie's head felt as if it might spin off, and he sat down on the floor.

"Delray!"

He wished the bird would shut up. When the spinning stopped, he got up and tried again. This time he lifted the arm and Delray wriggled his head out. He didn't have any hair on the top of his head, but it was him, no doubt about it.

"Get him off me! I'm dying under here!"

"Delray! Dying under here."

Ernie wanted to ask about the hair, but thought this might not be the time.

J.T. LOOKED UP the local hospitals and found the closest one to the motel where they'd last seen Sonja. Sam drove to it and waited to see if she would show up. He noticed the black Jag enter the parking lot a few seconds later. It turned the other way and parked about fifty yards away.

"Why do we want to see this Sonja person again?" Ruben asked. He had followed in his car, parked next to Sam, and now sat in the back seat.

"She's the only one who can get to the resort-deal money," Sam said. He knew Ruben didn't remember any of the details about the sale of the resort, so he laid it out for him.

"And Sonja has all that money in an account somewhere?"

"Afraid so."

"And you want to get it so you can trade it for this Jack fellow?"

"Maybe," Sam said. "The money is the only thing that will end all this nonsense. That truckload of pills is just a small link."

"Speaking of the truck, I want my stuff before you do anything with it."

Sam nodded, not worried about Ruben's stuff. He didn't know what Ruben's involvement in the resort scam might be, but he certainly hadn't been an innocent bystander, and if he lost his paintings he probably deserved it.

They waited almost an hour before seeing Sonja turn

into the driveway. They almost missed her because she drove a new Lexus instead of the wrecked car from the night before. Probably rented.

Sonja went directly to the front entrance and Morris came out the door and got in. He had a small bandage on his forehead, but other than that, he looked good as new. She drove away, and Sam started the car and followed. Ruben trailed behind him in his car.

ERNIE TUGGED AT the dead man's hands and arms for about twenty minutes, like trying to lift a mattress full of sand. Delray hadn't helped any with his constant complaints. He couldn't breathe. His head hurt. His arms hurt. His legs were numb. He thought he might have some broken ribs. And the bird just repeated everything he said.

Ernie's head pounded, and he popped a pain pill from his pocket and chewed it up.

Finally, he decided he needed to do something else and found an aluminum baseball bat in the big man's closet. He took off his belt, buckled it, and looped it around the big guy's armpit. With the bat hooked inside it and on the other side of the man's neck, he had a lever. Bracing himself against the kitchen table with his good hand, he pushed the bat with his foot, and lifted the great heft. It took several tries, but Delray finally squirmed out, struggled to his feet, and grabbed the piece of red hair from the floor.

"You see this?"

Ernie nodded.

"I can't believe it. My head's killing me. Dude threw that knife and scalped me. Would've hit me in the face if the bird hadn't saved me."

"What?"

"Yeah, Rolly over there saved my life. He said, Duck you moron, and I ducked, just in time."

"They only repeat what somebody says. The fat guy probably threw food at him and said that same thing to him. Birds don't think for themselves."

Delray's mouth pinched into a frown. "Hey, that ain't true, and you better shut up about it."

Ernie rolled his eyes. "Okay, whatever you say. Let's go."

"You go on out. I'll be there in a few minutes."

Ernie glanced at Delray's shiny red dome, and had to laugh.

"What're you laughing at?"

Ernie wiped the grin off his face. "Uh…nothing, just that bird."

"I'm warning you. I already told you not to talk about him."

Delray went back to the room where Needleman had worked on Ernie, his head on fire and pounding at the same time. He found a cabinet full of drugs and peered inside. Knowing his painkillers, he took out a bottle, swallowed four pills with water from the sink faucet, and stuck several of the bottles into his pants pockets. The other drugs looked like antibiotics, so he swallowed some of those, too.

Looking in the mirror, he stuck the piece of hair atop his head and wondered if he could attach it. He opened a drawer in the cabinet and found several needles, along with a spool of black thread. Usually squeamish of needles, for some reason these didn't seem to bother him. Actually, he felt pretty good, like he could do anything he needed to do.

After threading one of the bigger needles, he positioned the hair, stuck the needle in, and winced with pain. Also, he couldn't see where he needed to sew for all that hair and blood. That could be fixed. He located a razor, pulled off the hairpiece, shaved it clean, and rinsed it in the sink. It looked like a thin, egg white omelet, sprinkled with paprika. Thinking of an omelet made him hungry. When was the last time he'd eaten?

He shaved the hair on his head at the bloody edges, stuck the piece of skin back on top, and slid it around until it fit. There, looked pretty good. Nice big clean spot. Remembering how the needle stung, he took a couple more pills and started sewing. Didn't hurt a bit.

It took ten minutes to get it right, in and out, like lacing up a big shoe. Of course, he couldn't reach all the way around in back, but it'd keep his brains from falling out. He left with Needleman's sandwich and the big knife, and the bird perched on his shoulder. In the car, he put Rolly on the back seat, cut the sandwich, and asked Ernie if he wanted half.

Ernie looked at the bloody knife and shook his head. "Noooo. I think I'll pass."

Delray shrugged. "Suit yourself, I'm starved." He started the car and drove out of the yard onto the street.

"How's my hair look?"

Ernie chuckled. "Like Bozo."

Delray's face felt like someone had thrown hot oil on it. He pulled his gun and thumbed the hammer.

"You're the bozo! I shoulda let you die with that bullet in your shoulder, and I wouldn't have to splatter your brains all over this nice car."

"No, wait a minute," Ernie said, urgency in his voice. "I meant Bozo the clown."

"Clown!" His voice thundered inside the confined space of the car.

"Clown!" Rolly mimicked.

He jammed the gun into Ernie's ear and heard the blare of a truck horn.

"Duck, you moron."

Turning to look at the road, he saw the grill of an approaching semi only a few feet away. He jerked the steering wheel and a miracle happened; the side of the Mercedes nearest the truck rose off the highway, pulling away from the truck, and then slammed back to the pavement on the right side of the road. The semi slid by with only inches to spare.

Could Rolly be his guardian angel?

Delray glanced at Ernie, whose eyes looked the size of billiard balls, and lay the gun on the seat. Maybe he'd shoot Ernie later. Right now, he needed to concentrate on the road, which actually looked like two roads at the moment. He wondered which one he should take.

TWENTY-FOUR

SAM FOLLOWED SONJA to a hotel close to the airport. When she and Morris went into the lobby, he asked Ruben to stay in the parking lot and watch for the black Jaguar, while he and J.T. investigated inside. They went in and waited for Sonja to register, and when she and Morris got into the elevator, they strode over and stepped inside before the door closed.

"What are you doing here?" Sonja asked.

"I thought I might help you make your decision."

"Which decision is that?"

"About trading the money for Jack."

Sonja sighed and pressed the elevator button for the fourth floor.

"What do you think you can do to me if we disagree?"

"I haven't cut off any fingers lately. Maybe I'll start with those."

"Sure you will." She smirked, and Sam wondered what it might take to make her nervous.

They reached her suite, and Sonja went directly to the wet bar and made a drink. She offered them one and Sam declined, remembering the sleepy dust she'd blown into his face. J.T. and Morris said they wouldn't mind, and both went to the bar.

Sam sat down in a chair next to the window. Sonja took the chair across from him and sipped her drink.

Smiling, she set it down on a table and crossed her legs. A beautiful woman, and now she would try her charms on him.

"I decided to pay and called Jack to let him know. He said Baxter will set up a meeting to get the account information."

If she gave Baxter the information, he could still arrest them if he wanted to. He wouldn't be interested in the money for himself if he did that. That might be his intention, anyway…but Sam didn't think so. The more likely scenario would be for him to get the money and kill them both to cover his tracks. No one would know he had the money, and he could quit his law enforcement job and disappear with the fortune. With no crime reported, nobody would think he did anything wrong.

"Sounds risky," Sam said.

"Yes, my thinking, exactly."

"Are you really going to give him the money?"

She took a drink. "Absolutely."

"Just like that, huh?"

Sonja gave him a sweet smile, as if to convey that he'd judged her wrongly up to now. She re-crossed her legs.

"You two can take your drinks into the other room," Sonja said to Morris.

J.T. raised an eyebrow and Sam nodded, so they left.

"Sure you won't have a drink?" Sonja asked.

"No, no drink."

"Suit yourself."

"What if Baxter decides to kill both of you after getting the money?" Sam asked.

"Maybe you could make sure that doesn't happen. I

planned to use Morris, but he still seems a little loopy. I'm not sure he's up to it."

She reached across the table and placed her hand on Sam's. It felt warm on his skin, and her eyes glowed with a hypnotic intensity. A snake charmer, she probably always got what she wanted. Though Sam knew her act was less than sincere, that knowledge did little to diminish its effectiveness.

The phone buzzed in his pocket. He pulled it out and looked at the display. Mona.

"I'm going to take this in the other room," he said to Sonja.

When he answered the call, Mona said, "I'll be there in an hour. You still want to meet?"

"Uh, something's come up. Can we get together later?"

"Yeah, that's fine. I'll go on to the studio and call you when we finish."

DELRAY'S HEAD HAD a bloody four-inch track down the middle. It was like a gigantic part, bushy red hair on both sides, with stitches that looked like a first-grader's craft project. Ernie knew he didn't like the Bozo reference, but that's exactly what he looked like. Black eyes, red nose, and all.

Ernie remembered that his gun had disappeared after Mackenzie shot him. He would need to get another one, and the faster the better, because he'd had enough of Delray's tough talk. Ernie knew about all those people Delray had killed, so he had to be careful, catch him when he least expected it, not give him a chance. Thinking back, he'd wasted his golden opportunity when Delray had been pinned underneath the gigantic blob of a man with nothing but his head sticking out. He could have just smacked him good with the ball bat and it would have been done. But he wasn't thinking too clearly at the time. Too many pain pills. Had to get another gun, and the first chance he got he'd pop Delray and drop him off a bridge. Cut his losses and leave town. The loan shark didn't even know him.

A siren droned in the distance.

"Somebody must have called the police," Ernie said.

"Forget about the police."

"You left a lot of blood back there, and probably fingerprints."

"So? Nobody has my DNA, or prints either. They probably have yours, though."

After a long silence, Delray said, "We got to figure out how to get that truck back."

Ernie glanced at him. Mackenzie had the truck, and could be anywhere by now. They'd never get it back, but Ernie didn't want to mention that to Delray. He might pull out his gun again.

"What about the girlfriend?" Delray said as he sped down Interstate 95.

"What do you mean?"

"The news reporter woman Mackenzie was so cozy with."

"What about her?"

Delray rolled his Bozo eyes.

"If we had her, we'd have leverage."

"Yeah, but we don't know where she is."

"We know where she works. Call the news station and ask for her."

Ernie called telephone information and got the number. It took a while to get to the station manager, but when he finally did, he identified himself as Ruben Vale, and said he needed to talk to Miss Miles about the story she'd done on him. He said he'd already called her number and she didn't answer. The manager said she wasn't there at the present, and wouldn't give him her cell number, but did say she would be back at the station about five.

Though he didn't know how to get in touch with Mackenzie, something nagged at him about the guy. He'd first thought about it at Delray's place in Grand Cayman, but decided it wasn't important. Now, thinking again, he remembered that Mackenzie's voice had sounded a lot like the guy named Charlie, who had called on Reston's phone right after Reston went missing. He wondered if Charlie might actually be Mackenzie. He found the number on his phone, pressed the Call button, and sure enough, Mackenzie answered.

"THAT'S ODD," SAM SAID, closing his phone. It had buzzed immediately after talking with Mona, and Sam thought it might be her calling back, until he recognized the number. He said Hello and the line went dead.

"What's that?" J.T. asked.

"I think Ernie just called and hung up. He took Jack's phone the day Jack called for help, and Jack's number just showed up on my phone. I answered, but he didn't say anything. It had to be Ernie."

"So? Big deal."

Sam had a funny feeling. He remembered dialing up Ernie and calling himself Charlie. Maybe Ernie had put two and two together and wanted to see if Sam would answer.

"I don't know, but something's wrong."

"What could be wrong? We got the truck, and Ernie doesn't know where it is. Or where we are, for that matter. Forget about it."

Sam glanced around the room and said, "Where's Morris?"

"He went out a few minutes ago, headed to the lobby for some smokes."

"Go check on him."

TWENTY-FIVE

MONA MILES PARKED her car in the decks next to the TV station, got out, and went to the elevator. Before the door opened, she heard the roar of a car engine and saw a Mercedes speeding toward her with two men inside. The tires squealed as it slid to a stop a few feet away. The driver got out and pointed a gun at her head.

"Hold it there, babe."

He looked crazed, but familiar, like the guy who owned the place in Grand Cayman, except something had happened to his head, maybe some kind of surgery. He also had two black eyes, what looked like a broken nose, and blood on the front of his shirt.

She punched the button again and the elevator opened, but she heard him running, his feet slapping the concrete. He fired a shot that hit the metal casing next to her arm. It sounded like a bomb exploding, and she lunged into the elevator. Before the door could close, he grabbed her arm and jerked her back out.

"What do you want?" She barely got the words out, anxiety taking her breath.

"Just shut up and get in the car." He opened the back door and shoved her in, then handed the gun to the other man—she remembered his name as Ernie—and got behind the wheel.

"I don't know anything about what you guys are doing," she said.

The redheaded man put the car in gear and sped out of the parking decks, sideswiping a couple of other cars, and entered the busy Miami street.

"Where's Mackenzie?" Ernie asked.

"He left yesterday. I haven't seen him since." A true statement. She didn't know where he'd gone, and wouldn't tell them if she did.

"That's okay," the man with the bizarre haircut said. "We figured you wouldn't tell. But you don't need to. Ernie here has his phone number, and he'll come running when we tell him about you."

SAM WENT BACK into the room with Sonja and found her on the phone, probably talking to Baxter. He sat down and listened.

"All right," she said into the phone, "I'll meet you at eight… Yes, I know Jack's car… You just hold up your end of the bargain and everything will be fine."

When she hung up, Sam said, "So it's all set?"

"Yes, eight o'clock."

"What are you supposed to do?"

"I'm supposed to go alone. He'll have a computer in the car with him, and if the account checks out, he'll let Jack go."

He raised an eyebrow. "And you're supposed to trust him?"

Sonja smiled. "That's where you come in. You'll follow me in your car, just in case he tries a double-cross."

It sounded okay, but Sam still didn't trust Sonja to not double-cross everybody.

His phone buzzed. He didn't recognize the number. "Hello."

"Hey, Mackenzie, I owe you one for pounding my

nose with that door." It was Delray. He slurred his words, as if drunk.

"Yeah? Maybe you'll get a chance to pay me back."

"I'll pay you back, all right, b'first I want that truck back, and everything inside."

"Sorry, the truck's on its way back to its rightful owner."

"Rightful owner? I'm the rightful owner, you idiot."

"Yeah, well, that's too bad. Maybe this is a sign that you need to get into another line of work."

A silence stretched into several seconds, and Sam could see Delray in his mind's eye, his face turning as red as his hair, ready to pop a blood vessel. When he finally spoke, his controlled voice sounded on the verge of explosion.

"Okay, smart guy, try this on for size. I got your girlfriend, and you're gonna get me whatever I want, or she dies. How about that for another line of work?"

Mona? Sam had spoken with her just a few minutes before.

"I don't believe you."

"You don't, huh? Well, listen to this." After another pause, he heard a woman scream, and Delray came back on the line. "How's that, believe me now?"

Sam could hear his pulse hissing in his ears, his face hot. J.T. had been right; he should have put an end to Delray when he had the chance.

"Let me talk to her." Sam tried to keep his voice from shaking.

"No problem."

"Sam, is that you?" Mona sounded as if she'd been crying.

"Did he hurt you?"

"Yes. I mean, no, not really. He put a gun to my head and—"

"That's all." Delray was back on the line. "Now, you going to get me that truck, or do I put a bullet in this pretty face?"

"I'll bring the truck, just tell me where. And Mona better not have a scratch on her."

Delray laughed into the phone. "Yeah, or you'll do what?"

Making him angry might not be the best way to handle this. If Delray lost control, he'd shoot everything in sight.

"Just make sure she isn't harmed. Where do you want to meet?"

"Hold on, that ain't all. You got to bring me the fortuneteller, too."

Sam glanced at Sonja and she had a questioning look on her face. He wondered if she could hear from that distance.

"How do you expect me to do that?" Sam asked.

"Hey, I know she's right there with you, so don't waste my time. Just bring her to me and this girl won't get hurt."

Sam wondered how he could know about Sonja. *Morris*. J.T. had gone after him a few minutes ago and hadn't returned, which probably meant he couldn't find him. The guy had called Ernie and tipped him off. He had been Ernie's right hand before showing up with Sonja, which made it look like Sonja and Jack had planted him there. Now he seemed to be playing both sides of the fence. He probably knew Sonja planned to turn over the money to Baxter, and thought he would have a better chance of getting a piece of it from Ernie than from Baxter. Sam sighed and ran his fingers through his hair.

"Okay, where and when?"

"Warehouse on 41, 'bout a block west of I-95. Be there at seven."

Sam checked the time on his phone: almost six.

"That'll be cutting it close. It'll take at least that long to get the truck."

Delray laughed. "Then, you better get moving. And hey, nobody comes but you and the fortuneteller, both of you in the truck. I see any other cars around, I'm gonna shoot this pretty girlfriend of yours. You unerstan?"

"I understand."

Sam closed the phone as J.T. came in the door.

"I looked all over the place. Morris is gone."

Sonja looked at J.T. and turned her attention back to Sam, apparently, not too concerned about Morris.

"What was that about?" she asked.

"You're the fortuneteller; you tell me."

She surprised him with a smile. "Forget it. Your side of the conversation told me enough."

"Okay, then you know we need to leave right now."

Sonja was partly responsible for a lot of what had happened. If Delray wanted what she had, Sam would make sure he got it.

"Don't forget about the meeting with Baxter. He might kill Jack if we don't show up."

Jack had gotten himself into this situation, so he could take care of himself. Besides, Sam didn't think Baxter would do anything to Jack as long as he remained the key to getting the money.

"We'll worry about Baxter after we get Mona."

Sam handed the keys to J.T. and told him to take her

to the car. He thought about the angel dust, took her purse from next to her chair, and handed it to J.T.

"Better hold on to this. It's full of magic tricks."

He stayed behind and called Hector to tell him they were on the way.

J.T. and Sonja were already in the car when he went outside. He walked over to Ruben's car and asked about the black Jag.

"They stayed around for about an hour and then pulled out. Maybe they gave up."

Sam scanned the parking lot and didn't see the car. He hoped they *had* given up and left, but he wasn't too sure about that. It didn't matter, he had to get that truck. If they showed up, he would deal with them. He also didn't want Ruben going along, because he'd just get in the way or get killed.

"You can take off now. We've got some things to do."

Ruben shook his head, "No way. I'm following you until I get my stuff out of that truck."

"I'll get your stuff. Just let us handle it from here."

"Sorry, but I don't necessarily trust you guys."

Sam sighed and walked away.

BAXTER LOOKED AT the computer and glanced up at Jack.

"You sure this'll work?"

Jack nodded. He'd been through it several times, but the guy continued to be skeptical.

"Have you ever used a computer?"

Baxter gave him a smirk. "Course I've used a computer. I just never transferred any money, that's all."

"It'll be a breeze. You opened an account in the same offshore bank where she has the money. She'll give you her information and you can transfer the funds from her account to yours. Simple as that."

"It better work that way. I told you what'll happen if she double-crosses me."

"Yes, you did. It bothers me that you still don't trust me on this."

Baxter chuckled. "Trust you? That's a laugh. Anyway, *she's* the one with the money."

Jack smiled. Maybe this would work out after all.

"I just don't understand why she would be willing to trade the money for *you*," Baxter said.

THEY ROLLED INTO Hector's auto repair lot and drove to the bay farthest from the street. Hector stepped out of the office, removed the padlock, and pulled the garage doors open.

Ruben got out of his car and went inside. Sam entered and saw him bringing his belongings out of the back of the truck. He made several trips to the trunk of his car before he had everything. Hopefully, Delray wouldn't make an issue over Ruben's things. Sam went back to the car and told J.T. to put Sonja in the truck's cab.

They had only thirty minutes to get to the warehouse. That should be enough time, if rush-hour traffic had died down. Sam climbed into the driver's seat and started the engine. J.T. went back to Sam's car and followed them out of Hector's lot.

"You know what you have to do?" Sam asked.

Sonja smiled. "They'll want the account and PIN where the money is located."

"You don't seem to have a problem with that."

Sonja shrugged. "Things have gotten out of hand. I never expected anyone to get hurt. That newswoman didn't have anything to do with this, and I need to make sure she's safe."

Didn't sound like Sonja. Probably had something up her sleeve; maybe more knockout dust.

"You knew they were holding Mona?"

Sonja stared out the passenger window at the traffic.

"I *am* psychic, you know. I saw all of this happening yesterday."

Sam glanced at her; she seemed totally serious. Did she think he actually believed any of this?

He took the on-ramp to the Interstate and wedged the truck between two cars that had slowed to a crawl.

"The traffic should be gone by now," Sam said. "Somebody must've had an accident up ahead."

"We'll get there on time. The problem will be with Mr. Jinks."

Sam glanced at her and saw her eyes closed, her fingertips massaging her temples.

"What do you mean?"

"He plans to welsh on the deal. Even though he gets what he wants, he won't release your friend."

Sam's pulse thumped in his ears.

"You can save the fortunetelling routine for somebody else."

"Suit yourself."

"Okay, if you know so much, tell me how it comes out."

"The only thing I know for certain is that someone will die."

She had that part right. Delray, for sure, and maybe Ernie, too.

TWENTY-SIX

ERNIE'S PHONE RANG. Studying the caller ID, he recognized the number of the geek who took care of their websites. He never called unless he had a problem.

"Hello."

"Hello," Rolly screeched. Delray had brought the bird into the warehouse with them, saying it was his good luck charm. Rolly now sat atop a desk lamp next to Ernie's chair, his head bobbing up and down.

Maybe Ernie could wring its neck before Delray returned from the office in back. Tell him Rolly just keeled over.

"Hey, uh, Mr. Brent?" the geek said. "Sounds like we got an echo."

"Yeah, an echo. What's up?"

"Echo."

"Something's wrong with our sites. We haven't had a sale since last night. I think somebody sabotaged them."

"You said nobody could mess them up with all that new security you installed. What happened?"

"What happened?"

"There's the echo again."

"Forget the stupid echo and tell me what happened!"

"What happened?"

"I…I don't know. I've been working all afternoon and haven't found the problem."

Ernie felt his blood pressure rising. This guy spent

all that money on the firewalls and stuff, and bragged about it being bulletproof.

"Okay, figure it out, and you better do it quick."

Ernie closed the phone, dropped it into his shirt pocket, and leaned back in the chair.

Delray came up behind him and said, "Who was that on the phone?"

He would go ballistic if he knew what had happened.

"I just checked on some business."

"Do it quick."

Delray looked at the bird. "Rolly said Do it quick. What'd he mean by that?"

"He's a stupid bird. How do I know what he meant?"

"HE'S LYING TO you," Rolly said. *"That was the fortune-teller on the phone. She told him to kill you and they'd split the money. You better waste him before he gets the chance."*

Delray stared at Rolly, amazed, and replied to the bird, "But if I kill him now, I won't be able to transfer the money."

"What?" Ernie said, panic in his voice.

"You heard Rolly. He said the fortuneteller was on the phone and told you to kill me."

"Fortuneteller? You're looney tunes, Delray. Rolly didn't say nothing. You better quit taking those pills."

"Don't lie t'me; I heard the phone ring."

THE GUY SOUNDED like a lunatic, the bird telling him stuff nobody else could hear. He'd always been nuts, a homicidal maniac, but he seemed worse now. Ernie thought maybe he should just tell him about the call.

That would sound a lot better than what he thought the bird might have said to him.

"That was the guy who programs the computer sites that called."

Delray's eyes narrowed. "I don't believe you." He stared at the bird for a moment. "Come on, Rolly, tell him."

"I'm telling you the truth. It was the geek; he said all our systems are down. We're not selling any product, and haven't for a while. He doesn't know what's wrong."

That seemed to shock Delray back to reality. "What's going on here? First, you give away our money for that bogus hotel deal, and now our business is in the toilet."

"I don't know, I—"

"Shut up!"

"Shut up!"

In a blur, Delray swung the gun barrel at Ernie's face. He felt a numbing blow and fell out of the chair, his head buzzing like a hornets' nest, white lights flashing in his eyes. Then the lights went out.

SAM LOOKED AT his watch as he exited I-95. They would be on time, as Sonja had predicted. He turned onto Highway 41, started looking for the warehouse, and spotted it about a hundred yards down the road. The facility, which was newer than he had expected, had a sign out front that indicated it was a distributer of cleaning supplies. No other warehouses were visible, so it had to be the one.

A late model Mercedes sat near a door on the side, next to several truck bays. One of the bays opened as he turned in. Delray ambled out. His face looked black and blue around his eyes and nose, probably from the door hitting him, and something bad had happened to the top of his head, like he'd had brain surgery and the doctor had done a lousy job of putting everything back in. He just needed some floppy shoes, and he'd be ready for the circus.

Delray glanced up and down the road, to see if anyone had followed, and motioned for Sam to pull the truck inside. The big door lowered behind them after they'd entered, and Delray stood by the truck cab as they stopped and got out, holding his gun on them.

He checked both of them for weapons, and took Sam's gun and shoved it into his pocket. Sam decided he'd go along with it until Mona was safe.

"Give me the keys and go in that door over there," Delray said, his voice seeming slower, more controlled, like a drunk trying to seem sober.

They went into a large room with a half-dozen desks, each with a computer monitor on top. The air conditioning didn't seem to be running, the hot air stale and smelling of soap and chemicals. Perspiration beaded inside Sam's shirt.

"I want to see Mona," Sam said.

"She's in the back. You can see her as soon as I drive that truck out of here."

Sam looked around. "Where's Ernie?"

"Where's Ernie?"

A myna bird sat perched on a desk lamp.

"Ernie ain't none of your business." He hesitated for a couple of seconds. "He's outside making sure nobody followed you."

"Where's Ernie?"

"Shut up, Rolly," Delray said to the bird.

It sounded like he was hiding something. Sam wondered what it could be, since he already seemed to be in control of the situation.

Delray looked at Sonja and grinned.

"So, you're the dish that masterminded this deal. I can see why they mighta fell for your line." He snapped his fingers. "Gimme the bank information."

She reached inside her bra and pulled out a piece of paper. Delray grabbed it from her fingers.

"Is this the account number?"

Sonja smiled. "The web address for the bank is at the top. The long number is the account and the short number is the PIN."

"PIN, what's that?"

"Personal Identification Number. It's like a password for the account."

Delray looked at it again and jammed it into his shirt pocket.

"Okay, all I got to say is, it better be right."

"It better be right."

"I'm gonna lock you in a room in back and go transfer the money."

"It better be right."

Delray stared at the bird for a moment, as if listening for it to say something else.

"On second thought, you're going with me. Get in the back of the truck."

He motioned with the gun for them to go out the door.

"What about Mona?" Sam asked.

"Hey, tough guy, you better worry about yourself."

If Ernie had been there, he would have transferred the money using one of the computers. So something had happened to him, and Delray didn't know enough about computers to do the transfer.

They went to the back of the truck. Sam opened the cargo door, as instructed by Delray, and he and Sonja climbed up. Delray locked them inside, the cramped space completely dark except for a crack of light at the bottom of the door. As hot and stale as the air had been inside the office, this was far worse.

DELRAY WENT BACK inside and got the pretty lady. He wouldn't have any leverage over Mackenzie if he left her there, and he needed that.

"Let's go, Rolly." He picked up the bird and put it on his shoulder.

"Let's go, Rolly."

After taping Mona's mouth, he put her in the floorboard of the cab and tied her feet. He took Mackenzie's gun out of his pocket and stuck it under the seat.

Driving onto Highway 41, Delray wondered who he could get to transfer the money. He stopped at a traffic light and looked down at the blonde news reporter. Reaching down, he peeled the duct tape from her mouth. She took a deep breath and stared at him, her blue eyes wide. A beautiful chick, no doubt about it.

"She likes you," Rolly said. *"She'd rather be with you than Mackenzie."*

Delray chuckled and said to Mona, "You know anything about transferring money from offshore bank accounts?"

"Yeah, maybe."

"What do you know?"

"I went to the bank with them that day on Grand Cayman, remember. I saw what they did."

"Huh."

"Cut me loose and I'll help you."

A little too eager. If he gave her the chance, she would be out of the truck, running down the freeway. Besides, she might send the money somewhere he didn't want, and he'd never know the difference.

"In your dreams, sweetheart." He stuck the tape back over her mouth.

"In your dreams, sweetheart."

The light changed and he took off again. He trusted only one person to handle this: the man he owed the money to. Delray would go straight to the guy's place out on Biscayne Bay, hand him the fortuneteller's piece of paper, and say, *Here's your money, now get off my back or I'll make you sorry you ever knew me.* He sighed. No, that wouldn't work. The guy probably had, like, five goons there all the time. Better say as little as possible until he got out of there.

SONJA SAT ON a box and leaned against the wall, perspiration streaming down the side of her face.

Sam took out his phone and called J.T. "Where are you?"

"Following the truck. I got stuck in traffic, and by the time I got there, it had just pulled out. Where are you?"

"Sonja and I are in the back of the truck. Delray's driving."

He told J.T. what had happened.

"What about Mona?" J.T. asked.

"He might have left her in the warehouse, tied up in the back. Turn around and go look for her. Delray gave us a story about Ernie being outside somewhere.

It sounded like a lie, and we never saw him, but you should be on the lookout in case he's there."

"Are you and Sonja okay?"

"Yeah, don't worry about us."

Sam wondered where they were headed. He knew you could never guess at what might happen with a wild card like Delray. Nobody had died, yet, as Sonja had predicted, but the night wasn't over.

DELRAY WHEELED THE truck into the posh neighborhood and looked for the house, an old two story with a red tile roof. He saw it in the distance and remembered the gate. He wouldn't be able to get the truck through it, so he'd just park on the street. The woman would be okay while he went inside. Nobody could see her on the floor unless they stood on the running board and looked through the window.

He stopped at the curb, sauntered to the gate, and pressed the button on the intercom.

One of the shylock's henchmen said over the speaker, "What do you want?"

"It's Delray Jinks. I need to see the man about the money I owe."

"You got the money with you?"

"Yeah, just let me in."

The gate eased open and Delray strode inside and down the driveway to the big house.

He stepped onto the veranda, and a guy wearing a shirt decorated with pink flamingos opened the door.

"What happened to you?"

Delray waved the comment away.

"None of your business. Just take me to the man. I want to get this over with."

"You know the drill; I gotta have your piece."

Frowning, Delray pulled his gun from his pocket and handed it to him.

Flamingo put the gun in his own pocket. "Hold out your arms, I gotta frisk you, too."

Delray looked sidelong down the veranda and then fixed a stare on Flamingo. "You got to be kidding?"

"No, no exceptions."

Delray didn't like being without his weapon, and *hated* to be frisked. He shook his head and held out his arms. "I'm gonna tell your boss what I think about this."

"You do that." Flamingo smiled, patted him down and stepped back. "Okay, first door on the right. He ain't in a good mood, either, so you better be on the level."

Delray stepped into the office. The guy sat behind a big desk with a computer monitor on the corner. Mr. Buzzo. He stood from his chair and rose only a foot or so to a height of about four-feet-five, his width about the same. The name fit. Kinda like a big, fat bumblebee. He wondered how this shorty could get to be the boss. The guy hadn't seemed all that tough when Delray had dealt with him that one time before. But Delray had paid the money back, plus the vig, so he really didn't know how tough the guy could get. Could be a real tiger, for all he knew.

"You look like a train ran over your head," Buzzo said.

Delray had tired of everybody talking about his injuries. Every time he thought about it, his head started to hurt again. He remained silent for a couple of seconds and the boss shrugged.

"You got the money?"

"Yeah, I got it, but I want my gun back. Your guy out front took it."

Buzzo seemed to consider his request for a beat, nodded his head, and said into the intercom on his desk, "Bring Mr. Jinks his gun."

Flamingo stepped into the room, a sneer pinching at the corner of his mouth. Delray sneered back at him, took the weapon, and stuck it into his pocket. Flamingo left and Delray turned back to Buzzo. He handed over the piece of paper with the bank information.

"What's this?"

"It's where the money's deposited in a Grand Cayman bank. You just need to transfer it to your account."

The short man stared at him, then at the piece of paper, and pressed a button on the intercom.

"Tell Dom to come in here."

Delray sat down in a chair in front of the desk.

A teenager came to the door and stopped. He looked like an eighteen-year-old version of the boss.

"Jinks here said he's got our money in an offshore bank. He wants us to transfer it. Can you do that?"

Dom shrugged. "Yeah, I think so, if he's got the account information."

"It's all there," Delray said, pointing at the note.

The boss stepped away from the chair and handed the kid the paper. Dom sat down and worked his chubby fingers at the keyboard of the computer.

Flamingo stuck his head in the door.

"Jinks parked a big truck out front. Just wanted you to know."

The short man looked at Delray. "What you got in the truck?"

Delray shrugged. "Just some product I need to take to the Keys."

"Product? You mean drugs?" His voice rose with each word.

"Well, yeah, but it's just NewMood."

Buzzo waddled around the desk and stood a foot from his face. He didn't look too happy, and Delray wondered if this might work into a problem. He'd given the man the money, and he wasn't going to take too much from *anybody* about the lousy truck. Besides, his whole head hurt like a giant, throbbing toothache. He took three pain pills from his shirt pocket and chewed them up.

"Is it hot?"

Delray nodded. "Could be."

"Are you crazy? The Feds are all over me already." He turned and told Flamingo to go check it out.

Delray stood up and said, "Hey, don't be messing with the truck."

The short man stepped in front of him.

"Sit down."

Delray could shove him out of the way, or pop a hole through his fat head, but something in the man's eyes told him he ought to just take it easy and see what happens. He took the seat and watched Dom work the computer. The pain in his head had leaked away, but now it seemed warm in the room. Sweat rolled down his forehead and stung his eyes.

After a minute or so, the kid whistled and said he had access to the account.

"How much do I transfer?"

"How much is in there," Buzzo said.

"Ten million."

That's right, Ruben had five mil in there, too. He'd forgotten that.

The short man glanced at Delray.

"Do six million. That'll cover the vig."

"A million for the vig?" Delray said. "That's robbery."

"Yeah, well, you had the money several days. You expect me to do business for free?"

He didn't really care. If he could get somebody else to transfer the rest of the money to one of his accounts, he'd be four million ahead.

Dom pulled some papers out of the desk and keyed information into the computer.

"Okay, it's done." The kid leaned back in the chair and grinned, looking really pleased with himself.

"Get into our account," Buzzo said. "Make sure it's all there."

Delray heard footsteps coming down the hall, more than one person, and one of them had on high heels. The newswoman came through the door, her hands and feet free, the tape removed from her mouth. Rolly rode on her shoulder. Flamingo followed behind her.

"Who's this?" Buzzo said.

"She was tied up in the truck. This is the TV news lady."

The short man grinned.

"Oh yeah, she's a looker."

He turned to Delray, the grin drained away.

"Why you got this dame tied up, Jinks? You some kinda pervert?"

The last straw. Delray stood up and grabbed the paper with the bank information. He took Mona Miles by the arm and turned toward the door.

"You got your money. I'm leaving."

"Hold it right there," Buzzo said. "We're not finished yet."

"Some kinda pervert?"

Buzzo stared at Rolly. "A talking bird. Pretty cute. Where'd he come from?"

Flamingo shrugged. "He was standing on the babe's head, pecking on her hair."

"You look in the back of the truck?"

"No. I found the girl tied up and thought I ought to bring her inside, first."

Buzzo nodded. "Go do it." He looked back at Delray. "And you better not ever come to my place again with a hot truck. You're lucky I don't bust your kneecaps for pulling a stunt like that."

"Bust your kneecaps."

"Hey, Pop," the kid said, "there ain't any new money in the account."

Flamingo, who had started out the door, turned around and came back in.

"What do you mean?" Buzzo said. "It didn't work?"

"Noooo. You got the same amount you had this morning."

Buzzo's blubbery lips pinched together and his eyes narrowed as he turned and looked at Delray. This wasn't going too good. Had the fortuneteller scammed him?

"Maybe it takes a while," Delray said.

The kid shook his head. "It should've transferred immediately."

Buzzo moved faster than Delray thought possible. He took several short steps and his fat little fist became a blur as it struck Delray on the side of the face.

Delray fell against the doorway and dropped to the

floor. The short man stood over him like a bully on the playground and kicked him in the side. Springing to his feet, the gun in his hand, he pointed it at the man's stomach and pulled the trigger. *Click.* He snapped the trigger twice more with the same result.

Buzzo's lips peeled back in a grin. "We took your bullets."

Flamingo worked the slide on his gun and brought it up, but Delray spun and hit him in the face with the barrel of his 9mm. The man with the colorful shirt dropped to the floor as Delray ripped the gun out of his hand. Blood spurted from his face and he clapped his hand over the injury, but it did no good, and his eyes went wide before he passed out.

Delray tossed his empty gun to the floor and turned to see Buzzo and Dom huddled behind the desk.

"Don't shoot us," Dom said. "Please. I go to college."

That gave Delray a chuckle. He goes to college.

"Sorry, kid. Wrong time, wrong place."

He pointed Flamingo's gun, but heard footsteps coming down the hall, and as another goon came through the door, Delray turned and shot him.

Buzzo probably had more men, and the sound of the gunshots would bring them in. Delray grabbed Mona by the arm and headed out the door past the wounded man and down the hall toward the back of the house.

Rolly clung to Mona Miles shoulder. *"Wrong time, wrong place."*

TWENTY-SEVEN

SAM THOUGHT THEY had ridden in the back of the truck about a half-hour before stopping, and it sounded like Delray got out and slammed the door. A few minutes later, Sam heard one of the doors of the cab open and then close again. He also thought he heard a female voice that sounded like Mona. *Had Delray brought her along?*

He waited a few minutes and kicked the door a couple of times. It wouldn't budge, but then he heard someone working the latch and it opened. The airflow created by the swinging door felt like a cool breeze.

"What're you doing in there?" Ruben stood looking up into the back of the truck.

Sam was glad to see him, even more so now than when the guy had let him out of the car trunk. He climbed down, helped Sonja, and filled his lungs with the fresh air.

"I thought you left," Sam said.

Ruben shook his head. "Decided to follow the truck, just in case somebody needed me."

"I'm glad you did. Did you see Mona?"

"The redheaded guy drove the truck here and got out. Then a few minutes ago, another guy came out and got Mona out of the cab." Ruben looked at Sonja with concern in his eyes. "Are you okay?"

"I'm fine, but we need to go get Jack," she said, more to Sam than to Ruben.

"Okay, you two go," Sam said. "I'll check on Mona." He turned to Ruben. "You have a gun?"

Ruben nodded and pulled Ernie's gun from his pocket.

"Give it to me."

"What if I need it?"

Sam heard shots inside the house. He grabbed the gun from Ruben's hand and ran to the closed gate. It wouldn't budge, so he climbed over, sprinted to the front door, and went in. Leading with the gun, he hurried through a large living room to a hallway where a man lay on the floor. He looked dead, and the smell of spent gunpowder hung heavy in the air. Inside a doorway on the right, a heavy-set kid, maybe in his late teens, and a grown man who looked like an older twin, stood behind a desk.

"Don't shoot us!" the kid screamed.

"I'm looking for the girl."

"They went that way," the man said, "probably out the back."

Something made a slamming noise toward the rear of the house. Sam ran down the hall to a closed door on the left. Finding it locked, he stepped back and kicked. A jolt of electricity ran up his leg to his back, but the door splintered and swung open. It led to the kitchen, and a few feet inside and to the right, another door opened to a pantry and then to the outside. Bursting through the back door, Sam scanned the yard. Delray and Mona were nowhere in sight. The yard bordered on the waterway, and a boathouse the size of a small home perched over the edge of the water. A boat motor started up, and Sam ran to the boathouse, reaching it in time to see a Donzi scream out the far side, Delray at the helm. Mona sat low in the passenger seat next to him.

A second Donzi rocked in the wake against the dock. He untied the lines, started it and opened the throttle. The speedboat roared out of the boat slip and rose to a plane.

Expansive lawns and luxury yachts flew by in a blur, and the wake from the Donzi threw water over the sea wall. Sam knew this area well, his own marina only a mile or so away. Delray had about a half-minute lead, and had already traveled several hundred yards down the waterway, spewing a rooster tail into the sky behind him. Sam passed a boat that had overturned from Delray's backwash, and dodged others trying to get out of the way.

The waterway led to Biscayne Bay, and Sam saw Delray's boat in the distance, headed under the Venetian Causeway. He pushed the Donzi to full throttle, but gained little, if any, on his target. A few minutes later, Delray's boat sped around a yacht that looked at least a hundred feet long, ran under the MacArthur Causeway and disappeared from view.

LAMAR HINGLE SAT in the idling Jaguar a block away from the truck, watching the activity through a pair of binoculars. A man had opened the back of the truck and let a man and a woman out of the cargo area. The men were the ones who had interrupted the NewMood deal and took the truck; the woman he didn't recognize. Nobody seemed to be guarding the vehicle now, and he planned to take it.

He dropped the binoculars, drove up behind the ten-wheeler, and glanced at Earl, his muscle-bound helper.

"See if the keys are inside. If not, maybe I can hot-wire it." Lamar had hot-wired cars in his youth, but had gotten away from the art when he made it into baseball.

Earl got out and glanced both ways before easing to the driver's door and climbing into the cab. The truck started right away and pulled away from the curb. Lamar followed, chuckling. Who would have guessed these guys would be so stupid as to think somebody could turn NewMood into a street drug worth millions? Well, they had fallen for it, and that's all that mattered. Now, if he could just get this truck off his hands and collect his money, he would have enough to start a baseball franchise. Of course, he'd have to be a silent partner until he got his little misunderstanding with the FBI straightened out.

ERNIE WOKE WITH a jerk and sat up in the dark space, a sliver of light shining under a door a few feet away. His head felt like it had been crushed in a vise, the pain pounding with every pulse. He got to his knees and crawled toward the light. Grabbing onto the doorknob, he pulled himself up, went out, and recognized the warehouse office where they had argued. Delray had slugged him. That's why his head hurt so bad. He pulled the bottle of pain pills from his pocket, tossed a couple in his mouth, and swallowed.

Where had Delray gone? Ernie had decided even before the argument that he would have to kill him. To do that, he needed to get out of this place, go home, and get another gun. Pack a suitcase and clean all the money out of his stash, just in case the shylock knew about him. He'd never get the money back from the bogus resort investment. Live and learn. There are some real scoundrels out there. And he'd seen the last of the truck of NewMood. Even if he could get it back, the pale guy, Rime, probably would be too scared to buy the stuff after all the guns came out at their last meeting. The Internet sales were out, too. It would probably take too long for the computer guy to fix the sites to do any good. Time to go. Lay low for a few months. But first things first. Delray had to die.

Ernie staggered out of the office, his head still pounding and feeling as if it might go into a spin. A man stepped in front of him from out of nowhere and pointed a gun at his head. The big guy who'd been along with Mackenzie.

"YOU SAID THEY'D be here," Baxter said, "and it's ten after."

They sat waiting in Jack's Mercedes in the parking lot of the Holiday Inn on 57th Avenue, near Miami International.

Jack took his hands off the steering wheel and glanced out the window at the traffic passing on the street.

"Don't worry, she's just running a little late."

"Yeah, but I told her she better be on time."

Jack thought Sonja understood the situation. She didn't have to give up any money, just show up and go through the motions. Baxter wouldn't know the difference. He'd think the money had been transferred, and by the time he figured it out, it would be too late. But now, Baxter was more jumpy than ever.

The phone rang and Baxter took it out of his pocket and looked at the Caller ID.

"It's her." He flipped the phone open. "Where are you? You're late."

Baxter frowned. "Yeah, yeah… You got everything ready?… Okay, you better be here in ten minutes."

Baxter closed the phone. "Said she got delayed by an accident on the freeway."

Jack had a bad feeling. He glanced at the gun on the dash, wondering if he could grab it before Baxter.

"Hey, don't be eying the gun. I might have just one good arm, but I can still put a bullet in your head in the time it takes you to blink."

RUBEN STARED AT the fortuneteller driving the car. "What's this all about?"

She glanced at him, smiled and patted his hand. "Don't worry, it'll be over before you know it."

"You have the money from the resort sale, don't you?"

"Don't you remember *anything*?"

An image of the fortuneteller's face flashed in his mind's eye, only she looked younger, a lot younger, as she handed him a cowboy hat. Cowboy hat?

"How long have we known each other?"

She glanced and gave him a sad smile, but said nothing.

Ruben sighed and laid his aching head on the car's console.

SONJA TURNED INTO the Holiday Inn driveway and spotted Jack's Mercedes on the left. Parking a few spaces before reaching the car, she said, "Stay down. I'll be back in a few minutes."

She got out of the car and walked over to the Mercedes. Baxter opened the door, struggled out with the gun in his good hand, and nodded toward the rear door.

"We'll do business in the back seat, so I can keep an eye on both of you."

"Sure," Sonja said, "whatever you say."

They got in, Baxter on the right and Sonja on the left.

Jack had turned around to watch, and Sonja touched the backs of her fingers to the side of his face. "Are you all right?"

Jack grinned. "Never better, now that you're here."

A computer sat on the middle of the back seat, a web page displayed on the screen. Baxter laid the gun down and turned the computer so Sonja could reach the keyboard.

"Okay, show me the balance and I'll give you my account number to send it to." Baxter smiled and picked up the gun. "I know all about computers and offshore banks, so don't try any funny stuff."

Sonja glanced at Jack and he winked. She brought up the phony website using the same address she had given Delray, and entered the account and PIN. The screen indicated a balance of $10 million, and she turned the computer so Baxter could see it.

His face lit up, and he gave her a piece of paper with a number on it. "Do your thing. But keep the screen turned so I can watch what you do."

She selected the option for transferring funds, entered the amount to transfer and Baxter's account number, and pressed a button to complete the transaction. The website operated as expected, the words "Transferring Funds" flashing at the bottom of the screen while the program slowly painted a blue bar across the middle. A few seconds later, a box popped up containing the message "Transfer Complete."

When she turned the computer so Baxter could see, he said, "Hey, that's pretty slick." He took the computer.

"Maybe for you. You have all our money."

"Yeah, imagine that. Conning the cons out of their hard-earned cash."

He laid the gun on the seat beside him and pecked on the computer keys with his index finger.

Jack cleared his throat. "Can we go now?"

"In a minute, soon as my account information comes up."

Sonja glanced at Jack and raised an eyebrow.

SAM CRUISED UNDER the MacArthur Causeway, but didn't see Delray up ahead and pulled back on the throttle, slowing the boat to an idle. The other Donzi wouldn't have gotten to open sea in the minute or so it took Sam to get there. *Maybe hiding behind one of the bridge supports?* Sam stood up, pulled his gun, and nudged the boat around the concrete footing of the support closest to where Delray had gone under the bridge. Steering back toward the mainland, he saw the tip of the other Donzi sticking out from behind the footing. He pointed the gun toward the other boat and eased closer. Mona sat in the passenger seat, her hands tied behind her back, Delray nowhere in sight.

Mona's eyes grew large when she saw him. "Watch out!" she screamed. "He's up there!" She nodded toward Sam's right and above his head.

Delray, standing on top of the footing, swung an oar at Sam's head. He ducked, but not fast enough, and the blade of the makeshift weapon struck him above the ear. A hornet's nest buzzed inside his brain, and Delray's clown face turned sideways as Sam fell over the Donzi's low rail.

TWENTY-EIGHT

BAXTER FROWNED AT the computer screen. "Hey, this don't look right."

Sonja leaned forward and slid the tips of her fingers underneath the back of the computer. "What do you mean?"

Baxter glanced up at her, his eyes tiny slits. "My account's still empty. You tried to cheat me." He grabbed for the gun next to his leg and Sonja flipped the computer into his face. Jerking back, he dropped the gun to the floor of the car, and Jack back-fisted him to the temple. Baxter's eyes sprang wide for a split second and then slammed shut as he fell over against the seat.

"Get the gun," Jack said as he started the car.

Sonja did as he asked and handed it to him.

"I'll follow you." She opened the door and got out.

Jack drove a couple of miles down the street to a restaurant that had gone out of business, parked in back, and got out. Sonja pulled in as Jack tugged Baxter out of the back seat onto the ground. After retrieving his cell phone from Baxter's pocket, he spotted a rusty trash barrel that lay on its side. He dragged the unconscious man over to it, pushed him in head first, and stood the barrel on end. They left him there sleeping with his face pressed against the rusty bottom.

J.T. DROVE out of the warehouse parking lot and tried to reach Sam on his phone. No answer. That didn't sound good.

Ernie squirmed in the passenger seat, his hands tied behind him. J.T. had found him in the warehouse, but there had been no sign of Mona, anywhere.

"Hey, why don't you untie me?"

"Quiet," J.T. said, "I'm trying to think."

"I'm not going anywhere. I couldn't escape if I had to."

"I know you won't, because I'm not untying you."

"Yeah, but my shoulder's killing me where Mackenzie shot me."

J.T. looked at him and grinned. "Hey, that's too bad. I remember you talked pretty tough when you had the gun on us. Don't be such a wimp. You keep it up and I'll put you in the trunk."

Ernie narrowed his eyes, probably thinking how he would kill him when he got a chance.

"You're a funny guy, you know it." Ernie peeled his lip back in a sneer.

"Okay, I'll play fair. Tell me where your stupid partner took Sam and the women and I'll cut you loose."

The car hit a bump and Ernie grimaced with pain. He took a deep breath and let it out. "Like I know where he went. He hit me on the head before Mackenzie even got there. When I woke up, they were gone."

"You and Delray had a spat?"

"You could say that. I'm getting pretty sick of him pushing me around like he's some kind of big shot."

J.T. glanced his way. "I bet you'd like to put a bullet in his head. I know I would."

"The thought has occurred to me."

"Why'd he get mad at you?"

Ernie remained silent for several seconds, probably trying to decide if he wanted to talk about it. Finally, he said, "Things were going great until Ruben came up with the plan to buy that hotel, talking big about what a great investment it would be. 'We could go legit,' he said. It was bad enough that the hotel turned out to be bogus, but I didn't have the money so I brought Delray into the deal. Biggest mistake I ever made. He said, 'If we can double our money, I'll get it for you.' He didn't mention he would be getting it from a loan shark who had to have it back in a week or two."

"So the loan shark has been after you?"

"Well, not me personally, but he's been calling Delray. Delray's been on my case for losing the money."

J.T. chuckled. "Then it sounds like all you need to do is pop Delray and your troubles are over. I can help you out with that part if you tell me where he went."

"I told you, I don't know where he went." Ernie groaned. "Believe me, I'd like to know, myself."

Had J.T. been doing the shooting back at that warehouse, instead of Sam, he would have put the round right in the middle of Ernie's chest, and Ernie wouldn't be whining to anybody. End of story. He would've also put an end to Delray back on Grand Cayman. But did Sam? Nooooo. When would he learn?

"Sam and the fortuneteller went to see Delray," J.T. said, "to give him the resort money she scammed."

"Maybe they did. I was unconscious. But Delray wouldn't have been able to do the bank transfer by himself."

"Okay, where would he have gone to get it done?"

"Maybe to the loan shark, since the money would be going to him."

They might be getting somewhere.

"You know where this shylock lives?"

"I went there about a year ago with Delray when he paid a debt. He went inside and I stayed in the car. I think I can find it again." Ernie squirmed in his seat. "But I'm not going to unless you cut my hands loose."

J.T. sighed, steered the car to the shoulder of the road, and stopped.

"Okay," J.T. said, picking the gun up from the seat next to him. "I'm going to untie you. If you try anything, anything at all, you'll be a dead soldier. You understand?"

Ernie narrowed his eyes and nodded.

J.T. opened his door, stepped out and looked back in. "Scoot over here. You're driving."

Ernie struggled across the front seat and squeezed in behind the wheel, groaning in pain with every move. J.T. walked around the car and got in where Ernie had been sitting. He pulled out his knife, held the gun tip to Ernie's side, and cut the rope he'd used to tie Ernie's hands. Ernie drew a deep breath and let it out as he leaned back in the seat. He reached into his shirt pocket, pulled out a pill, and popped it into his mouth.

Buckling his seat belt, J.T. said, "Get going."

"My shoulder feels like it's going to drop off. It might be bleeding again, too."

J.T. jabbed him on the arm with his fist.

"Ow!"

"Yeah, bet it hurts even more, now. Stop your whining and get moving."

JACK CALLED SAM'S number and no one answered. Sonja had told him about the meeting with Delray and everything that happened after that.

"He went inside the house when he heard the shots, and we drove away to find you."

"What about J.T.?"

"I saw him following us out of the mechanic's shop, and kept him in sight until after we got on the Interstate. I lost him some time after that, with all the traffic, but he must have been there when Delray drove us out of the warehouse, because Sam called him from the back of the truck and told him to go back and look for Mona Miles."

TWENTY-NINE

SAM WOKE ON the deck of the Donzi, his clothes wet and head pounding. Tingles ran up his arms and he realized his hands were bound behind him. Mona sat on the deck next to him, her hands behind her back as well. She didn't seem to be injured. The myna bird from the warehouse sat on her shoulder, peering down at him.

"Are you okay?" Mona asked.

"Yeah, I think so. How about you?"

Mona nodded and cut her eyes toward the front of the boat. Sam pushed himself up to a sitting position and saw Delray at the helm. A patch of his bloody scalp in back flapped up and down in the fifty-knot wind. The Donzi engine roared, and Sam felt the bump of rippled water passing underneath. Sharp pains shot through his head with each jolt.

Delray pulled out his phone and punched in a number.

"Where are you?" Delray asked, his voice loud, audible over the Donzi's engine noise. "Okay, change of plans. I'm outside Miami, headed for the island. You know the place… Yeah, that's it. Bring the boat there."

He closed the phone, opened it again, and punched in a number. After a pause, he said, "Where are you on moving that piece of merchandise I told you about?… Yeah, well, you better find a buyer fast, or I'm gonna get somebody else, and I'll come looking for you after this is all over." He flipped the phone closed without a goodbye.

Turning around, he saw Sam watching. "What're you looking at?"

When Sam didn't reply, Delray frowned and went back to steering the boat.

Sam looked at Mona and she leaned over and said into his ear, "Do you know where this island is located?"

Sam shook his head. He saw what looked like Key Biscayne in the distance to their left. Delray's destination could be any of several small islands in the bay.

They rode for about fifteen minutes, racing a dying sun, before the Donzi engine slowed. An island lay ahead, no more than fifty yards away. It looked small and uninhabited, dense with palms, mangroves and undergrowth. They neared land and Delray turned the boat into an inlet that looked like a small cove. It curved and led at least another hundred yards inland.

A tent the color of green camouflage rose in the distance. The setting reminded Sam of jungles where he'd worked in Central and South America. Delray eased the boat up to a crude dock, constructed of wooden cargo pallets, and cut the engine.

"Okay, Mackenzie, take a good look at this place. No electricity, no running water, no air conditioning." Delray chuckled. "This is where you'll be staying until I get my money back from your thieving friends." He grabbed a rope and a flashlight, jumped out of the boat, and wound the rope around a cleat in the makeshift dock.

Sam wondered if he still had his cell phone in his pocket, and if it would work after getting wet from his fall into the water. He tugged at his bindings and the effort sent shock waves through the spot where the oar had struck his head.

The boat secured, Delray took out his gun and said, "Okay, get out. Take it real easy so I don't get nervous and start shooting."

"Okay, get out." The myna's head bobbed up and down as he scrambled back and forth on Mona's shoulder.

They struggled to their feet and stepped out onto the rickety conglomeration of pallets, Delray backing up as they did. Something large slithered through the underbrush a few feet away, rustling the weeds and dried leaves.

Delray glanced down and grinned. "Lots of snakes on this island. I killed four big ones the last time I came here."

"Four big ones."

"Shut up, Rolly," Delray said.

"Shut up, Rolly. Rolly wants a cracker."

They trampled through the brush toward the tent, Delray behind them with the gun, sunlight leaking away by the second. Near-darkness surrounded them by the time they reached their destination, and Delray clicked on the flashlight. He shone it on the tent, unzipped a canvas door and pulled it open for them to enter.

Inside, Delray reached down and flipped on a battery-powered lantern, illuminating the drab interior. The space looked about twenty feet square. Its floor was elevated a couple of inches off the ground to keep it dry. Cots sat in each of the two back corners, both with dingy, rumpled sheets on top. Steel poles supported the tent on the four corners and in the center.

"Sit down on the floor so I can keep an eye on you."

Sam did as instructed.

Mona sighed. "What about a bathroom?"

"Rolly wants a cracker."

"You got the great outdoors, sweet cheeks."

"You're joking."

"I don't joke."

Sam wondered if this might be the time to escape. Mona glanced at him, maybe thinking the same thing.

"I guess I don't have any choice."

"Okay, go ahead." He untied her hands. "I'll be watching you through the doorway. If you're not back in a couple of minutes, I'll shoot your boyfriend in the leg."

Rolly hopped off Mona's shoulder and fluttered down to the floor.

She went out. Delray held the canvas door open and aimed the flashlight beam outside, glancing back at Sam every few seconds to make sure he stayed down.

He would be distracted when Mona came back, and that might be Sam's only chance. The person Delray had called from the Donzi would be on the way in the yacht, and the phone conversation didn't reveal when it might get there. After that, though, the window for escape would be shut and locked down tight.

Sam edged his feet in close to his body and braced himself. It seemed like a long wait, but Delray finally backed up to let Mona through the canvas door. Sam pushed himself onto his haunches from behind with his bound hands and sprang to his feet. Delray spun around and pointed the gun at Sam's head. Mona crashed into his shoulder, knocking him off balance, and the gun fired wildly, the shot sounding like a bomb exploding in the closeness of the tent. Rolly screeched, flapping his wings, fluttering around the inside of the tent. Sam swept his right leg up and to the left, bumping Delray's gun away from him, then pivoted and side-kicked him in the stomach. As Delray doubled over, Sam stepped in and brought his knee up to smash against the man's chin. The clown head snapped back. He hung there for a split second, his eyes half-open, before crumpling to the floor, unconscious.

"Get the gun," Sam said.

She pulled the weapon from Delray's fingers, laid it on the floor several feet away, and untied Sam's hands. Sam fished the boat key and cell phone out of Delray's pocket. He looked down at the unconscious man and said, "Okay, what do we do with you?" Faced with this same decision a couple of days before, he'd let him live and regretted it. He picked up the gun from the floor.

Two POLICE CRUISERS sat in front of the posh Miami Beach house, blue lights flashing. The gate to the driveway stood open. Yellow crime scene tape stretched across the entrance. A group of what looked like curious neighbors stood around talking behind the police cars, trying to get a peek inside. Ernie turned off the car, and J.T. took the keys from the ignition.

"Better not try to run," J.T. said.

He got out of the car and ambled over to a woman in a tight skirt who stood alone, peering toward the house.

"What's going on?"

The woman turned and smiled, as if trying to place him. Her smile leaked away. "You live around here?" A looker, she had black hair that hung to her shoulders and large blue eyes.

"In the next block," J.T. said. "I saw the flashing lights on my way home."

The woman nodded. "Somebody fired a shot in there and took off up the waterway in their boat."

"You're kidding?" He wondered if Sam had been shot.

"No," the woman said, shaking her head, her eyes wide. "My ex-husband thinks they're criminals." She held J.T.'s eyes.

"Criminals." He shook his head and sighed. "And I thought we lived in a respectable neighborhood."

"Oh, we do." She touched J.T.'s arm. "They're the only ones, at least that we know about."

"Huh. So the guy just sped off in a boat?" J.T. peered over the hedge that lined the yard to get a look at the waterway.

"Yes, and he had a woman with him. A pretty blonde, according to the neighbor next door. And another man chased him in a second boat."

Could that be Sam? That would fit. Delray speeding away with Mona, Sam chasing.

J.T. glanced at the woman, who seemed to be checking his fingers for a wedding band. "When did all this happen?"

"About thirty minutes ago."

If Sam still lived, J.T. wondered why he hadn't answered his phone. Maybe out of range? He supposed he could follow the streets next to the waterway and see if anything turned up. If Sam caught up with Delray, there likely would be fireworks, and that might leave a trail.

This woman looked pretty hot in the cop car lights, and she seemed to be giving him the eye.

"How about getting a drink later?" J.T. asked.

She smiled, this time more brilliantly than before. "I don't know you."

"Sure you do. John Templeton Smith III." He stuck out his hand.

The woman glanced down at his outstretched hand and took it. "Okay, then, I'm Heather… Heather Simmons." She seemed to add the last name with some reluctance.

J.T. smiled. "Where do you live?"

Heather pulled her hand away and chuckled. "You can call me. I'm in the book."

"I'll do that," J.T. said, pointing his index finger at her, thumb up, as if aiming a gun.

Back in the car, he said, "It looks like Delray might have killed the shylock and escaped in a boat on the waterway. Let's go toward the bay."

Ernie shrugged, started the engine, and steered around the police vehicles. They reached the edge of Biscayne Bay as the sun reclined on the Miami horizon. Though there had been many boats along the way, J.T. hadn't seen any speeding, and hadn't seen anyone who looked like Delray or Sam.

"This is like looking for a needle in a haystack." Still scanning the water, J.T. spotted a boat near the causeway that looked as if it might be grounded. "Pull over. There's a Donzi down there and nobody's in it. It looks like it's wedged into the bank."

Ernie turned onto an access road, drove down under the causeway and stopped. J.T. turned off the ignition and took the keys.

They stepped down the incline toward the water's edge. The Donzi appeared to be stuck in a crevice of the bank, its engine idling, the propeller churning up mud and bottom debris. A handgun lay on the console.

"I wonder where the other boat went?"

Ernie glanced up at the car, probably worried about the police. "What other boat?"

"The chick back there said a second boat chased the first one. I think that might have been Sam doing the chasing."

Maybe Sam had caught him, but why would he leave the boat here with the engine running? And the gun? J.T. called Sam's phone again. No answer. That didn't sound good. He probably didn't answer because he couldn't. That meant Delray had gotten the drop on him.

"You know any place Delray would go in a boat?"

Ernie scratched his head, grimaced, and peered down at the water. Moments passed before he looked up, a half-smile on his face. "He set up a hideout a few months ago when he got worried about some guys he'd stiffed coming after him."

"Where is it?"

Ernie glanced south on the bay. "It's a small island not far from Key Biscayne. Nobody lives there. Delray found it while out cruising in his yacht. There's a little inlet where he pulls in and hides the boat. He set up a tent on the island for his men."

"You know how to get to it?"

Ernie shrugged. "I've never been there, but he told me where it is in case he ever needed help."

"You think you can find it?"

"I don't know. Maybe."

MONA GRABBED SAM'S ARM. "You're not going to kill him, are you?"

Sam smiled and popped the clip on the weapon: only a couple of rounds left. "No, just checking the ammo."

He put the gun in his pocket, picked up the pieces of rope they'd dropped on the floor, and tied Delray's hands and feet. Lifting the unconscious man, he threw him over his shoulder.

"Grab that lantern and flashlight, and let's get out of here."

With Mona in the lead, they left the tent and eased down the path to the dock. Sam dropped Delray into the bottom of the Donzi and unwound the line from the dock cleat. They boarded and he started the engine, turned the boat around, and headed toward the bay at low throttle. They made it about ten feet out of the channel, and the engine sputtered and died. Sam glanced at the fuel gauge: empty. He tried the starter a couple of times without success. Mosquitoes buzzed around his head.

"We're out of gas," Sam said. "See if there's an emergency tank in the back."

Mona stepped over Delray into the rear of the boat, lifted a couple of panels, and pulled out a red tank. "This looks like a gas tank, but it feels empty."

THIRTY

J.T. HEADED THE Donzi south at dusk, leaving the car parked under the causeway. Ernie said Delray's island lay somewhere off the coast of Key Biscayne. Visibility proved to be a problem within a few minutes, and J.T. flipped on the running lights.

"I don't know if I can find it in the dark," Ernie said, shaking his head.

"You can find it," J.T. said. "You better, if you know what's good for you."

"Hey, lay off. I'm tired of your threats. You're as bad as Delray."

J.T. glanced at him. Pretty bold talk for somebody in his situation.

He punched Ernie on his sore shoulder. "It's no threat. Just count on dying if you don't find that island."

Ernie stared straight ahead, his lips pressed together tight as a Tupperware seal.

Darkness descended upon them as they reached a land mass to the east.

"According to the GPS, that's Virginia Key," J.T. said.

"Yeah, yeah, I figured that. Delray said the island is another few miles south."

SAM PULLED OUT his cell phone and opened it. Water dripped from the keypad. He tried a couple of keys and got nothing. Delray's phone had a one-bar signal, but when Sam entered J.T.'s number, no one answered. Sticking the phone back in his pocket, he sighed and looked at Mona.

"No luck, huh?" Mona said.

Sam shook his head, wondering who else he could call. If not for the boat being borrowed from a murder scene, he might have tried 911. The only other number he knew from memory was for Jack's old phone, the one Ernie had taken. At least Ernie wouldn't call the cops. Maybe Sam could make some kind of deal with him, since he had Ernie's business partner. He punched in the number and waited for the phone to ring five times before someone answered sounding more like J.T. than Ernie.

"J.T.?"

"Who is this?" J.T.'s voice had an edge.

"It's Sam. Man, I'm glad it's you. I expected to have to negotiate with Ernie to come get us."

"I took Ernie's phone; I'll tell you about that later. Where are you?"

"Mona and I are on some island Delray brought us to. He's unconscious in the bottom of the boat, but we're out of gas." Sam told him about Delray getting the drop on him.

"Yeah, I found the boat…" The phone went dead for a couple of seconds, and then came back, J.T.'s voice choppy with breaks in the signal. "…Ernie remembered the island…isn't having much luck remembering the directions."

A GPS monitor on the console indicated Sam's location. "J.T., listen, you're breaking up. I'll give you our location." He read the coordinates into the phone and asked if J.T. had heard them. No response.

"J.T.?"

Dead. He hung up and turned to Mona. "He's looking for us. I don't know if he heard the coordinates or not."

The boat had drifted and Sam decided they would be better off anchored back at shore. He found an oar, got onto the point of the bow on his stomach, and began paddling. It took a few minutes, but the boat finally slid into the edge of the mangroves around the corner from the channel, the bow wedged between two limbs.

Sam pulled out the cell phone. No signal.

"Untie me!" Delray had awakened.

Shining the light on his face, Sam said, "Forget it."

Delray yelled out, "Help!" and repeated it several times, as if someone else might hear him.

Sam found a hand towel in one of the storage compartments, stepped into the rear of the boat, and stuffed it into Delray's mouth.

Back in the seat next to Mona, he gazed off into the distance. The neon of Miami glowed in the west like the last remnants of a setting sun. Frogs croaked somewhere onshore. A few minutes later they stopped, their music replaced by the sound of an engine. Though he hoped it might be J.T., he knew better; the engine had a more muffled sound than that of the Donzi.

"This is worse than driving in a strange neighborhood in the dark," Ernie said. "At least streets have signs. Out here everything looks the same."

J.T. sighed and pulled back on the throttle to an idle; no sense in wasting fuel. He took out the phone and tried again. Still no answer. A real shame. Sam had been ready to say the GPS coordinates when the connection dropped.

"You know anybody else who can tell us how to get there?"

Ernie scratched his head. "Cal, the guy who works for Delray on Grand Cayman, would know. I put his number in the phone when we were down there."

J.T. handed Ernie the phone. "Call and tell him Delray wants you to meet him there but you can't find it, and Delray's phone doesn't answer."

Ernie found the number and pressed the Call button.

"Yo, Cal. This is Ernie…you know, Ernie Brent, Delray's business partner… Yeah, that's right… Oh, yeah? Huh. That's the reason I'm calling. Delray wanted me to meet him at the island, but I got lost and I can't get him to answer his phone. Must be out of range… Yeah, that'd be great, the GPS coordinates. Hold on."

Ernie put his hand over the phone and said he needed something to write on. J.T. opened a compartment in the console and found a notepad and a pen. He handed the items to Ernie, and Ernie wrote down the numbers as Cal read them off to him.

"Okay, you're a life saver, Cal. I should see you there in an hour or so." Ernie closed the phone and handed the coordinates to J.T.

J.T. compared them to those on the GPS monitor. "Yeah, we went too far south. Why'd you say you'd see him there?"

"Cal said he and Joe are almost to the island in the yacht. They were on their way to Miami, but Delray called a couple of hours ago and told them to meet him there instead."

SAM LISTENED TO the engine noise just around the bend of the island. It slowed and revved a couple of times, probably the driver negotiating the mouth of the inlet.

"They're in the channel, headed for the dock," Sam said.

The thugs would realize something had happened to Delray after a while and would head toward Miami looking for him. He and Mona would still be out of gas, and J.T. might not be able to find them. So Sam decided he would go after Delray's boat. He pulled the gun from his pocket, thumbed the hammer, and handed it to Mona.

"What's this for?"

"I'm going ashore for a few minutes and check things out. Stay here and watch Delray."

"What if they come around here before you get back?"

"They'll probably wait there for Delray at least an hour before giving up. I'll be back before then. But if something goes wrong and you see those guys, put the gun to Delray's head and threaten to kill him. You could hold them off until J.T. finds us."

"What do you mean if something goes wrong?" Mona asked, her voice pitched higher than normal.

"Don't worry. It'll be okay. I just said that as a precaution."

Apparently unconvinced, Mona grabbed his hand. "What if I have to shoot somebody? How do I do it?"

"Just point and pull the trigger. You have two shots left in the gun."

Sam couldn't see her face in the moonlight, but imagined her eyes wide and teary. She would be all right, he told himself.

"Okay, just hurry back. I don't want anything to happen to you."

Sam kissed her on the lips, and she leaned into him, extending it for a couple of beats. Tears rolled down her face and wet Sam's cheek. He broke away, gave her Delray's cell phone, grabbed the oar and flashlight, and climbed out of the boat onto the shore.

The foliage became dense after about ten feet, the oar providing little help as Sam weaved his way through palmettos and scrub oak. The distance between him and the channel where the yacht sat would be only about a hundred feet, so he had to be as quiet as possible and use the light sparingly.

What looked like a raccoon's eyes shone in the light at one point, and the creature scampered away. A few feet before reaching the channel, Sam heard something slither on the ground ahead of him. Not wanting to use the light that close to the yacht, he waited several moments, and the noise stopped. He hoped the snake had passed by. Taking a step, twigs crackled under his shoe and the slithering noise started again. He stopped and waited. The noise ceased. After a minute or so, he squatted as quietly as possible, shined the light onto the ground for a split second, and then turned it off. The snake lay directly in his path.

If it struck him, he would die. It posed a greater threat than Delray's men, who might not even have guns handy. Sam shined the light on the head of the snake and it rose up, its red eyes bouncing into the light like laser beams from a night scope. He tried to move the creature to one side with the oar and it wended its way around it, sliding toward him. Laying the light on the ground, Sam lifted the oar and chopped down at the creature's neck. The blow didn't seem to connect, but the snake hissed and hurried into the underbrush. Sam plodded on, hoping he wouldn't have to come back that way.

Reaching the channel, he saw the yacht moored next to the makeshift dock. A muffled generator motor ran somewhere on the vessel. Lights illuminated the deck and the windows of the salon.

Sam laid the oar and flashlight on the ground, slid into the black water, and pushed away from the bank. The water felt cool under his clothes. Wondering if creatures lay underneath the surface waiting for fresh prey, he reminded himself that he'd dived in far more exotic and dangerous places than this and had lived to remember them. He swam to the stern, pulled himself up, and slid over the rail onto the smooth wood deck.

THIRTY-ONE

J.T. STOOD BEHIND the wheel of the Donzi, studying the GPS. "We're getting close."

Ernie had taken his seat a few minutes earlier and had buckled himself in, complaining of dizziness and an aching head. He'd been quiet. In his peripheral vision, J.T. saw him reach under the console for something. The gun still lay in a pocket atop the console on J.T.'s side, so he wasn't worried about Ernie getting his hands on it.

The engine abruptly shut down, and the Donzi pitched forward, its bow dipping into the water, dropping in speed from fifty miles per hour to near-zero almost instantly. *Ernie had yanked out the kill switch!* J.T. fell against the wheel, grabbed for something to hold onto, and reached for the gun. Too late. Ernie popped the buckle on his seat belt and kicked J.T. over the side.

J.T. went into the water, head first. It happened so fast he didn't have a chance to think about the ramifications. Now, coming up out of the cool water, his ears burned with anger, at Ernie and himself. He had been so preoccupied with the GPS, he'd become complacent about the danger Ernie posed.

The new boat captain peered over the rail, a smile pinching the corner of his mouth in the glow of the console lights. He started the engine.

"Hey, don't leave me out here!" J.T. yelled over the burble of the big engine. "I won't hurt you, I promise."

Ernie grabbed the gun and pointed it at him. He said, "You got that right," and fired.

SAM EASED TO the yacht's cabin and peered through the windows into the salon. It appeared to be empty.

"What's your name?"

Sam jerked. It sounded like Delray's voice, coming from the direction of the tent, but Sam knew it couldn't be him. Rolly. They'd forgotten about him after sacking Delray. The shot had probably scared him and he'd hidden.

More voices. Squatting next to the rail, Sam peered over the edge. The two men who worked for Delray, Joe and Cal, trampled up the path toward the dock, a flashlight leading their way.

"He said he'd be here," the older guy, Joe, said, "and that was a coupla hours ago. Something happened to him."

"Try his phone," Cal said.

"Okay, soon as we get back on the boat. These woods give me the creeps. No telling what's out here."

"Give me the creeps."

"This is the neatest bird I ever seen," Joe said. "I wonder how he learned to talk, out here on this island."

"You shoulda left him in the tent. He'll peck your eyes out."

"No, he won't."

Sam crouched next to the gate in the rail and sprang to his feet as Joe stepped through onto the deck.

"What the—"

Sam kicked him in the stomach. He fell back against

the other man onto the dock, gasping for breath and hugging his midsection, as if trying to keep it from falling out.

"Get off me!" Cal said. "I can't reach my gun."

Jumping onto the dock, Sam jerked Joe to the side and slammed his fist into Cal's face. The blow smacked like a ripe melon dropping on concrete, and the flesh yielded as bone and cartilage tore loose under Sam's knuckles. Cal's mouth flew open, and his eyes rolled up as he lost consciousness.

Sam took their guns, put one into his pocket and held the other on Joe.

"Get up."

"Where's the boss?" Joe asked between labored breaths, still clutching his stomach.

Sam undid one of the tie lines and tossed it to him, ignoring the question. He didn't want to take them with him, but they might cause him trouble later if he left them here.

"Tie your friend's hands and feet, and drag him onto the boat."

Joe struggled to stand. He rolled Cal over and bound his wrists and ankles like a rodeo calf. Still out of breath, he wheezed as he wrestled the unconscious man onto the deck of the yacht.

"Put him in the wheelhouse."

When Joe finished dragging the man, he remained bent over, resting with his hands on his knees, gasping for breath.

"You'll pay for this."

"You'll pay for this," Rolly said. He'd fluttered away when the action started, but now sat perched on the rail.

Sam sighed. "You might be right, old timer."

Sam tied Joe to the helm and unwound the remaining line from the dock.

"Okay, start it up and back us out of here."

They had moved only twenty feet or so when three gunshots discharged somewhere in the distance. Sam reached around the old boxer and cut the throttle so he could listen. Maybe Mona had shot someone, but who? The direction didn't seem quite right, though. Unless the foliage played tricks with the acoustics, the noise had come from somewhere in the bay, rather than around the point of the island. Maybe J.T. had shot Ernie, or vice versa. Sam hoped J.T. still had the gun; otherwise, they could be in for some trouble, especially if the Donzi reached Mona and Delray first.

"Were those gunshots?" Joe asked.

"Yeah," Sam said. "Speed it up."

Joe rammed the throttle forward and the propellers churned the water behind them, the yacht picking up speed. Seconds ticked away as they backed toward the mouth of the channel.

ERNIE EYED THE island directly ahead, an ominous black glob in the night. Something white lay off to the left side. Maybe the other Donzi. J.T. had said they'd run out of gas. He drew nearer, and the other Donzi came into focus. Pointing a flashlight at it, he saw only two people aboard. The newswoman was in front, and Delray was in back, his mouth gagged with a piece of cloth.

Ernie stuffed the gun into his pocket, stood up, and called out to Mona Miles, "Where's Mackenzie?"

"He's coming right back," she said, her words too loud and shaky. "Where's J.T.?"

"Ah…he got seasick. He's throwing up back there in the bottom of the boat."

Ernie pulled to within a couple of feet of the boat, close enough to see the woman's eyes. They were large with fear. Delray yelled something through the gag, but his words were unintelligible.

Mona turned and peered at him, then back at Ernie, seeming unsure what to do. After a couple of beats, she stood up and pointed a gun at him. "If J.T.'s back there, tell him to stand up so I can see him."

Ernie hadn't expected her to have a gun. He didn't think she would have the guts to shoot him, but accidents happen, so he needed to get that gun out of her hand.

"Oh, he's back there, all right, puking his guts out." Ernie turned and spoke to the vacant space behind the seats: "The woman wants you to show your face. She's got a gun and looks like she might shoot me if you don't get up."

Ernie didn't want to kill her, the only key to getting the money. He glanced back at Mona. "He wants me to help him up." Stepping into the back of the boat and bending over, Ernie searched for something he could hit her with. Spotting an oar and a flare gun, he developed a plan: he would startle her with the flare and knock the gun out of her hand with the oar. He stood with them in his hands and swung around.

MONA WATCHED AS Ernie bent over in the back of the boat. When he stood up with the oar in his hand, he looked suspicious, as if he might be up to something. Sure enough, he had a gun in his other hand. She thrust her pistol out in front of her, closed her eyes, and squeezed the trigger. The gunshot exploded and the weapon bucked from her hands and dropped to the deck.

There had been another pop, maybe right after her shot, or before, she couldn't be sure, and even before she opened her eyes she knew something had gone bad wrong. The night turned into day, and her back felt as if it might be on fire. Delray screamed through the gag, and she pivoted to see flames engulfing the seat close to him. She wondered if she had killed Ernie with her shot, and glanced back, but didn't see him. His boat, still idling, had pushed into their craft, nudging it sideways to the bank.

Delray continued making noise, motioning with his bound hands. Mona tried to undo the knots Sam had tied in the rope, but they were like rocks. The fire roared larger and had migrated to the seat next to her. She just wanted to get out of the boat and run, but a fiery image of Delray burning to death would surely burden her conscience for the rest of her life. A quick search of the compartment where Sam had found the towel produced a box cutter. It sliced through the ropes and freed his hands and feet.

Delray jerked the gag from his mouth. "This tub's gonna blow up!"

SAM NUDGED THE yacht around the corner of the island as one of the Donzis sped away from a burning boat next to the shore. Their boat had run out of gas, so it wasn't the one in motion. *It had to be the one on fire!* Hurrying out of the wheelhouse to the bow, Sam saw only the shine of Delray's red hair as he piloted the speeding craft. He didn't see Mona anywhere. His heart pounded, and an aching knot blossomed in his stomach and in the back of his throat.

Tentacles of flame grew higher. The resin in the boat hull popped as it melted and the fire consumed it. Sparks scattered into the air like the Fourth of July. Sam saw nothing moving inside the inferno, and no one on the bank, which was illuminated for several feet inland.

Could Mona have gotten onto the other boat? The fiery mass exploded, broadcasting debris fifty feet or more into the air. A curtain of heat hit the side of Sam's face, and he turned away. Nothing could have lived through that. His pulse hissed in his ears like a viper, his heart seeming on the verge of bursting from his chest.

Sam reached for the spotlight on the rail and snapped it on. It cast a beam at least a hundred feet, but it couldn't reach the fleeing Donzi. Something had happened to J.T., of that he had no doubt; otherwise he'd be at the boat's helm instead of Delray.

THIRTY-TWO

SAM HAD TO believe that Mona had made it out alive. Delray would make sure of it, so he could use her as leverage to reclaim his yacht. He would be back soon, and Sam would need to be ready. Leaving Joe in the wheelhouse, he went on a quick search for weapons, and whatever thing Delray had stolen from the New-Mood truck. He had thought about the item, and decided that it had to be one of two things: a large gem of some kind, probably a diamond, or a trade secret, Seams being in the pharmaceutical business. A diamond seemed the most logical…maybe the blue diamond J.T. had read about on the computer. He'd said that Seams hadn't owned it, but what if the old man had stolen it? Then Delray stole it from him? That would explain why Seams transported it using an armed courier in the back of his truck, rather than in an armored car. He didn't want anybody to know he had it.

Searching the salon and the rest of the upper deck, he combed through several tackle boxes containing lures, lead weights, leaders, and hooks. The storage compartments held rods and reels, life preservers, nets, ropes, and knives. No diamond.

Progressing to the cabins below, he found Joe and Cal's travel items and clothing, strewn throughout the forward cabins by two guys not accustomed to cleaning up after themselves. The only thing of interest was a sawed-off pump shotgun stowed in a compartment beneath one of the bunks.

He saved the master stateroom for last. Much larger than the others, Delray would have reserved that room for himself. Jerking open the bulkhead compartments and drawers, he dragged everything out onto the floor. After a few fruitless minutes of sorting through clothing, shoes, a travel bag that Joe or Cal probably had packed for Delray, and a medicine cabinet filled with the usual items, he stood next to the bed for one last look. *Running out of time.* What had he missed? The item hadn't been in his safe at his home, and he didn't have it on his person. This was the only other likely place.

Sam's face felt hot. He turned and kicked the nightstand next to the bed. It tumbled onto its side, a lamp on top crashing to the deck. A childish act, no doubt. Maybe he'd sink the boat, too, when all this ended. An easy way to dispose of all the bodies.

Sighing, he took a deep breath and started to go back topside, when he noticed a tiny gap in the deck boards where the nightstand had sat. He got down on his knees, worked his fingernail into the gap, and pulled the board loose. It lifted out to reveal a space underneath about the size of a shoebox. It was filled with cash. Sam pulled the money out and found nothing else underneath. If Delray had hidden something valuable on the boat, this would have been the place. And it wasn't here. The stacks of cash looked like about $10,000. More running money.

Sam had an idea, in case Mona did come back with Delray. He went back to the medicine cabinet, took out one of the disposable razors, and separated the head of the plastic housing with his fingernails. The small metal blade fell free. Wrapping three-quarters of its length with a finger-sized Band-Aid gave him a handle for a makeshift cutter. It would need to go into his pocket, so he pulled a wad of tissue from the bath roll and wrapped that around the sharp end to keep from accidentally cutting himself.

Leaving the cash on the floor, he hurried up the ladder with the shotgun. No sign of Delray yet. As he stepped into the wheelhouse, Joe jerked his free hand back to the helm and frowned, like someone caught with his hand in the cookie jar. Rolly hopped onto Sam's shoulder as he entered, startling him, until he realized what had happened. He picked him up and put him onto the console, but the bird ran back up his arm.

"Gun in the console."

Sam glanced at Rolly.

"Gun in the console."

Birds only repeated things people said. They didn't make up statements like that on their own.

"Did you hear that?" he asked Joe.

Joe stared straight ahead and said, "I didn't hear nothing. How about cutting me loose. This nylon thing is cutting my wrist."

"Rolly wants a cracker."

Sam glanced at Cal on the floor. He'd regained consciousness and lay there peering up at them.

"You and Cal been talking about a spare gun in the console?"

Joe turned and glared.

Sam opened a drawer that was just about within Joe's reach, if he really tried, and found a 9mm handgun. In a matter of seconds, Joe might have had it, and Sam would have returned to a slug in the heart.

"Stupid bird," Cal said from the floor. "I told you, you should've left him on the island." Sam scrounged through the rest of the compartments and found only a pack of oatmeal cookies. Setting the bird atop the console, he crumbled a cookie in front of him. Rolly bobbed his head as he pecked and ate.

"You can forget about the guns. I'm throwing all but one of them overboard."

Stepping outside where Joe could see him, he tossed the shotgun and one of the handguns into the water, then turned and paced aft, out of Joe's sight, took the ammunition from one of the two handguns he'd kept, and dropped it into his pocket. He stuck the remaining loaded 9mm in a locker behind a tackle box, and went back to the wheelhouse.

Within a few minutes, the pale shape of the Donzi rose in the yacht's beam. Sam told Joe to shut down the engine and went out onto the bow. Delray stood at the helm, with Mona near his elbow. Drawing a deep breath and letting it out, a feeling of relief and elation coursed through Sam's chest. The scalped man still had the upper hand, but not for long.

Ernie didn't seem to be aboard, unless he lay on the deck out of sight. Sam held the empty 9mm in one hand down by his side.

Delray eased the Donzi close to the yacht and turned off the engine. He worked one-handed, the other hand holding a pistol aimed at Mona's head.

"Okay, wise guy, we're going to try this again, but my patience is running low. You so much as make a face at me and I'm going to shoot your girlfriend. I don't think you want to see any blood on this pretty blonde hair."

"Okay," Sam said, "just tell me what you want."

"Lay your gun on the deck."

Sam stooped, put the 9mm at his feet, and stood up.

"Where's Joe and Cal?" Delray asked.

"They're both tied up in the wheelhouse."

Delray dragged Mona up the ladder and clambered aboard. Holding onto her arm, he stepped over and picked up the gun from the deck. He eased by Sam to the wheelhouse door where he cut Joe loose.

"Where're your guns?" Delray asked Joe.

"He threw them overboard."

Delray turned to Sam. "You think you're pretty clever, don't you." He handed Joe the gun Sam had laid down and told him to untie Cal.

A minute later, Cal staggered onto the deck and sat down in a chair, his head in his hands.

Sam turned to the side, eased the cutter out of the tissue in his pocket, and palmed it.

Ernie appeared at the top of the ladder, breathing deeply. Blood and sweat glistened on his face. He said to Delray, "Hey, you need to take me to the hospital."

Delray snorted a laugh. "Take another pain pill. You'll be okay."

"I'm bleeding to death where that witch shot me."

Sam caught Mona's eyes and winked. A smile teased at the corner of her mouth, and something fluttered inside his chest. She still looked beautiful, even after all she'd been through.

"We'll get there when we get there," Delray said. "You're the one that caused all this trouble, so you better keep your mouth shut."

"I'm dying. I got blood leaking out of me."

The grin slid off Delray's face, and his facial features

pinched into a frown. He pointed the gun at Ernie, held it there for a couple of beats, then sighed and dropped his hand to his side. "Wait'll we get settled here, and I'll get Joe to take you to the mainland."

Ernie sat down on the deck and closed his eyes.

Reaching into the locker where Sam had hidden the gun, Delray grabbed two nylon ties and handed them to Joe.

"Here, tie Mackenzie up. Hands and feet. I don't want him walking around."

"Hey," Sam said, "I'm not going anywhere. You've got two guns on me."

"Shut up and turn around."

Sam sighed, turned his back to them, and crossed his wrists behind him, careful to conceal the cutter underneath his fingertips. Joe laid his gun down, took the ties and wrapped one of them around Sam's wrists, locking and snugging it down. He told Sam to get down on the deck next to the bulkhead. Sam sat, and Joe bound his ankles as well.

"What about her?" Joe asked, nodding toward Mona.

"Don't worry about her."

Leaning against the bulkhead, Sam began work with the cutter. He had little slack in the binding, and cut his hand trying to insert the small blade underneath the nylon tie. The incision stung, but he didn't feel any blood on his fingers.

A couple of moments later, Delray pulled out his phone and stepped over to Sam. Unsure whether or not Delray could see his hands, Sam palmed the blade.

"Okay, time to get the show on the road. What's the fortuneteller's number?"

"I don't know her number."

"Don't lie to me. You were with her when she stiffed me on the bank transfer."

"Yeah, but the only way I ever got in touch with her was through Ruben. Call him. He'll know it."

Delray frowned. "Hey, Einstein, how am I supposed to call Ruben? He ain't exactly on my speed dial."

Mona spoke up. "I might have it."

Delray turned and peered at her.

Mona took out her phone and punched some keys. "Here it is. I called Ruben for an interview before all this started."

"Call him and get the fortuneteller's number."

She pressed a button and held the phone to her ear. Several seconds passed before she spoke. Ruben apparently answered, and after identifying herself, she asked him for the number.

"Okay, put her on." Mona handed the phone to Delray. "She's there with Ruben."

Delray took the phone, waited a couple of beats, and said, "Okay, dragon lady, this is Delray Jinks, the guy you stiffed on the money transfer. We got your pal Mackenzie and the pretty television lady, and if you don't figure out a way to get me that money, they're going to die."

He listened another moment, took the phone from his ear and turned to Sam. "She says I can kill you both for all she cares."

"Let me talk to her," Sam said.

Delray frowned, then stepped over and held the phone to Sam's ear.

"Sonja, this is Sam. Tell Jack I found the prize."

The line fell silent for a moment, and then Sonja said, "What prize is that?"

"I think you know."

Delray jerked back the phone and closed it. "What are you talking about, 'the prize'?"

"You know, the blue diamond worth $30 million."

Delray stared for a couple of beats, and something seemed to click in his eyes. "You didn't find it. It's in my safe on Grand Cayman."

"Not anymore. It's in the room below decks where Joe and Cal sleep. You might want to ask Joe how it got there."

Delray's eyes grew large. He turned to the old man, his lips pressed together like a vise, and then raced to the rear hatch leading down.

Sam worked the blade, sawing the nylon. The seconds ticked away, and perspiration beaded on his face. Pressing hard on the blade, he felt a sting as it cut into his finger, but he shifted his grip and tried again. The blade finally cut through, freeing his hands. He reached down, sliced the tie on his ankles, and sprang to his feet.

"Hey, what are you doing?" Joe said, pointing the gun at Sam.

Dropping the cutter, Sam reached him in three long strides and grabbed the gun by the barrel. Joe pulled the trigger. *Click*. He tried again with the same result.

The old man's eyes grew large and his mouth dropped open as he stared at the impotent weapon.

Sam jerked it from his hands and said, "Sorry, old timer."

Joe swung a right hook, faster than Sam thought possible, but Sam stepped back in time for it to pass his jaw with a *swoosh*. Pivoting, he swept a kick behind Joe's knees, knocking his feet out from under him.

Cal stumbled toward him as he turned around,

swinging a haymaker. Sam stepped back and kicked him in the stomach. He slammed against the steel bulkhead, his head rapping it with a *thump,* and sat heavily onto the deck.

Footfalls pounded the steps on the ladder coming up from the rear hatch.

Sam popped the clip, pulled two cartridges from his pocket, and thumbed them into the clip. He rammed it into the gun and chambered a round. "Get down!" he yelled to Mona.

As he raised the gun to a firing position, Delray's head appeared in the hatchway, his face red, eyes bulging. He saw Sam and reached for his gun in his waistband.

Sam pointed the 9mm at his face. "Stop right there."

He didn't stop. Instead, he pulled the gun, charged through the hatchway onto the deck, and thrust his gun in Sam's face. "Where's the diamond? Tell me, or I'll blow your head off right now."

"He's crazy enough to do it," Mona said, panic in her voice. "Tell him what he wants to know."

Delray wouldn't shoot, because he thought Sam knew the location of the diamond. He also thought Sam wouldn't kill *him*. Sam lowered his gun, as if to give up, and shot Delray in the kneecap. Delray screamed, and Sam kicked his gun hand with the toe of his shoe. The weapon tore loose from his grip and landed a couple of feet away. He fell to the deck and moaned as he clutched what was left of his knee, watching blood seep between his fingers and drip onto the varnished deck boards.

THIRTY-THREE

"I HEARD WHAT you said about that diamond," Ernie said.

Sam had forgotten about him, but he now stood at the stern, pointing a gun at Delray.

"You've been holding out on me."

Delray glared, still clutching his bleeding knee. "You didn't have anything to do with it. I had to kill a dude on the NewMood truck to get it."

"You should've told me about it. We could've used it to settle up with the shylock."

"Like I said, the diamond is mine. I wouldn't give it away to settle a debt that you caused." Delray grunted with pain, grabbed the gun on the deck, and jerked it in Ernie's direction.

Ernie fired three times. The first two shots went wild and punched holes in the deck. The third hit Delray in the chest. The doomed man's eyes widened in a moment of shock and disbelief before they rolled up out of sight behind his lids. He fell back on the deck, the gun clattering out of his hand.

Delray Jinks was dead. Sam would never have guessed a lightweight like Ernie could have taken him down. Of course, Delray did have a blown-out knee and had to scramble to pick up his weapon. No telling how many men he had killed in his career, but he wouldn't be killing anyone else, not tonight, not ever.

Ernie grasped Mona around the neck and turned

the gun to her head. "Okay, Mackenzie, toss the piece over the side."

Sam threw the gun and heard it splash in the water below.

"Do the same with Delray's gun."

He complied.

Joe struggled to his feet, holding onto his lower back as if it might be injured, and distanced himself from the armed man.

"Okay," Ernie said, "where's that diamond?"

"It's in one of the lockers over there." Sam nodded toward the area where he'd stashed the other gun.

"Get it and bring it to me."

Sam strode to the locker, opened the tackle box, and pulled out a chrome fishing lure with treble hooks. Palming it, he also retrieved the 9mm and stepped back out toward Ernie, holding the gun behind his back.

Ernie grinned, took his arm from around Mona's neck, and held out his hand. "Give it to me."

Mona pushed away from him, frowning, and rubbed her neck.

"Here you go." Sam tossed the lure, just out of his reach.

"Hey!" Ernie lunged to catch it, and the lure bounced off his free hand and tumbled to the deck.

Sam fired the gun, a head shot, but Ernie must have jerked at the last moment, the round striking high on his forehead. The man with nine lives cursed and staggered back, his eyes a mixture of anger and confusion. Sam stepped forward and twisted the gun from his hand.

Glancing at the boxer, Sam said, "Tie him up."

Joe eased toward his boss's killer, a frown on his face. "I got a better idea."

The old guy grabbed Ernie's head in both hands and twisted. *CRACK!* Ernie dropped like a sack of potatoes, his neck contorting at an unnatural angle, eyes staring skyward at something in the next galaxy. Life number nine: over.

Mona gasped, staring down at him, her hands clutching the sides of her face. "Is he dead?"

Joe looked at her and smiled. "He better be."

Rolly flew out of the wheelhouse and lit on the rail, then flapped his wings again and landed on Mona's shoulder. He screeched and pecked at her flaxen hair.

"You have the diamond, Joe?" Sam asked.

"Nope."

Sam stared at him for a moment, wondering if he was telling the truth.

"What about Cal?"

"You'll have to ask him."

Cal, still passed out, wouldn't be telling anybody anything for a while.

"Can't we just go?" Mona asked.

Her eyes seemed hollow, glistening in the deck lights. Tears streamed down her cheeks.

"Can't we just go?"

She turned and looked at the bird, managed a teary smile, and reached to pet the top of his head.

"Can't we just go?"

"We're taking the Donzi," Sam said to Joe. "You'll have to figure out what to do with your friends here."

Joe nodded. "That's okay. We're going back to Grand Cayman and get our stuff. We'll drop them in some deep water along the way."

"He's got my phone," Mona said, pointing at Delray

on the deck, probably thinking she didn't want something belonging to her left on the dead man's body.

Sam rolled Delray over and pulled the phone from his pocket.

They climbed down the ladder to the boat below and Sam started the engine. Joe untied the line and threw it to them, and they sped away, leaving the gloom of the yacht, along with its two dead passengers, in their wake.

Bright stars shone in the night sky, the moon a waning crescent, its cusps as sharp as sail needles. A dying moon…and a moon for dying. First J.T., then Delray and Ernie. And maybe others Sam didn't know about. He hoped that would be all this moon would get.

The Donzi cast a beam at least fifty feet ahead of them, and in its glow, Sam saw something moving in the water.

Mona grabbed onto Sam's arm. "It's J.T.!"

Sam pulled back on the throttle, eased the boat over to the waving arms and cut the engine.

"You okay?" Sam asked as he pulled him into the boat.

J.T. collapsed onto one of the seats, took a deep breath and let it out. "Yeah, I think so." He reached down and massaged his lower leg. "Ernie tried to kill me, but he's lousy with a gun. He only hit me once."

"Let's see," Sam said.

"Let's see."

J.T. pulled the cuff of his wet trousers up almost to the knee and Sam examined the injury.

"Where'd the talking bird come from?" J.T. asked.

Mona picked Rolly off her shoulder and held him in her lap. "Delray had him when he kidnapped me."

"You were lucky," Sam said to J.T. "It looks like

the bullet cut a groove in the skin. The bleeding has stopped."

"I was too busy treading water to worry about it."

Sam glanced around the area. They were only a mile or so from the island where Delray had taken them. Sharks probably patrolled the area, but he didn't see any need to mention that to J.T.

"How long have you been in the water?"

"I don't know, maybe an hour." J.T. took another deep breath and let it out. "I still can't believe I let that knucklehead get the best of me. He kept whining about his injuries, and I guess I thought he was harmless."

"Don't worry about it," Sam said. "It worked out okay."

"Did he cause you any trouble?"

Sam described what had happened on the yacht.

"So Delray stole the blue diamond," J.T. said, a gleam seeping into his eyes.

Sam nodded. "Looks that way."

"Huh. I just wonder how Seams got his hands on it. Since he wasn't the guy I read about who owned it."

"I'm guessing he had somebody steal it for him, maybe Earl Bates."

"Man," J.T. said, "I'd like to get my hands on that baby. Somebody in that house must have taken it out of the safe before we got there. Could've been Joe, or Cal, or even that tattoo guy. I say let's go back over there and pay them a visit. Sweat it out of them."

"Maybe."

"We wouldn't get the whole thirty million out of it, but it'd be a pile of cash. We'd never have to work again."

Sam studied him for a couple of beats. "Let me think about it."

"You wouldn't be able to keep that diamond," Mona said, her tone sharp. "You'd be arrested."

J.T. chuckled. "You mean, like we were criminals?"

Mona turned in her seat, a frown on her face, probably thinking that was exactly what they were. And she might have been remembering the faraway look in Ernie's disconnected eyes.

"You okay?" Sam asked.

She nodded. "I just want all this to be over so I can get back to a normal life."

Sam understood. The resolve he'd seen in her face earlier had disappeared, probably wiped away by the two deaths on the yacht.

He reached for the ignition. "It *is* over. I'll take you home as soon as we reach shore. We'll sort the rest of this out after that." Starting the boat, he asked J.T. where he'd left the car. J.T. told him and they headed that way.

They were quiet for the next hour as they made their way toward Miami Beach. Idling under the causeway where Delray had slugged him with the oar, Sam spotted the car in the distance, parked about twenty feet from the shore. He motored the Donzi to the water's edge, cut the engine, and climbed out over the bow. J.T. threw him the line and he tied it to a bush. As they reached the car, a stretch Cadillac limousine screamed into the parking lot and slid to a stop just a few feet from them. Pulling his gun from his waistband, Sam realized he had been premature in telling Mona it was over.

The Caddy's front doors opened, and two men carrying automatic weapons stepped out. The armed men rushed toward the car, their Uzis pointed at Sam and J.T.

Both looked like bodybuilders. They had G.I. haircuts and wore button-down oxford shirts and khaki pants. One had a goatee and the other wore glasses.

"Lay the gun on the car," Goatee said.

"What do you want?" Sam was pretty sure who these guys were.

"Lay it on the car!" He said it louder this time, his face pinched into a frown.

Sam glanced at J.T. and Mona, and put the gun on the hood of the car.

Glasses kept his weapon pointed at them. Goatee slung the Uzi over his shoulder, stepped over and picked up Sam's gun, and handed it to Glasses.

He told them to assume the position, and then patted them down, taking his time with Mona.

Mona looked at Sam as they stood straight again, her eyes wide, lips pressed together.

"Don't worry," Sam said. "It'll be okay."

She just stared, his words not seeming to register.

The back door of the Caddy opened, and a chubby young man stepped out. It was the kid Sam had seen at the house where Delray shot the man.

Glasses caught the door and closed it behind the teenager. "They're clean, Dom. No stone."

Dom sauntered over to Sam. "What happened to the diamond?"

"Beats me. I don't have it."

"Where's the redheaded dude? I believe his name is Delray Jinks."

"He's dead. His partner killed him."

Dom stared for a couple of beats, a frown growing on his face.

Nodding toward the Cadillac, Dom said, "Get in the car."

Sam, Mona, and J.T. rode in the back of the limo facing the front, and Glasses rode in the seat facing them, his gun held at the ready. Goatee drove, and Dom rode in front with him. A glass window separated the front seat from the passenger area. Sam saw Dom stick a phone to his ear, but couldn't hear any of his conversation.

They rode across the MacArthur Causeway, continued on the Dolphin Expressway and got off at 42nd to light traffic. A few minutes later, they turned into Coral Gables. Sam thought he knew where they might be headed.

The house had a gated entrance, and beyond it stood a Mediterranean mansion, probably one of the original homes of the Miami rich. Sam knew the place, having visited a couple of months before with Jack Craft. The gate opened as they approached, and Goatee drove into a winding driveway and stopped at the front portico of the house. As they got out of the car, a short man, almost as wide as he was tall, stepped out onto the portico wearing a bathrobe. Frankie Buzzo. Sam remembered him from another situation about as bad as this one.

Dom got out of the car and stepped to the front door. "Uncle Frankie, this is the guy I mentioned on the phone."

Frankie glanced at Sam and smirked as he stuck his pudgy hands into the robe pockets. "Yeah, I know Mackenzie. Get 'em inside."

THIRTY-FOUR

Dom led Sam, Mona, and J.T. into a dining room and told them to wait there. He left and closed the door behind him. They took seats on one side of a table configured for ten people, Mona to Sam's right.

"What's going on?" Mona asked.

Sam shrugged. "Hard to say, but I'm guessing these are the guys Delray stiffed for the money to buy the resort, and they want it back. The kid didn't look too happy when I told him Delray was dead."

She nodded, her eyes glistening.

Sam looked over at J.T. "I don't know what they expect us to do about it. Jack and Sonja have their money, and they probably won't be inclined to give it back."

"Yeah," J.T. said, "that worries me a little."

Glasses brought in a coffee service and a tray of pastries and left again. J.T. reached for a cheese Danish. Sam looked at Mona and nodded toward the plate. She frowned and said, "No thanks." He took a pastry and poured a cup of coffee, trying to remember the last time he'd eaten.

About an hour passed before the door opened again. Mona, who had put her head down and fallen asleep, sat up as Jack Craft stepped into the room, impeccably dressed in a blue suit and striped tie. Sonja followed him, with Frankie and Dom behind her. She looked like a rich heiress. Frankie wore a suit and tie himself, which obviously had been custom tailored to fit his medicine-ball shape.

Jack pulled out a chair across the table from Sam and sat down. Sonja took a seat next to Jack and glanced from Sam to Mona, and then turned toward Frankie. Her composure seemed much the same as the last time Sam had seen her: difficult to read. The odd thing seemed to be that no one looked under duress.

Frankie grabbed a bear claw from the tray and climbed into the chair at the head of the table. Sam knew his feet would be dangling above the floor. Dom sat at the other end, staring at the breakfast treats.

"Okay," Frankie said, talking around a bite of pastry, "Mr. Craft asked for this meeting. I'm just providing the refreshments." He nodded to Jack, "So go ahead any time you get ready."

Sam looked at Jack and raised an eyebrow.

Frankie wolfed down the rest of the pastry and licked his fingers. He motioned for J.T. to slide the plate closer so he could get another.

"Thank you, Frankie," Jack said, smiling. "First, I want to apologize to Ms. Miles, who has suffered a great deal of hardship these last few days."

Mona frowned and looked away.

Jack's smile faded, and he turned his gaze to Sam. "When you called Sonja, you mentioned you had found the prize. Would you care to elaborate on that?"

Sam's face felt hot. He'd signed on to help Jack, and here Jack was interrogating him in front of a bunch of mobsters. "I knew you wanted the blue diamond, and I only said that on the phone because Sonja told Delray we were on our own. What did you expect me to do?"

Jack frowned. "You're saying you don't have it?"

"That's what I'm saying."

Jack rolled his eyes. "Well, do you know where it is?"

"I have no idea."

"You told Dom that Delray is dead. How do you expect us to find it now?"

Sam shrugged. "That isn't my problem. You never even mentioned the diamond to me. We had to figure that out on our own."

"Yes, well, I intended to do that, but was unable after Baxter took me at gunpoint."

"I don't know what to tell you, then. J.T. and I got a look inside Delray's safe in Grand Cayman, and I searched Delray himself and his boat. Those are the places I would expect him to hide it, and it wasn't there when we looked."

Jack stared for a moment, as if trying to decide something. Then he leaned back in his chair and sighed. "Well, Seams did pay the expenses, so I suppose it isn't like we lost any money."

"Aren't you forgetting about the money you scammed Ruben for the resort? I know you got five million from Ernie and Delray, too, but I suppose that actually belongs to Frankie."

Glancing at Frankie, Jack smiled and said, "I know it might seem that way, but I'm afraid there never was any resort money. It was all bogus, even Frankie's loan."

Sam turned and gave Frankie a look. "You were in on it?"

Frankie closed his eyes and nodded. "Yup."

"What about the guy Delray shot at Dom's house? Was that part of the plan?"

Frankie shook his head. "No, Sal shoulda been more careful. Hazard of the business. He's gonna live, but I'll probably replace him because of what happened. That redheaded maniac could've killed us all."

Sam sighed and shook his head. "All of us could have been killed."

Jack poured a cup of coffee and took a sip. "I knew you wouldn't let that happen, Samuel. Frankie and I were partners, and we wanted a reason for Delray to need a lot of cash, which we knew he didn't have. That's where the Outpost Mariner came in. Actually, Seams, the pharmaceutical man, owns it. We proposed to sell it at a price too good to pass up. Of course, the place was never really for sale. We just made Ernie and Delray think it was. One of Frankie's men offered Delray a loan, and he took it, thinking he couldn't lose. We made it look like the money had been transferred to us for the sale, but that was just a sham. No money ever changed hands, everything orchestrated electronically with bogus bank sites."

Mona spoke up, her eyes narrow slits: "That was an ugly scene with the bank manager in Grand Cayman. You couldn't have fixed that."

"All a big show," Jack said. "Henry Wells is an old friend."

"What about Ruben?" Sam asked. "I thought he had a part of the supposed purchase?"

Jack shook his head. "Ruben was with us, until he lost his memory. We worried about him compromising the operation after that."

It all fell into place. Jack and Sonja had created an illusion. Delray owed Frankie five million for his and Ernie's investment, and Frankie's people put pressure on him to pay it back, hoping he would bring the diamond out of hiding and offer it up in settlement of the debt.

The fact that Jack had omitted the part about the stone irked Sam. He probably would have opted out early on had he known all the details. And that was precisely why Jack hadn't told him.

"I do have one more question, though," Sam said.

"Sure, shoot."

"Why didn't you just hire some guys to go to Grand Cayman and take the stone?"

"Well, for one thing, we didn't know where he had it hidden. His safe would be the most logical place, but you said yourself that he didn't put it there."

"Actually," Sam said, "I said it wasn't there when we *looked*. Someone might already have taken it out by then."

Jack nodded in concession. "Yes, I suppose we could have taken that approach, but I fear the body count would have been higher, given Delray's background and the people working for him."

Sam nodded and said to Mona, "Let's go. Jack's going to take you home."

Jack glanced at Frankie. "Okay, I guess we're done here." He stood, buttoned and smoothed his suit coat, and said to Frankie, "We can talk about where we go from here in a couple of hours if you're free."

Frankie brushed crumbs from his suit. "The sooner the better."

On the way to drop Mona off, Jack told her that she couldn't say anything to her TV people about what had happened. "If word gets out about Ernie and Delray dying on that yacht, the Feds and the locals will still be investigating it a year from now. No one will be safe."

Mona didn't respond. Jack tried to make eye contact in the rear-view mirror, but she looked away.

Everyone remained quiet until they reached Mona's condo. She got out of the car without a word.

"Wait for me," Sam said to Jack, and followed Mona out.

At the lobby door, he said, "I'm really sorry how this turned out."

"Come in for a while."

Sam just looked at her. She probably wanted to talk more about the news aspect, and he wondered what they would gain by hashing it over again.

She gave him a pout, lips puckered. "Please?"

"Okay, hold on." He went back, got his car keys from J.T., and told Jack he'd catch a cab from there.

Jack smiled. "You're okay on how this turned out, aren't you?"

Sam gazed at Biscayne Bay in the distance. "No, I'm a little steamed about it. We'll talk later."

Jack looked away. "Okay, whatever you say."

The window went up with a whir, and the Mercedes glided away.

Inside the townhouse, Mona made scrambled egg sandwiches, and they sat at a dinette table overlooking the bay.

She ate a bite of her sandwich and touched a napkin to her lips. "He expects me to just forget about the last week and go back to my job like nothing happened."

"I knew you wouldn't like it, but you really can't put this business out on the six o'clock news."

"You agree with him?"

Sam sighed. "It's not that I agree with him. But if you go on TV and tell about this stuff, cops are going to swarm the station and ask a lot of questions. I know you're clean, but you never know how things will turn out when the Miami PD and the FBI get into it. There could be some big players who want to make names for themselves. And with the kidnapping angle, the tabloids will be all over it."

Mona laid her sandwich on the plate and pushed it away. "So you're saying I should just leave it alone?"

Sam stared at her for a long moment, stood and sauntered to the window. Sails of all colors dotted the bay. The scene looked like a still-life painting, a portrait in tranquility. A power yacht cut through the center headed toward open sea, its wake roiling the water beneath the sailing vessels, spoiling the perfect picture. However, the boat, with its avant-garde lines, embodied a perfection of its own, as it silently glided past the smaller crafts, their hulls bouncing on the man-made crests. A paradox of nature, one beauty destroying another.

What Mona could do with this story would be a career-making event for her, but it might destroy Jack Craft and a few others, and anything they had going. If some bad things hadn't happened, there might be less conflict between the two sides of the situation. But bad things *had* happened…at least in the eyes of a handful of people.

Perhaps the script could be rewritten, if the audience didn't know what happened in the first place. Probably happened all the time in history books.

THIRTY-FIVE

THE TAXI DROPPED Sam at his car and he drove home to the marina. With only a few hours of sleep during the last two days, fatigue dragged at his legs like twenty-pound weights. He ambled down the dock to *Slipstream*, got a beer from the reefer, and settled into the big chair in the lounge. After taking a couple of swallows, he leaned back, closed his eyes, and fell asleep.

A dream carried him back to Grand Cayman, where he stood next to Delray's garage. Even though night had fallen, the sky glowed yellow, tinting the palms around the estate a brilliant green. Finding the back door ajar, he pushed his way in, but this time he already knew about Earl Bates doing his dirty work inside. Down the hall, he saw the tattoo man on the floor, unconscious, bound. Easing around the corner, he heard Bates open the safe and swing the door open. Sam scraped against the doorway and the sound stopped. Then, he heard the subtle noise as he had before, s*nick...snick*, and he stepped into the room with the gun leading the way. Bates stood by the window, and when he turned around, he pointed his silenced handgun at Sam's head and pulled the trigger.

Sam woke with a jerk and glanced at the clock: twenty past midnight; he'd slept about six hours in the chair. He went to the head, showered, and dressed in clean clothes. Back in the lounge, he picked up the phone.

"Yeah?" J.T. answered, sleep slurring his voice.

"Where are you?"

J.T. told him the hotel where he had a room.

"Okay, get dressed. I'll pick you up in fifteen minutes."

"Pick me up? For what? I'm sleeping, man."

"We're going to get the diamond."

After a moment's silence, J.T. said, "Bring some coffee. I'll be in the lobby."

TWENTY MINUTES LATER, they headed for the MacArthur Causeway. They sped across Biscayne Bay to I-395, and then veered onto I-95 South, which changed to US-1 somewhere north of Coconut Grove. On the way, Sam asked J.T. to turn on his computer and bring up the information about the theft of the diamond.

J.T.'s fingers clicked on the keyboard. After a few moments he said, "Here's the story. I'll pick out the high points and paraphrase. It says the owner, Luger Stevens, had the diamond on display for a party at his home. Three men armed with automatic weapons entered the house sometime after midnight and took it. The dead bodies of three men fitting the description of the robbers were found later that morning about a mile from Stevens' home. The police had no leads at the time of the story."

"Sounds like whoever engineered the robbery killed the help so he could keep everything."

"Yeah, and at the same time, eliminate anyone who could talk about it."

Sam changed lanes and passed a semi. "I'd bet Earl

Bates got greedy, tipped Delray about Seams sending the stone to Florida on the NewMood truck, then double-crossed him, too."

"But we searched him, remember?"

"I think the diamond was there all along. When Bates heard me in the hall, he got really quiet, except for a subtle noise he made. I tried to identify it, but I must have had too much adrenalin blasting my brain to think, because it didn't occur to me until a little while ago." Sam didn't want to say it came to him in a dream. "I think he knew he might run into trouble when he went to check out the noise, so he opened the window and dropped the diamond outside."

J.T. glared at the dash. "Right outside the window. Man, I hate to hear that. Just a few feet away, in plain view, if we had only looked."

"Yeah…but I guess I could be wrong, too," Sam said. "This is all just speculation at this point."

J.T. still had Bates' wallet with his address inside. They arrived at his condominium ten minutes later, and Sam spotted an empty parking space for number 35.

"Must be a night owl," J.T. said.

They parked several spaces away, went to the stairway, and eased up the steps to the second floor. Sam worked on the door lock with his pick. It took less than a minute to open.

Pushing through the door, guns and flashlights leading the way, they stepped into a small foyer. No lights on anywhere. They continued past the living room and down the hall toward the bedroom. There appeared to be only one, its door wide open. Sam peeked inside and saw an empty, unmade bed.

"Let's wait and see if he comes home before we tear the place apart," Sam said.

They ambled back up the hall into the living room, and Sam stopped with a jerk, a buzz running across the back of his neck. A silhouette of a man traced against the window's drapes. He had a weapon in his hand.

"I don't think I have to ask why you two are here." Jack Craft, his tone sharp.

Sam took a deep breath and let it out, dropping his gun to his side. "How did you figure it out about Bates?"

"I put it together from something Cal said. No help from you; you never mentioned anything about Bates being at Delray's."

"What did Cal tell you?"

"He told Ruben that Bates slugged the guy with tattoos and robbed the place. I assume you saw Bates leaving there, and would have to know he had the diamond."

"How did Ruben get so chummy with Cal?"

"Cal is the one who told Ruben about Delray stealing the diamond in the first place. He wanted to get into movies, and tried to ingratiate himself with Ruben every chance he got."

When Sam didn't say anything, Jack continued: "I have to say, it disappoints me to learn about it from him, rather than you."

"Yeah, sort of like how we had to find out about the diamond on our own."

Silence. Tension hung in the air like a burning fuse.

J.T. finally spoke up: "Hey, Sam didn't tell you about it because he didn't have anything to tell. We caught Bates in the process of trying to steal the diamond, and we slugged him and searched his pockets. He didn't have the stone on him, so we looked in the safe, and it wasn't there, either. That's the truth."

"Then why are you here?"

Sam told him his theory about the window.

Jack seemed to mull it over. "Okay, I'll buy that. I guess that makes us even."

They waited in the dark. The window provided a good view of the lighted parking lot below.

At 2:20 a.m., Earl Bates swung a new Porsche Carrera into his parking space.

"Looks like he's already spending the money," J.T. said. "That car costs about a hundred grand."

Sam stepped into the foyer to the hinge side of the entrance. He heard Bates insert the key in the lock, and waited for him to come in. When he stepped through the door, Sam rammed it with his shoulder. It knocked Mr. Rivets off his feet and he crashed to the threshold. J.T. grabbed him by the ankles and dragged him into the room. Sam pointed his gun at the man's face, and Jack flipped on the light switch.

Bates blinked his eyes a couple of times and looked at Jack. "You! What do you want?" He tried to sit up, but J.T. pushed him back down.

J.T. searched the pockets of his suit coat and pants, and found only keys and a wallet.

"Not here," J.T. said.

Jack held out his hand. "Let's see those keys." He examined them and held one up, dangling the rest on the chain. "This is a bank deposit box key." To Bates he said, "Is the stone in the box?"

"What stone? I don't know what you're talking about."

Jack grinned. "We'll see."

AT 9:00 A.M., when the bank opened, the four men strode through the front door to the desk of a loan officer. His nameplate identified him as Fred Weems.

"Yes?" Weems said, standing. "Can I help you?"

When Bates didn't say anything, Sam jabbed him in the side with the handgun in his jacket pocket. Mr. Rivets held up the key.

"Need to get into box 410."

Weems stared at him for a moment, than glanced at Sam.

"Nice day, huh?" Sam said.

"Uh…yes." He looked briefly through the glass entrance doors. "A very nice day. Follow me, please."

They went into the vault where Weems asked for Bates' ID, then checked a list on the computer and pulled a key from a box on the wall. After signing a log, Bates put his key into one of the two slots on box 410.

The bank man inserted the second key, turned them both, and opened the door. "You can use one of the private rooms to your right if you want." He stepped away.

Jack pulled the box out and carried it into one of the rooms.

An ivory case the size of a Rubik's Cube sat inside. It had star-shaped windows carved into its sides and top. Jack lifted off the ivory top. The gem lay there on a small satin pillow, like a sleeping princess, awaiting a kiss. The Seamont diamond. Holding it up in front of him, its facets grabbed the bright bank lights and bounced them back like a thousand tiny, glistening blue eyes.

Jack smiled, put it back into the ivory case, and stuck it into his blazer pocket. The four of them left the bank and took their time walking through the parking lot.

J.T. told Earl to get into the back seat and followed him in. Sam sat in front, and Jack got behind the wheel.

"You might have the stone," Bates said, "but I'll find you and make you pay."

Jack started the engine of his Mercedes. "You think so?"

"You better believe it, old man. And you other scumbags, too. We'll see how tough you are when I catch you without a gun. You're all dead men."

"Like those three guys who stole the stone for you," J.T. said.

Bates looked surprised for a moment, and then grinned. "You got it, Sherlock. Just like them."

"You sound pretty upbeat for a man on a one-way trip to the Everglades."

Bates' grin leaked away, and his eyes grew large. "You wouldn't do that."

THAT AFTERNOON, Jack, J.T. and Sam sat in Jack's yacht, *The Clipper*, sipping cold beers. Jack told them that he'd never had any intention of giving the diamond to Seams.

"I pretended to work for him so he would front the expenses."

"So, what are you going to do with it?" J.T. asked, his eyes glowing. "I can get a buyer. It won't bring the whole thirty million, but we can get about half that."

Jack glanced at him. "I've spoken with the insurance company. They're willing to pay ten percent, no questions asked."

Sam smiled, took a long drink of beer, and leaned back in his chair. He knew what would come next.

"You're kidding?" J.T. said. "I can get...maybe five times that much."

Jack closed his eyes and shook his head. "The longer we hold onto this thing, the more likely somebody will come for us. This is the cleanest way. Besides, I already made the deal. We turn it over this afternoon and they give us a satchel full of cash."

J.T. took a deep breath and let it out. His eyes narrowed, and his lips pressed together like a clamshell.

"Who said you could make that decision? You wouldn't have that diamond without us."

When Jack didn't reply, J.T. set his beer down on an end table, sprang from his chair, and stamped out.

Jack looked at Sam and grinned.

"He'll be back," Sam said. "You didn't use your real name with the insurance company, did you?"

Jack rolled his eyes. "Please. You insult me."

THIRTY-SIX

THAT EVENING, SAM sat on a barstool in the Marina Bar and Grill, watching the news on television while eating a fried crab sandwich.

"This is Mona Miles, reporting to you from Key West, at the home of Ruben Vale, star of the hit television series, *Vogue Detective*."

Mona looked radiant, the stress of the last few days gone from her face. Her eyes were warm and inviting, her hair like spun taffy. She turned to Ruben, who sat in a wingback wicker chair, resplendent in cream-colored linen slacks and a pastel designer shirt. His handsome face looked flawless, hair combed in a retro style reminiscent of a young Errol Flynn, sans the mustache. The head wound had healed, or he'd concealed it underneath his slicked-back hair. The nagging feeling Sam had experienced before, that the actor looked like someone he'd met, flickered behind his eyes and skipped away.

"Ruben, this is a beautiful home you have," Mona said. "You are certainly living the life of a famous screen star. I loved you in your role as Mason Vogue, solving the mysteries and charming us ladies."

"Thank you, Mona. I enjoyed that role and hope to reprise it very soon."

"Oh?" Mona glanced at the camera, flashing a mischievous grin. "Do you have some news for us?"

Ruben winked at her. "Just be on the lookout for Mason Vogue this fall."

"That's terrific, Ruben, we'll certainly do that. But that isn't why we're here today. I understand you've done some real-life detective work as Ruben Vale."

"Yes, I have."

"Tell us about it."

"Have you heard of the Seamont?"

"It sounds like an exclusive hotel."

"No, not a hotel. The Seamont is a very large blue diamond. It belongs to a man named Luger Stevens. Mr. Stevens purchased the stone not long ago for $30 million, and had owned it only a month or so when armed robbers broke into his home and took it."

"That had to be a frightening experience for Mr. Stevens."

"Yes, I'm sure it was, Mona. And even worse, three men were found dead later that night, only a mile or so from Mr. Stevens' home. The police think they were the robbers, but, of course, the diamond was never found."

Mona shook her head. "That is tragic."

Ruben shrugged, like this might be everyday fare for him.

Mona continued. "Okay, now tell us how you became a true-life detective in this high-stakes case."

"Probably not many people know this, but I do some amateur detective work on the side, from time to time. I read about the robbery in the newspapers, and then, a week or so later, someone—let's call him an informant— told me he'd heard the stone had ended up in South Florida. I was intrigued, to say the least, and decided to do some investigating. Being a TV personality, I'm in touch with a lot of people in Miami, so I made some calls and visited a few places. That led only to dead ends, I'm sorry to say, and I started losing interest. Then, a few days later, I hit pay dirt. The phone rang, and the man wouldn't identify himself, but said he'd heard I was looking for the Seamont. He said he knew who had it, and could get his hands on it for the right price."

"He wouldn't tell you his name?"

"No, he was adamant that he remain anonymous, because of the potential threat to his life."

"That's scary. What did you do?"

"I did some research to learn what company insured the diamond, and put Mr. X in touch with them."

"I assume an insurance company would gladly pay a finder's fee for something so valuable."

"You bet, Mona, and I learned yesterday that the stone had been recovered."

"So the Seamont is back in the hands of its rightful owner?"

"Yes, it is." Ruben winked. "Another mystery solved in the casebook of Mason Vogue." He used the Bogart voice Sam had heard him use before.

Mona grimaced for a split second, but caught herself.

Ruben continued in his normal voice. "Maybe this will be one of the episodes in my new show that I'm not officially announcing yet."

"Okay, Ruben, that's very exciting." She faced the camera. "We'll have more in-depth coverage of this amazing case from our network offices in New York, tomorrow night at 9:00 p.m. Central Time. This is Mona Miles reporting for Channel 5 News."

Turning back to Ruben, she said something, her voice muted and overlaid with the news program theme song. Ruben nodded and continued to smile for the camera.

Sam asked the bartender if he could freeze the picture on the TV. The man picked up the remote and pressed a button, stopping the action. Sam studied Ruben's face for a few moments.

A HEAT WAVE had blanketed South Florida, and the temperature hovered around ninety, even though nearing sundown. The few steps down the dock sent beads of perspiration down Sam's neck. He turned at Jack Craft's slip and stepped aboard *The Clipper*.

"I thought you'd drop by," Jack said when he opened the door.

"Did you see the news?"

"Yes, I saw it. It actually sounded believable." He made drinks and they sat in the big easy chairs of the salon.

"Do you think you'll have any problems with Seams?"

Jack shook his head, an odd look on his face. "No, I wouldn't worry about him."

Not wanting to know any more, Sam just nodded.

"Something occurred to me while I watched the news," Sam said.

Jack's eyes widened a fraction. "What's that?"

"I think you know."

"Indulge me."

Jack leaned back in his chair and crossed his arms.

"This situation seemed out of kilter from the start. You always pull the strings, but you never work the front lines, and here you are dealing directly with the marks. Then there's the diamond, something so valuable it's bound to attract national attention. Now it all makes sense: you did it for Ruben. He probably looks the way you did at his age. I figure Sonja dropped that bombshell on you before all this started."

Jack's eyes locked on Sam's for a couple of beats, a

frown pinching at the corner of his mouth. He got up and made another gin and tonic, and drank half of it before turning around.

"Who else knows this?"

"Nobody, that I know of. I'll bet Ruben doesn't even know."

Jack sat down again and shook his head. "He doesn't. As I told you before, she disappeared almost thirty years ago. Then, out of the blue, she calls me on the phone and tells me about the Seamont diamond, and about Ruben. I've seen him on TV, of course, but I never had any idea he could be my son. She told me how he got hooked up with Ernie when his show got canceled, and she wanted to free him of that burden and get him back on his feet in Hollywood. It took me by surprise, and I didn't want any part of it. Like you said, this isn't the way I normally operate. But she laid a guilt trip on me and I relented."

He sat there and stared at a painting on the wall of a lone sailboat on Biscayne Bay, probably thinking his life had gotten a lot more complicated than it had been just a few weeks ago.

"What about Sonja? She going to hang around?"

Jack shook his head. "She's already gone."

LATER THAT NIGHT, Jack sat in the salon, a metal case full of cash sitting open on the coffee table before him. Hearing a noise from the main hatch, he closed the case and set it on the deck next to his chair. Before he could get up, Baxter, his former captor, stepped through the doorway with a gun in his hand pointed at Jack's face.

"I bet you thought you'd never see me again." Baxter grinned, no longer wearing the sling on his arm.

"I knew you'd be back. Just wasn't sure when."

He thumbed the hammer on the gun. "Then you know I'm here for the money."

Jack settled back in the chair. "There never was any money."

"Good try. I was there when Ernie transferred it to your bank account. I saw it with my own eyes."

"You just thought you saw it," Jack said. "It was all a scam. No money ever changed hands."

Baxter frowned. "I'm not buyin' it."

Jack shrugged. "We made it look real. We were after a diamond Delray had stolen."

"What diamond?"

"It was on the six o'clock news."

"I don't know what you're talking about."

"Here." Jack reached for the remote and flipped on the TV. "I recorded it. See for yourself."

Baxter watched the interview, but glanced back every couple of seconds, the frown frozen on his face. Jack thought about the gun he kept stuffed in the crevice between the cushion and the chair arm.

When the program ended, Baxter said, "So you helped Ruben get back this Seamont diamond?"

"That's right."

The frown morphed into a smile. "Then you got a finder's fee from the insurance company."

His eyes homed in on the metal case.

"What have we here?" He grabbed the handle and opened the case on the table, careful to keep the gun pointed at Jack.

"How much is in here?"

"I don't know. Why don't you count it?"

He reached into the case and fingered the stacks.

Jack got his hand on the gun, but pulled back when Baxter closed the case and glanced up at him.

"It looks like a lot. I'll count it later."

"I did some checking on you," Jack said.

"Yeah? What'd you find out?"

"You work for the Feds, and you'll serve some time if you take this money."

The dirty cop shook his head. "There's no way they'll find out. You're the only one who'll know, and you'll be dead." He gripped the gun with both hands and pointed it at Jack's face.

Jack's pulse drummed in his ears, and he felt a bead of perspiration roll down his cheek. A door squeaked behind the would-be killer, and he turned his head to look. Jack snatched the gun from the crevice in the chair, but before he could fire, Lamar Hingle burst from the galley with a baseball in his hand. Baxter swung around with his gun, and the former pitcher drew the ball back over his shoulder and hurled it, as if pitching a major league game. *WHACK!* It struck the standing man between the eyes, snapping his head back. He fell to the floor next to Jack's chair and lay still, the space between his eyes already swelling.

Jack stood and pulled the gun from his hand.

"You took your time making that drink."

The pale man grinned, stepped over, and picked up the baseball.

Jack stared down at the unconscious man, and pulled out his phone.

SAM STEPPED ONTO *The Clipper* holding a 9mm down by his side.

Lamar Hingle exited the door and hesitated as he passed Sam, a wary look on his face.

"I heard you pitched a shutout," Sam said.

Lamar grinned, the uneasiness seeming to leak away.

"You could say that. Look…sorry about how things went. I didn't know who you were at the time."

Sam shrugged. "Don't worry about it. I was in the dark, too."

Jack opened the door and stood there as the pale man strode up the dock.

Following Jack inside, Sam ambled to the salon and peered down at Baxter, who remained dead to the world. "Got any ammonia?"

Jack disappeared into the galley and returned with a plastic bottle. Sam opened it and splashed some of the liquid into Baxter's nostrils.

Baxter jerked to life, coughing and covering his nose with his hand. He sat up and glared at Sam, mopping his nose with the front of his shirt, tears racing from his eyes. "You trying to kill me?"

Jack took the bottle and looked at it. "You think this stuff could kill him?"

Sam shrugged. "I don't know. Maybe."

When Baxter stopped coughing, Sam pointed the 9mm at his face.

Jack came closer. "What are you doing?"

"I'm going to put a bullet in his head," Sam said.

Baxter squirmed backwards on the floor, terror in his eyes, still holding his hand over his nose.

"You can't just kill him," Jack said.

Sam nodded. "You worried about messing up your boat? I'll take him out to the Glades and do it." He thumbed the hammer on the gun and said to Baxter, "Get up, scumbag."

Baxter pled to Jack, "Don't let him kill me! I can just walk away and you won't ever see me again."

Jack stared at him for a couple of beats, and then

turned to Sam. "Maybe he's telling the truth. Besides, I have a video."

Sam raised an eyebrow. "A video?"

"Yes. I have a motion activated camera over there that turns on automatically after midnight, in case somebody breaks in, like he did."

"You ever heard of Frankie Buzzo?" Jack asked Baxter.

"Sure, everybody knows about Frankie." Baxter looked at Sam, then back at Jack, a hopeful look on his face.

"I tell you what. Frankie was in on this scam. So I'm going to give the video to him. If anything ever happens to any of us, Frankie will pop you and send the video to the Feds. They'll look it over and think you just disappeared with the money."

"Okay, whatever you say. I won't ever bother you again."

Jack stared at Sam. "What do you think?"

Sam shrugged. "Up to you. It'd be cleaner if I killed him."

Seeming to consider that, Jack said to Baxter, "Get outta here."

Baxter glanced at Sam, then struggled to his feet and staggered out of the salon.

"That should take care of it," Jack said.

"Yeah, I don't think he'll be back."

"How about a drink?"

THIRTY-SEVEN

"YOU WANT TO go ashore for lunch?" Sam asked Mona as they climbed the ladder from their morning swim. Cool seawater dripped from her skin, like crystals glistening in the sun. It had been three weeks since the deadly night on Delray's yacht. Sam had replaced the bad water pump on *Slipstream*, and they had motored down the coast, spending the last two days anchored off Key Largo. They swam, fished, and drank wine while soaking up the rays.

"I'd rather stay aboard and have those lobsters you caught," she said, toweling off. "Do we still have fresh water for a shower?"

She looked stunning in a white bikini.

"Maybe enough for one more...as long as we take it together."

Mona grinned. "That's what I had in mind."

TWO HOURS LATER Sam placed the lobsters on the grill. He put rolls wrapped in foil and a bowl of butter in the corner over low heat. Mona set out a container of coleslaw from a Miami deli and opened their last bottle of Chardonnay. She had remained quiet since coming onto the deck, as if her mind might be somewhere else.

Ruben had gotten the green light on his TV show the week before. An anonymous investor had agreed to fund production of six episodes, and a major network picked up the show for a trial season. Sam pegged the investor as Jack Craft.

Immediately after getting the good news, Ruben asked Mona to go to Hollywood with him for a recurring role on the show as a TV news reporter. Though she had no formal acting experience, she had logged many hours in front of the camera, and was intrigued by the idea. Sam didn't care much for it, but he understood why she might be interested. Besides, he knew she had questions about the viability of their continued relationship, considering their vast differences. She was a celebrity with a bright future, and he was a violent figure with a murky past, and maybe an even murkier future. Mona wasn't the only one with questions.

They ate the lobsters and rolls with melted butter, and finished off the pint of coleslaw. Sitting back, sipping her wine, Mona fixed him with a stare, as if trying to decide whether or not to say something.

"What is it?" Sam asked.

"I think I'll take Ruben's offer."

Sam drained his wineglass and poured another for both of them. He would have liked it better if they could just lose all the tension and continue things as is, but deep down he knew that would never work. Even if she stayed, she would always wonder what she might have missed, and maybe blame him. Sam had his own issues to consider: his work didn't exactly fit the nine-to-five mold, and he doubted if she could stand the risky situations he placed himself into. But what worried him most was the possibility that someone might target her to get to him, as Delray had done.

Sam took a sip of wine and smiled into the sun,

eyes squinting behind sunglasses. "I'm excited for you. You'll be a movie star."

"It's television, not the movies."

"Okay, then, TV star. Let's just enjoy the rest of our trip and forget it for now."

"You'll come out for a visit, won't you?"

"Of course."

A gentle breeze raised goose bumps on Sam's skin, and he smiled as she gazed in the distance at nature's artwork of sky and sea, maybe dreaming about the red carpet and the Hollywood Walk of Fame.

They stayed the night and left early the next morning, arriving at the marina a little after 2:00 p.m. Sam had agreed to drive her back to her condo for her bags and to freshen up, and then take her to the airport. They sauntered up the dock and swung by Jack's boat to pick up Rolly. One of Frankie's men had returned him to Mona the day after their meeting at Frankie's house. She'd become attached to him, and decided to take him to California with her. Jack had agreed to watch him while they cruised to the Keys, but he seemed pretty relieved when they picked him up. On the way to Mona's condo, the bird kept saying, *"You don't know Jack."*

At the airport, after they said their goodbyes, Mona went through security and headed for her gate. Sam watched her leave carrying the birdcage. He felt something in his chest drop into his stomach.

Back on his boat, Sam changed into shorts and a tee shirt, uncapped a cold bottle of beer, and ambled out onto the deck where he took a seat in the shade of the stern. It seemed nice to be back at the marina. A pelican sat on a timber awaiting a jumping fish. Sails of all colors dotted Biscayne Bay. Jets droned as they left

Miami International for the Caribbean. A cool breeze washed over his skin. He tried not to think about Mona traveling to the other side of the continent.

The phone chirped, and he studied the display, recognizing the Washington D.C. number. He considered ignoring the call, but knew the man would keep trying, or send someone.

He pressed the answer button. "What do you want?"

"A guy took something belonging to us. We want you to get it back."

"Sorry, I'm out of that line of work."

"You remember Simone? You'll be working with her."

Yes, he remembered Simone: tall, shapely, beautiful blue eyes.

"You have other people. Get one of them."

"Sorry, the admiral insisted on you. Besides, you shouldn't have wasted Jinks. We still used him every now and then."

"*I* didn't kill him."

"Sure, you didn't. Simone will pick you up at midnight." The line died.

An old rock song played nearby, the notes floating on the breeze, probably signaling the beginning of a party somewhere in the marina as the sun reclined on the horizon. Sam thought about getting another beer and heading that way. Then Simone's image flashed behind his eyes. He smiled and went inside to prepare for his mission.

* * * * *

Get 4 FREE REWARDS!

We'll send you 2 FREE Books plus 2 FREE Mystery Gifts.

Harlequin Intrigue books are action-packed stories that will keep you on the edge of your seat. Solve the crime and deliver justice at all costs.

FREE
Value Over
$20

Get 4 FREE REWARDS!

We'll send you 2 FREE Books plus 2 FREE Mystery Gifts.

Harlequin Romantic Suspense books are heart-racing page-turners with unexpected plot twists and irresistible chemistry that will keep you guessing to the very end.

FREE
Value Over
$20

YES! Please send me 2 FREE Harlequin Romantic Suspense novels and my 2 FREE gifts (gifts are worth about $10 retail). After receiving them, if I don't wish to receive any more books, I can return the shipping statement marked "cancel." If I don't cancel, I will receive 4 brand-new novels every month and be billed just $4.99 per book in the U.S. or $5.74 per book in Canada. That's a savings of at least 13% off the cover price! It's quite a bargain! Shipping and handling is just 50¢ per book in the U.S. and $1.25 per book in Canada.* I understand that accepting the 2 free books and gifts places me under no obligation to buy anything. I can always return a shipment and cancel at any time. The free books and gifts are mine to keep no matter what I decide.

240/340 HDN GNMZ

Name (please print)

Address   Apt. #

City   State/Province   Zip/Postal Code

Email: Please check this box ☐ if you would like to receive newsletters and promotional emails from Harlequin Enterprises ULC and its affiliates. You can unsubscribe anytime.

Mail to the **Reader Service:**
IN U.S.A.: P.O. Box 1341, Buffalo, NY 14240-8531
IN CANADA: P.O. Box 603, Fort Erie, Ontario L2A 5X3

Want to try 2 free books from another series! Call 1-800-873-8635 or visit www.ReaderService.com.

Visit ReaderService.com Today!

As a valued member of the Harlequin Reader Service, you'll find these benefits and more at ReaderService.com:

- Try 2 free books from any series
- Access risk-free special offers
- View your account history & manage payments
- Browse the latest Bonus Bucks catalog

Don't miss out!

If you want to stay up-to-date on the latest at the Harlequin Reader Service and enjoy more content, make sure you've signed up for our monthly News & Notes email newsletter. Sign up online at ReaderService.com or by calling Customer Service at 1-800-873-8635.